Advance Praise for

The Mountain & The
Vortex and Other Tales

Stephen Vessels is one of those rare artists who effortlessly—or so it appears—cruises through genres, equally comfortable in science fiction, dark fantasy, and his own brand of emotionally-charged weirdness. He skates gracefully on the thin ices of genius in this superb collection.

Elizabeth Engstrom,
Author of *Lizzie Borden*,
The Northwoods Chronicles, and *Baggage Check*

The Mountain and The Vortex is a tour-de-force of the imagination, and a book of many worlds: some scary, all wondrous, all original. Exotic and intensely human, these stories will stay with you and leave you waiting eagerly for Stephen Vessels' next book.

Lorelei Armstrong,
Author of *In The Face*

From his portrayal of the consuming isolation of a teacher's power in "The Burning Professor" to the payment of a ghostly father's debts during his son's redemption in "Doloroso," I was enthralled by Steven Vessels' debut collection of sometimes surreal, sometimes hyper-real, and sometimes purely mystical, mythical tales.

Eric M. Witchey,
Author of *Beyond the Serpent's Heart*,
To Build a Boat Listen to Trees, and *Bull's Labyrinth*

The Mountain & The Vortex and Other Tales
A Muse Harbor Publishing Book

PUBLISHING HISTORY
Muse Harbor Publishing hardback edition published October 2016
Published by Muse Harbor Publishing, LLC
Los Angeles, California
Santa Barbara, California

Previously published
"No Night, No Need of Candle," *Spectrum*, Vol. 29, 1987
"Verge Land," *Cause & Effect Magazine*, November, 2008
"Doloroso," *Ellery Queen's Mystery Magazine*, November 2013
"The Butcher of Gad Street," *Equilibrium Overturned*, Grey Matter Press, 2014

Illustrations
"No Night, No Need of Candle," Jean "Moebius" Giraud, collection Stephen T. Vessels,
 all rights reserved
"The Butcher of Gad Street," "The Fourth Seven," "Dining Strange;" © Steven C. Gilberts
"Lighter Than Air," "Bulbous Things," "Doloroso," "Significance," "The Mountain and
 The Vortex," "Curious Black Substance," "Two Flowers," "Cog and The Gentleman,"
"Cutting the Eye;" © Alan M. Clark
"The Burning Professor," "Verge Land;" © Cheryl Owen-Wilson
"The Alchemist's Eyeglasses," and sigils © Stephen T. Vessels

Cover art: Stephen T. Vessels
Cover design: Dave Workman
Author photo: JoBeth McDanial

ISBN 978-1-61264-206-2

Visit Muse Harbor Publishing at www.museharbor.com

The Mountain
& The Vortex
and Other Tales

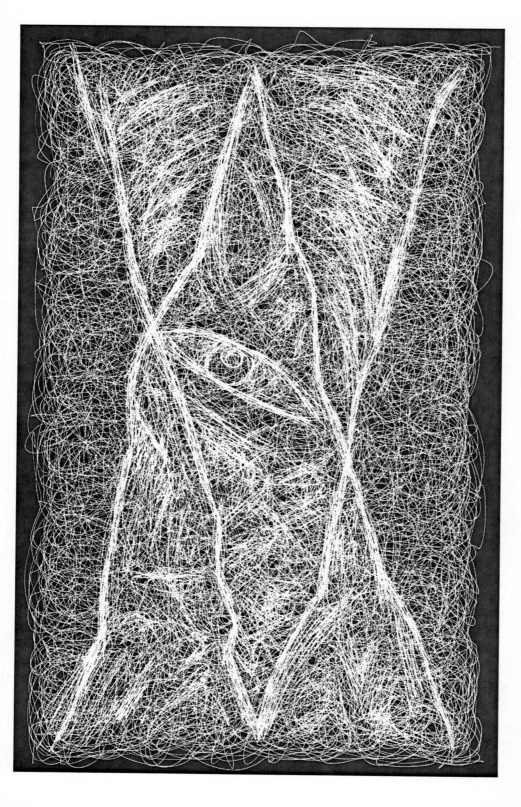

The Mountain
& The Vortex
and Other Tales

Stephen T. Vessels

Contents

Illustrations

Foreword

THE STORIES IN Stephen Vessels' first collection show us strange creatures from fantastic worlds who are all recognizable as quintessentially human.

The irreverent narrator of "Bulbous Things," relating an outrageous anecdote, quips, "If you can wrap your head around a warm, foamy mug of animal urine for a recreational beverage, you're good to go." In "Lighter Than Air" the main character makes an incredible discovery after at last forgiving himself. "No Night, No Need of Candle," Vessels' earliest published story, is about the existential horror of abandonment; set in a bizarre, haunting reality, it pays off in the currency of basic human emotion. Acrid, the gigantic "Butcher of Gad Street," engages in an epic battle against evil, told in the deeply personal terms of a desperate race to save his daughter's life.

All these tales, as fantastic as they may be, depict, at root, characters tortured by fierce emotions, engaged in what we recognize as universal human struggles. Therein lies the power of this work.

"Dining Strange," "Bulbous Things," and "The Mountain and The Vortex" are all textbook examples of the world-builder's art. Concrete sensory details bring their fantastic worlds into sharp focus, make us believe:

Unimaginable monsters cavort over an ice bridge arching through space, where God takes a shiv in the eye.

A character inserts his fingers into another's brain and finds: "The neural canal . . . surprisingly cool."

Odiferous (though tasty) black goo inundates the narrator as he hacks his way through a world-sized alien life form.

These stories deliver what Marianne Moore called, "Imaginary gardens with real toads." Though "The Mountain and The Vortex," the novella that gives this collection its name, is a complex tale, intricately interlaced with historical allusions and genre-jumping subplots, it remains imminently *readable*. This is the work of a true storyteller.

In the years that I've known Steve, as his teacher, mentor and friend, I've seen his work grow in power and scope. Now, given the cumulative effect of this remarkable collection, one thing seems clear: a new literary eagle has landed.

John R. Reed
March, 2016

For Rex Owen Waide.
You are missed.

No Night, No Need of Candle

And there shall be no night there; and they
need no candle, neither light of the sun.

REVELATION 22:5

HE HEARD, WITH a ghostly sense that was not really hearing, the voiceless scream of the Mad Train, welling up far across the barren land. The fused mob of souls swept fast over the horizon, wrecking the careful cycle of his thoughts. With a sudden jolt of recognition he remembered: escape. He had to escape. Quickly. He remembered: never merge.

He tried to conjure the image of his absent body, to remember the feel of the old living thing the earth had held onto, standing, legs joined to feet planted firmly on the ground, legs that could stretch and run and carry him to safety. But they were not there; the memories were gone. Where? The memories. Where were they? Had he neglected them for so long they were lost, dissipated like steam? Or had they been stripped from him the last time one of the Trains passed too near? Horribly, it grew clear they *were* gone, really missing. He searched frantically but there was nothing to draw on, no memory of sense strong enough to mimic.

He faced the invisible, looming madness. It would eat

him, chew up the remnants of his identity and endlessly re-digest them. The lingering hell he had drifted through these many centuries would seem paradise by comparison.

No. He was not going to be sucked into the mad thing. He imagined himself blended with the tormented throng, racing without direction until their group became too heavy with grieving souls to break their plunge, and too void of identity to cling any longer to the land. He had witnessed it over a hundred years before, and *that* event remembered clearly: the searing shriek of a hoard of ghosts boiling helplessly into space. No. Not yet. Let it not be so. Not for a hundred thousand more years. Not for a million. Please, never.

This train, by far, was the giant of all the Mad Trains he had encountered. It was incredible that it was still earthbound. It churned hundreds of feet high. Panicked, he strained again for a method of escape. He needed to flee, and flight required all the talents of the body long dead and blended with the dust and sand and hardened clay. Legs. Feet. He could only hazily recall their form, let alone the method of their function. For too long he had drifted, more like a cloud than a being, and his sense of legs had left him. He recognized it had been so long since he last tried to conjure the memory of body that now it was beyond him. Reluctantly, he resigned himself to having lost his best method of transport through the physical realm, and with this resignation his desperation grew.

What was left? He tried to calm himself. He was dimly aware of his physical surroundings and, threatened as he was, his sense of them grew rapidly clearer. He could still judge distance and location. Focusing on a spot nearby, he could imagine himself there and use his imagination as a grappling hook to pull himself to the place. It was the slowest way to go but it was the best he could manage. Burdened with a growing sense of futility, he drew slowly away from the onrushing flood of ghosts.

As he pulled himself along, here to an outcrop of rock a few feet ahead, there to a crack in the dry earth, he gradually became aware, for the first time in he knew not how long, of the appearance of the land around him. Winds blew down the barren slopes of distant mountains, spreading their cargoes of dust and sand in wispy sheets sent flapping like threadbare flags across a bone-white plain. The sky, cloudless, was evenly slate-grey. It was a panorama of utter desolation, where no living thing had stirred for centuries. The sight of it wounded him. It generated a sense of despair in him that threatened to send him hurtling back into the maws of a doom infinitely worse than the one he was already fated with, and so burdened him with another torment to struggle against.

The mountains—perhaps if he could make it to the mountains he could find refuge. They were so far away. Nearer, a shallow ravine twisted lazily towards the foothills. He decided to make for that, first, and then decide what to do next. Focusing his attention on the eroded surface of the interior wall of the ravine, he wrapped his consciousness in its details. He was there. He was *there*. He felt himself dragging towards the spot. But his progress was too slow. How would it look if he were really close to it, inches from it? Yes, the picture resolved more clearly for him. He drew closer. Then he had it; he was in the ravine, flattening his thin essence low against its bottom.

The effort had weakened him. But he knew he had not traveled far. Not far enough. He could not rest. A little ways ahead, towards the foothills, the ravine wormed its way to the left. That was it. He would draw himself down the dry stream bed one bend at a time. He would move like the ghost of a river, upstream towards its source.

He remembered rivers —the deep blue rushing of water shielding schools of swimming fish and banked by high trees: pine, cedar, ash, birch and willow, yes! He could see it clearly. It could work. It was a good plan.

The walls of the ravine were streaked with orange strata, frosts cracks in which delicate, white crystals puffed like foam. Five bends further on he detected traces of moisture in the sands beneath him. So it *was* a stream bed. He was glad. It helped him support the illusion of his imaginary persona. There, in the bed of a stream, water could stimulate memories of life. If he had been caught drifting over the oceans, it would have been different; there the water elicited no memory but death. But here it helped. His speed through the winding gully increased, and for a moment he felt a flicker of an ancient exaltation. But then he felt the drag of the Mad Train upon him, felt it suck at him like a vacuum sucking air, and hope left him. He was caught. Trapped. He had not been quick enough.

Still he dragged himself along, clinging to the damp ravine bottom. He could feel bits of himself being scraped away, as if thin layers of his consciousness were being peeled back and removed, memories he could not spare his concentration to retain, elements of his identity he had not the strength to hold onto. What was the use? If he escaped he would be less. So much less. Would it be worth it? Would he even have enough consciousness left to recognize he existed? Then it came to him: it might be better if he did not. It might be perfect. Escaping with his being intact but his consciousness and identity stripped away would be the condition nearest freedom from suffering he could ever hope to attain. He could drift through eternity, then, ignorant of his plight. But even as he formed the idea it was stripped from him and he had to let it go. He was almost lost, his ability to resist nearly spent.

He would have let go and been devoured but for a presence he sensed just as he was about to give up. For an instant it stunned him, thoroughly distracting him from the hideous force bearing down. Then alert again to his peril, he clutched madly towards the thing that had saved him. Something alive! A miracle! Merely detection of it quadrupled his strength. Something alive! His energy so increased he even managed to retrieve bits of himself not yet sucked beyond reach. He moved faster and faster towards the live thing, practically zooming around the bends of the deepening ravine. He was a river, rushing forward to feed the new life.

As he sped towards its source, he bathed in the strengthening aura of the life force. There was hope on the Earth again. There was a present that heralded a future. There was life!

Finally, where the ravine, grown deep and wide enough to contain a true river within its banks, entered the lowest foothills, the source of the living energy he had sensed came into view. A little plant huddled in the lee of a great stone. It was a little dandelion, reaching forth its first blooms. Elated, he dove into the plant, absorbing its life, bathing in its delicious energy. He crammed himself into the tiny weed, straining to compact his essence, to jam his being into the little leaves. He grew roots, sprouted a young flower for a face. He was no longer a river, he was a dandelion. A living being! He had survived the centuries of the reign of death!

Then the Mad Train caught up with him, and wrenched at him so powerfully that he did not know if he could withstand its draw even shielded by the life force of the plant. The mangled souls wailed and shrieked at him. There were thousands of them; in their close-ness he experienced a greater terror than he had ever known. Recognizing his bounded sense of being, they called to him, hungry; they begged him to save them, not with words but emotional barrage. They would unite in a final bond of love and be liberated. He knew the offering was a lie, had withstood the lie before, but never at such close range. He concentrated on their pain: they were lost within each other, helpless to pull apart. It was obvious and clear. There was no salvation amid their turmoil. But even from the most plainly deceitful, loathsome hoard, the call to unite was seductive. It had always been so. And the Train was by nature alluring. He clung fiercely to the dandelion with every measure of his will. The Mad Train raked at him, as if with long claws, in a final, clutching attempt to claim him, and even shielded within the aura of the life force he felt wounded. Then it was past, plung-ing up into the high reaches of the mountains, expelling its foul spirit breath so loudly over the land that it almost altered the currents of wind it passed through, that it almost, itself, stirred dust.

The struggle left him drained, exhausted beyond any prior experience. He released his hold on the plant and felt its leaves fall from him. Immediately, he knew that it should not be so. He nuzzled the wilting leaves of the dandelion, probed its collapsing roots, and found every spark of life extinguished. It was dead. He had killed it.

The recognition thoroughly dispelled the sense of elation that had swelled so vigorous within him, and dropped him deep into the despair to which he had long ago become grimly accustomed. He did not tor-ment himself over the loss. Time, he knew, would punish him more thoroughly than he could ever hope to punish himself. Briefly, a thought dimly rekindled his hopes—

possibly there might be other plants about, or even other types of organisms protected by some local phenomenon; he might search them out and do what he could to defend the thin hope they inspired. But he rejected the idea, knowing with a final and absolute certainty that there had only been the one. Searching for others would be repeating a process of self-torture to which he had already submitted for hundreds of years. The planet had embraced death, and was content. Even if he found something, a microbe, a tenacious bit of fungus, or even something as grand as another plant, he knew he was powerless to do anything more than linger in its presence until death subdued it. So he let his concentration collapse, and set about reconstructing the colorless, cyclical considerations with which he had learned to occupy his attention, so that he could remain as detached as possible from the passage of time, and attentive to the land only to the minimal degree necessary to remain close to it. Soon his long-practiced sense of detachment began, by gradual degrees, to return to him, and he began again to drift, moved not by wind or will but because it required less concentration to drift than to remain still.

In the middle of that night she found him. The winds had died away and the air was quiet. A three-quarter moon illuminated the vast plain in pale light. She could read the guilt in him. The fading aura of plant life lingered about him. She moved into his path to block his way, while he remained oblivious of her presence, deep in trance.

"What have you done?"

He felt the question's intrusive fire burn into him, and brought himself to attention. He became aware of her, and recoiled. She pursued him.

"What have you done?"

He knew why she was confronting him. Her essence was rich with the aura of the plant. After merging with it he knew he must, himself, reek of green life, so it did not surprise him that she had found him so quickly.

"The live thing?"

"What have you done?"

"Saved myself."

"You saved nothing!" she shrieked at him, advancing dangerously close. He was repelled back from her, without thought.

"I know," he admitted. He understood her grief, and the rage she was powerless to vent against him. She began to circle about him, slow and menacing, but he was not afraid of her. She could exact no punishment against him without equally endangering herself.

"You followed it long?"

Again she pressed perilously close to him. "Ages! Centuries!" Her responses were fired like projectiles. She was taunting him, daring him to question further. He asked nothing more, backing away again until a comfortable space spread between them. This time she kept her distance and they remained there, fixed in relation to each other until morning shed its grey light upon the silent land.

Gradually she became calmer, and her anger gave way to a larger remorse. The shift nevertheless made him wary, and frightened him. At close quarters instability was dangerous.

"In a glacier, I found it." Her words surprised him. She was going to explain? Why? He understood what she felt. To describe it was pointless and painful. But it could prove disastrous to try to escape. She was no aimlessly lunging Train of Souls. She was a bounded, self-directed being, who could follow and might well catch him, and then horror would have its way. He steadied himself. Very well, if she wanted so badly to expose her grief to him, he would indulge her. The plant had died because of him, and it had been a monstrous loss. He would listen. Perceiving that she had his attention, she continued.

"A great wind must have carried it high, and time buried it deep in the ice. I stayed with the glacier, followed it, its hateful slow movements. It carved a valley. Do you know this torture? I waited forever. The glacier broke, melted; the seed washed free. But even then it did not open. For years it remained wedged in a crack in a great wall of stone. I knew it must have been infertile. Still I sensed life in it. Then a storm washed it down from the rocks and it opened!" Her words, again, became imbued with a venomous tone. "It had waited as if it knew a moment would come for it! It lived! And you murdered it! It lived! The hope! You killed the hope I protected!" Her anger was fully regenerated, and again she lashed dangerously close to him. It was a hideous lie. He had listened enough, hurt enough. He wanted to return to the dull suffering he had learned to endure. And she had to be stopped before she risked too much. So he spoke the truth.

"You did nothing."

She recoiled from him, wounded, the strength of her anger stripped away.

"It would not have been enough. Even if it had lived. We are nothing. It is too late. We were something once and now are not. It serves nothing to punish ourselves with what could have been. We are less than dust. Even the air does not acknowledge our presence. It is over. Time punishes us enough. You cannot make it more. You did nothing. You are nothing."

She was rigid with suffering. "I know," she murmured.

He understood her. He had dedicated himself to the way of a sentinel for time so long he lost the measure of it. Many ghosts had done so, after the last mutated life forms had gagged in the foul poisons of the seas. Some had followed spores around the globe, others, like her, monitored seeds trapped in ice for millennia. Nothing grew, or if it started to, did not survive. In the end he had recognized the futility of such vigilance, that one could either torture oneself with the futility of their tragic fall or accept it. The dandelion had been a cruel joke. It had saved him the endless horrors of space in the clutches of the Mad Train but it was best to let it go, to push it from thought, eliminate it from consideration. It only held more grief for them, and their grief was already eternal.

"We could have been more."

He was shocked and revolted. "You still dwell on this?"

"We could have been more!"

He would not consider it again. He knew where the considerations led. It was painful self-abuse. More, it was dangerous. "We could have evolved!"

He drew away from her, preparing for flight. He thought he could escape her. The strength of the plant had not yet completely left him. Perhaps he could not run, but he could still move. Maybe he could still flow like a river. She might not know that trick, might never have thought of it.

"Wait!" she called out to stop him. He hesitated, uncertain whether to try to reason with her. "How can you stand it? It will never end. Do you know it? It goes on and on and will not let me choose that I cannot endure! I died a hundred and fifty years before the end, saw my future swept away, powerless to resist. Do you know this pain? I had hope in that little plant. Stupid hope. Vain hope. But it sustained me and I have nothing to replace it with, and I do not think I can rebuild the hope, and yet must go on!"

For a long time he did not respond. He did not want to hurt her more, or be any longer in the presence of a pain not his own. But she compelled him. "Then let it go," he said finally, and she sank away as from fire. "You will suffer less without it. You will drive yourself mad trying to keep it because anything it promises is beyond you."

It wounded him to destroy her so, even though he knew he attacked her most dangerous delusions. And he knew he should not let it pain him, not on her account or any other because his account was already full. It was the death she spoke of, her death before the end, which he found so compelling. Ghosts of the pre-apocalypse had known that humanity's spirit could not evolve without the endurance of physical being. They had known the dead had no future without the living. Near the end, many had even tried to warn the living, to send them messages in their dreams. But too few messages were received, fewer heeded. Then all, too late, knew the truth, and even he, who had done his best to ignore his dreams was powerless to wake up.

"We could have been more!"

It was the torment ghosts were never free from. But no. He reconstructed his defenses. In the moment the ancient sense of guilt snared him, she had advanced on him again. She would not get another chance like that. She would not draw on his guilt, nor elicit from him a desire to comfort her. Those who craved company were eaten by the Trains. Only the solitary spirits remained free from that horror. And anyway it was all the same. It did not matter when one had died. Now they were all the same. It was too late to be special, or unique, too late to reclaim an individual's infinite depth, to explore and know it apart. All this he had observed and reasoned through long ago, shortly after the end, when the divine emanations extended to humankind had been withdrawn, and the best had been doomed along with the worst, and the majority of spirits from all ages had come together in insane convulsions and mushroomed into the void. It made no difference. All were fallen. Those who remained separate on the earth retained the best that was left. All would suffer eternally. All were equal.

"We have nothing for each other. If you pursue me you destroy us both." He resumed his slow retreat from her.

"We are already destroyed!"

"We are lost. But we can suffer more than we do."

"How suffer more? To scream plunging through the hell of space, looking for our lost selves? That is worse? Worse than this nothing? This eternal haunting?"

"Yes, worse."

"How!"

He had to move carefully. She stayed right with him wherever he shifted. They could not touch.

"Worse because one never sleeps, because one is never free of grasping after one's lost self that is ever further and ever less. And one is never free of knowing that one is ever less."

"How do you know? How can you . . . ?"

"I know!" Now he was angry in return and held his ground. "I know, and so do you! No one has escaped confrontation with the mass-mutilations of the Trains! I am doomed! Not stupid! Not blind! I can read the scars of their tracks straight through you!"

Once more she retreated, this time into an abject depression and remorse that pulled on his sense of pity like a magnet, so strongly that he was nearly overcome.

And he thought of his own needs, to comfort, to connect, to hold. No! It was too late for that. Too late to come together and grow because there had been too much coming together, herding and corralling, hiding and denying. And now there was nothing to grow into, nothing to do but continue or become less. And she knew this. But it had been too long. She had waited for life but it had been too long. And he drew a little nearer, with no offer of comfort or embrace, confronting her with responsibility. But she had spent too long hoping the world would bring forth some hint of a new evolution of life, too long waiting to bask in the glow of embracing beings. And he was here with this painful joke, this truth, *the* truth: that the most a spirit could do to ease the pain of eternity was to take responsibility for the self, after there was nothing left to be responsible for, and submit to a solitary existence. But she needed and there was nothing that could fill her need. He could not fill it. But he was there, and she could feel his resistance. She knew he could not fill her but she needed. And she could feel his resistance, could feel him telling her to let go, not to hurt herself more, that there was nothing to be gained, no hope, no hope. But she needed, and he was there, drawing closer and closer, imploring her not to hurt herself more, that it was useless, closer, and she knew he was right, closer.

"I don't care!" she was upon him. He had not expected it, tried to gather himself together, to pull away from her but it was too late. She was through him like a million knives, severing the lines of concentration that held together his separate being. Her cry of vengeance echoed through him. "I don't care!"

"But you must, you must." And beneath her cry, within him now, he heard the deeper plea, "I need . . ."

Yes, but it was hundreds of years too late for that. "You must care. You must." Then she recognized the severity of her mistake and tried to withdraw but could not find her way. She gathered herself together with clumps of him, straining away with portions of her, pulled together with part of their struggle to pull apart.

For a moment they froze, terrified. Then as one they panicked and flailed through each other, clutching after pieces of themselves; were reduced to fragments clutching after ever smaller pieces, and with every raking move severed more of the connections that kept them separate.

And they began to spin. They began to roll across the plain, their effort to gravitate apart blending them together ever more thoroughly, creating a stir within their merged field of being that moved them over the land faster and faster. Soon their communication was reduced to a single impassioned plea for release, and then to a long, moaning, tormented denial.

They raced over the land, a whirlwind disturbing no grain of dust. They passed over sand dunes and vast hilly ranges, along shorelines thick with brilliant blue crystals, through red and gold canyons and wind-sculpted fields of stone. For a time the dead sea was a blur beneath them, reflecting rainbow colors from its iridescent surface. Wherever they went, solitary ghosts fled from their path, and with a hungry instinct they pursued, but their pursuits were like drunken lunges, wild, poorly aimed shifts of direction, and for a long time they gathered no prey, no others to companion their misery.

Then, in an ancient, petrified forest they claimed their first victim, one who had died old and had for millennia been trying to merge with the broken stone trunk of a fossilized tree. They felt his separate, bounded being like a craving too lost between them to identify, and they scraped his thin, dull consciousness from the rocks just as he was aware of their presence. His identity was churned up with theirs before he felt the first responsive tremor of fear. It was not long, then, until there were others, and their speed and power to feed increased. Their hatred of themselves grew ever more, and their sense of themselves ever less. And as their mass increased, their hunger expanded, and they gained the power to draw ghosts into their roiling midst from greater and greater distances.

And when they had become a giant, and feared by the diminishing numbers of solitary ghosts as a mad machine, a derailed Train of lost souls, an invisible, raging loco-motive, one day they could hold no longer to the land. The earth was indifferent to them. They released their voiceless shriek as one, pleading to the globe that had long ago given them birth to grab hold of them and keep them before they churned, plunging into space. But the earth did not hold onto them. It was indifferent to their plea, no less magnificent or beautiful for having shed its mantle of life. It did not miss them, would not call them back.

The Butcher of Gad Street

WITH THE TOLLING of the bells riot police poured into the ghetto. The Chinese bakery was in flames across the street and down the block so was the laundromat. Looters pushed in and out of the liquor store on the corner. The noise was a madness, with the old cathedral's bells crowning the din.

From the landing in front of his shop, Acrid the butcher, the six-foot-nine giant of Gad Street, watched the chaos unfold. People he had known since childhood jostled and howled, transformed into caricatures of themselves. Acrid gripped the rail at the edge of the landing and clenched the handle of his cleaver. This was Maul's doing. For weeks the butcher had sensed a dire conjuration at work somewhere under the city but hadn't been able to pinpoint it. He was glad his wife was not alive to see this. Tomorrow, the denizens of the neighborhood would tell themselves it happened because a boy none of them knew had been killed by a policeman. The truth would sour in their bellies. The demon's art would leave them scarred in ways that they would never understand.

Twin stairs flanked the landing, making Acrid an easy target. He would have been surprised if anyone tried anything. People praised him for his soft-spoken manners and the quality of his meats, in private traded rumors about him in hushed voices. Children gave him names like Grinder and Red Boots and fled when he drew near.

The police had formed a shield wall and were pressing down the street. Rioters jeered and hurled bottles and garbage at them. A big cop in full riot gear approached, saw the butcher and chose another route.

Acrid spotted his daughter in the crowd and his revulsion turned to shock. Even under his protection the demon's spell had reached her.

"All right, that's enough!" he bellowed. Those nearby were startled, civilians and police alike. But the mob was too great and determined to be mastered by voice.

The bells rang without pattern, the number of the hour long exceeded. Had the priests gone mad, too? To either side of the cathedral, other buildings burned. Acrid caught sight of a figure, high on the east tower, hanging by an arm from one of the gallery columns.

"Maul," Acrid growled.

The demon was not even cloaking himself. His broken, twisted horns glinted in firelight; his tail whipped in glee. He was laughing at them.

A clawed shadow stretched down the tower and across the faces of the old brownstone tenements lining the street. It snaked in and out of windows, arched high above Acrid's shop and swooped into the crowd. Before the butcher understood what was happening, the shadow closed on his daughter.

"Aria!" he cried. Three young thugs, Maul's unwitting minions, seized her and pulled her to the nearest alleyway.

Acrid plunged into the rioters. Both the hysterical and the enraged parted in fright before him; those too crazed to react he flung aside or batted with the flat of his cleaver. By the time he made it to the alley, the thugs had dragged Aria to the next street. "Let her go or I'll split your skulls!" he yelled after them. They disappeared around the far corner.

Timid souls and some who still had their wits about them clung to the alley, trapped by the violence, unsure which way to go. They shrank against the walls as the giant stormed past.

Palimpsest Street was quieter than Gad. Loose-knit groups of youths dashed about, shouting, breaking windows, tagging walls with spray paint. Loners and couples scurried in search of safety. Cars were on fire.

Here in the old part of the city the grid of streets was irregular. Aria's abductors had made it to the next alley, a block distant diagonally. Even encumbered by his daughter they were faster than Acrid. But they lacked his stamina.

The alley entrance was next to the defunct Rialto Theater, now an evangelical meeting hall. The message on the darkened marquee read, GODS GOT MAD SKILLS. Window light glistened on old cobbles in the alley. Far down, Aria struggled with her captors. Anguish strangled outrage in Acrid's throat when one of them slugged her. She went limp, and the thug threw her over his shoulder. The others pulled down crates and trash cans to impede the butcher's advance.

The clangor of the bells faded in the distance. The chase zigzagged toward the center of the city, the hoods keeping to alleys where they could. Acrid realized that Maul was guiding them, feeding them false power, pushing them beyond their limits.

They passed into the domain of skyscrapers, where traffic was heavy and sidewalks were crowded. People seemed unaware of the violence unfolding elsewhere, spreading towards them. The butcher stuck his cleaver in his back pocket and pulled his shirt out to conceal it.

Passersby gaped at the three men carrying an unconscious woman and the giant who pursued them. Two big fellows challenged Aria's abductors, and one of the hoods pulled a gun. A beat cop across the street saw it and made a call on his radio. He saw Acrid too. The hoods ducked into another alley.

The one with the gun pointed it back at Acrid. He ducked behind a parked panel truck, heard a shot. Someone behind him cried out. He peered around the truck. Maul had joined the thugs—cloaked, now, costumed in a wide-brimmed hat and greatcoat, his horns and tail invisible to common sight. He threw his hand up. Scraps of paper burst into the air and fluttered down. The hoods scrambled to collect them. Money.

They collapsed, then, like their plugs had been pulled. With one hand, Maul lifted a manhole cover and pitched it aside. He snatched up Aria, lightly, as if she were a pillow, sneered at Acrid and dropped into the hole.

Acrid screamed and rushed forward.

The manhole was a well of darkness; he could see nothing. He looked around frantically and roared in frustration. He needed light! He grabbed the hoodlum who had hit Aria and lifted him against a wall. The boy hung limp and drained in his hand, unable even to show fear. The demon's power had left him. Acrid dropped him, resisted the urge to kill him. The young fool's exhaustion was so profound that he would probably die anyway.

Onlookers had gathered at both ends of the alley. At the north end, the cop who had made the call was in the lead. He had his hand on his gun, but the gun was holstered. Acrid went toward him and the cop raised his free hand in warning.

"I need your flashlight. My daughter's been taken and I'm going after her." He held the policeman's gaze and let the man see his inner nature. The series of reactions was familiar, phases of fear and confusion that culminated in awe.

"What *are* you?" the cop asked. He gave Acrid his flashlight.

Acrid checked it. "A man, like any other."

The cop shook his head. "Man, maybe. Not like others——"

"No one should follow me," Acrid told him.

The flashlight showed a passage about thirty feet down. He had to hold his arms over his head to fit through the hole. He climbed down the access ladder. The passage extended indefinitely in both directions, ranks of pipes and conduits lining the walls. The air smelled of rust, steam and rot. Acrid listened. The reverberations of subway trains and overhead traffic obscured subtler sounds. He couldn't see footprints. To the left there was a sense of absence, like the void where someone has died. Acrid took a few steps that way and noticed something more— among the odors of metal, concrete and decay, a faint floral scent that was familiar. His daughter's shampoo. He inhaled sharply and ran again. Her scent grew stronger, as did the taint of the demon's shadow. He tracked them down a long staircase, through a door that opened onto a subway platform where people were alarmed and confused. Acrid grabbed a man in a business suit.

"Which way did they go?" Acrid shook him.

"That—that way!" The man pointed down the tunnel.

Acrid jumped off the platform and ran along the tracks. He sensed demon craft somewhere ahead. He had no time for clearing spells. He heard an echo of wild laughter and shouted Maul's name. The laughter died.

The rules had changed. Maul could not flit about through veil cracks burdened by a live human body. He was on foot, the same as Acrid. The butcher now recognized the demon's strategy. Their ordeal would begin in earnest, with Maul fresh and Acrid worn.

Acrid pursued them down other tunnels, maintenance passageways, flights of stairs. He had to break through a couple of locked doors. Eventually he found himself in a vast tunnel where several rail lines ran parallel across a broad distance, separated by rows of iron columns. The odors of decay were less but those of staleness and machinery greater. Aria's scent had been dispersed by passing trains.

The light was dim, from uncertain sources. Acrid smelled sweat and human waste. Something moved on the far side of the lines. He waited for a train to pass and went over, found about fifty people living in boxes and makeshift tents. The tunnel dwellers were agitated and wary. The spell Acrid had sensed earlier itched at him from somewhere close. He asked if anyone had seen a man carrying a young woman. No one answered. They were afraid of him.

A young boy pointed to the left.

Acrid started that way but stopped. Demon craft throbbed from a big pipe that crossed above the tracks. It was a killing spell and bore Maul's signature. Something was wrong with a flange that joined two of the pipe segments. Acrid's foot kicked a bolt. He saw others scattered about and shined the flashlight up again. The bolts had been removed.

A shudder reverberated through the ceiling as a train passed on a higher level. Acrid played his light along the length of the disjoined pipe. The stirrups supporting it had all been loosened; hardly anything was holding it up. The end of the unsupported segment slipped several inches.

Acrid heard a train approach. The tunnel dwellers were watching him. The pipe dropped lower. There was no time to clear the spell. He set his cleaver and the flashlight on the ground, climbed a vertical I-beam near the disconnected joint and positioned his shoulder under the pipe. The weight, when it came loose, forced him down the beam. Acrid braced his feet and stopped his slide, roared from the strain. The train passed under the pipe, inches from his ass, and another one came from the other direction. It felt like his shoulder would burst.

The second train passed and Acrid threw himself away from the beam. The loose end of the pipe swung to the ground with a hollow boom.

Acrid twisted where he lay, bit down against the pain and got up. He could barely move his left arm. The flange had caught him as it fell and opened a gash in his chest. He fingered the wound gingerly. It penetrated muscle. The pipe now hung diagonally across the tracks.

"The next train will derail," he told the tunnel dwellers. "You have to get out of here." The boy was maybe ten years old, filthy head to foot. "Lead them out," Acrid told him, pointing across the tracks at the door he'd come through. "Keep going until you see the sky."

The boy took off and the others followed.

Acrid found a call box mounted on a column between the lines. It was locked; he broke it open. There was no keypad. He lifted the receiver and heard auto-dialing. A woman answered and he reported the fallen pipe.

"A pipe?" she asked, incredulous.

"A big one, about three feet wide and fifty long. Train hits it, picture the end of the world."

He dropped the phone and glared down the tunnel. "You *should* be afraid, demon." He removed his shirt, tore off a piece and packed it in the gash on his chest, tied the shirt around his torso to hold the bandage in place. Using his left arm made him growl—the shoulder felt like an aching wad of dough.

He found the cleaver where he'd left it, but the flashlight lay crushed under the end of the fallen pipe. Acrid touched the place where he had braced the pipe with his shoulder, detected curse work crafted to blind him.

Maul's powers increased terribly where no light reached. Acrid had met their full force only once and had no desire to revisit the experience. There was still light here, faint as it was. The advantage was not yet won.

His legs ached, now, as he ran, and his breath came heavier. He forced himself to work his strained arm. He came upon a stopped train. The operator and passengers stared as he ran by. Farther on there was a station, with platforms in the middle and on both sides of the tracks. Acrid ran past a startled audience. *That's right, get a good look.* Chatter on the platforms swelled, drowned an announcement made over the PA. Several people photographed Acrid with their cell phones.

He left the station behind, wondered if Maul had been photographed. It would be unlike the demon to expose himself so. Maybe his plan was big enough, this time, that he didn't care. Acrid began to worry that he was going the wrong way. He might have missed a passage or a hiding place. Maybe Maul had doubled back.

Acrid made out two bodies on the tracks ahead. Transit cops. One was dead, eviscerated, the wound prematurely necrotic. Acrid had never known Maul to commit murder. Other demons killed, sometimes, if they went mad, or felt threatened. But Maul always pursued his ends by proxy, setting traps, pitting people against each other. These men hadn't been a danger to him. This was a message: Endgame.

The surviving cop mumbled incoherently. Acrid dragged him and his dead partner off the tracks. Both of their flashlights were broken. Acrid made the survivor as comfortable as he could and ran on.

Past a long bend, he entered the full darkness that he dreaded. His fears and doubts wrapped around him, lent magnitude by Maul's influence. Acrid's breathing was too labored for him to chant and run at the same time. He would have to endure the assault unmitigated. It was not as severe as he had expected, which was a dubious boon, leaving open when a harder blow might fall.

The thing Acrid struggled with most, in the depths of his soul, was loneliness. He knew there were others like him in the world. He had never met any of them but he sensed that they were there, and sometimes he dreamed about them. None of them traveled; they all stayed where they were. They had to, and Acrid was pretty certain they didn't understand their circumstances any better than he did his.

The cop in the alley, all the others he had permitted, over the years, to see his inner self, they'd had the same question in their eyes, every one. Acrid knew what they wanted to know. They wanted to know if he had been created by God. He couldn't tell them because he didn't know. His own opinion was that people had made him. Out of unconscious need, maybe, through some inchoate exertion of collective will. If there was a greater mind behind his existence, he wanted, some day, to have words with it. If that mind had a plan, he wasn't impressed. There were too many times when too much was required of him, too many days when he was more alone than he should have been. Just one person to stand with him, one other, who could see the demons and recognize their works—that would have been enough. But even his wife, who never needed to understand the things about Acrid that made him different, had been taken from him with the birth of their daughter.

Light from a distant source filtered into the tunnel,

and Acrid's thoughts became less burdensome. Fatigue, on the other hand, took deeper hold. If he had to keep going like this he might come to favor the distractions of Maul's psychic attacks.

He ran on through the night, past other platforms, through other darknesses and halls of dim light. Trains went by with diminishing frequency. People were fewer on the platforms, as the hours wore on, until there were none at all. At some stations, Acrid saw things that made him wonder what was happening in the city above. Trash cans were on fire at one, and the walls of another were smeared with blood.

His toils through total darkness were plagued by escalating mental torment. The demon's assault was not weak but measured, bound to an objective and layered with elusive intrigues. It seemed no logic existed to answer Acrid's fears. He questioned as never before the role he had accepted in life. There was never time to do anything well, no real chance to make things better. He chased off demons and countered their curses and spells, but the vestiges of their works lingered everywhere, and their cumulative influence grew. One day his efforts would be irrelevant.

The irony was that it was Maul and his kind who had made Acrid aware of his nature. Always there had been Maul, most powerful of the demons, most cynical and rotten with malice. That was the second most painful memory, recognizing Maul for what he was—not another adolescent boy like himself, who by some miracle understood and accepted the differences in Acrid. Maul had been no more young than human. He was thousands, maybe millions of years old. His only interest in Acrid had been to pervert him. When he saw that he had failed, he quit the illusion of friendship with swift finality—eons of storm and eruption, savagery beyond measure, unmasked in a single scornful leer.

A being so old must possess knowledge and wisdom beyond measure. Maybe Acrid was at war with forces to which he ought to submit. The thought ate at his mind. Even his love for his daughter seemed too trivial to counter it, too selfish. Beyond love was the sprawl of nature and time, a darkness that swallowed suns. What right had he, what power, to resist that?

Faint light again drove potency from enervating reflections. But the cursed darkness had penetrated, and insinuated an unclean will among Acrid's pains, a doubt like poison in his muscles and skin. He reached an intersection. Concrete barricades spanned the entrances of a cross tunnel. He climbed over the right hand barrier and ran toward the light, not because he was sure of the direction, but because he needed to. When, for the first time in hours, he detected Aria's scent, he stopped and let relief wash through him. Never had he been stretched so near to his limits. He was dehydrated and pouring with sweat. His legs trembled and it hurt to breathe. Sharp pains shot from his strained shoulder down through his arm and spine. The wound on his chest throbbed like fire. But knowing his daughter was ahead of him gave him strength. Maul would be hurting too.

Echoing machine noise resolved into the drone of a generator. At a fork in the tunnel, where scaffolding and floodlights had been erected, Acrid encountered a grisly scene. Some unmanned tool or electrical fault showered sparks from high in the scaffolding. Several workmen lay strewn about dead like broken toys. One of them was nearly as big as Acrid. His arm had been torn from his shoulder, the hand still gripping a pipe wrench.

Acrid dropped to his knees, heaving for breath. What

purpose did these deaths serve? To taunt him and feed his doubt? Men like these had built this city. Maul wanted him to feel responsible.

He never knew the rules; there was never anyone to tell him the rules. Maul knew the rules. All Acrid had to go on was instinct and intuition. He wondered if the others of his kind, around the world, were experiencing similar trials this night.

The big man's hard hat was fitted with a miner's light. Acrid took the hat, ripped out the bumper straps and forced it onto his head. He found a bottle of water by the generator and drained it.

The demon's taint was strong here. There was no question which way he'd gone.

About a half mile down the left tunnel Acrid came upon a mound of rocks, earth and gravel. The darkness seemed to thicken as he moved toward it. The air was filthy with curses. He began chanting.

The countering sounds sent vibrations through his body that intensified his pains. He did not know how the sounds worked, or if they had meaning. They were fashioned from will and instinct deep within him. The heaviness lifted an increment from the darkness, but these curses weakened too slowly. They were clustered around a central component to obscure its purpose. Many demons had labored here.

Acrid climbed the mound and leaned on his knees. His body felt like a burden. On the other side there was a hole in the floor of the tunnel. A crude shaft burrowed down at a steep angle.

He started down the demon tunnel, fell, slipped, rolled, found his footing, went down and down. There was nothing to do but meet Maul on his own terms. All Acrid cared about was saving Aria.

The demon tunnel twisted into the earth. Something red glistened in the composite matrix of the walls. In places it had the character of veins. As he made his way deeper, the walls became solid stone, smeared with a red, gelatinous substance.

The grade steepened. Acrid slipped and slid down and down and down, unable to arrest his descent. The walls were too smooth and slick, the passage too broad for him to wedge himself sideways. Hundreds, thousands of feet he slid, faster and faster. He saw that the tunnel was plugged below by a white and red mass, twisted about frantically trying to slow himself. He raised his hands to shield his face, burst through a fleshy membrane into a vast, cavernous chamber, landed roughly and tumbled to the cavern floor. He lay still, aching and disoriented, startled to be alive.

His hard hat had come off and landed a few yards away. Acrid crawled to it, rolled on his back and shined the light around. The cavity was maybe a hundred feet high. Everywhere the light touched, surfaces glistened red. Ranks of strange red lines spanned irregular cavities in the cave walls.

Acrid dragged himself to his feet. He spotted the opening he had fallen through, high atop a steep slope. Maul and Aria were nowhere in sight. He searched the perimeter of the cave but found no other way out of the place.

A grinding noise drew his attention upward. The opening he'd fallen through closed like a rocky sphincter. Acrid blinked, not understanding. Then everything that had happened that night made sense. He fell apart, laughed until he wept. Aria was lost; there was nothing left to fight for.

He stumbled sideways against the cavern wall, touched something fleshy and recoiled. The sensation brought him back to himself. He'd touched a group of red cords stretched taut across a depression in the wall. They appeared to grow out of the stone at both ends. They looked like animal veins but thicker, more like umbilical cords. What had he felt? Something bright and confused—

People.

It was a link with humanity that he'd felt. He peered at the cords, seized two groups in his hands and again felt the people in the city above. Their hopes, fears, desires, regrets, pains, frustrations. Glimmers of mercy—someone pulled to safety, a sheltering embrace. Everyone was suffering and terrified. Their lives were coming apart, and they were angry. Enraged. Hateful. Blaming each other. Acrid released the cords and staggered back.

He was on the other side of the veil. He had penetrated the demon reality. The cords connected humanity to the earth, to the natural world.

Acrid had searched for this place a long time. This was where the demons played on the minds and emotions of humans, prodded them to distrust each other, kept them at odds. Here they stroked and plucked humanity's heart strings, broadcast their sordid spells and composed the music of apocalypse.

And there was nothing Acrid could do about it. This was why he had been brought here, not just to die, but to perish in despair. Maul knew the rules. He needed Acrid to see that his whole life had been an exercise in futility.

Acrid picked up his cleaver and looked at his reflection in the blade. His face was slick and blackened with grime, his eyes so hard and wild that he didn't recognize himself. He thought about all the tragedy he had witnessed, the murdered workmen, the homeless boy, his rioting neighbors on Gad Street. He thought about the unspeakable things his daughter would experience before she died. He thought of his wife. Was this what it was to be bound to nature? To be forever at the mercy of invisible forces that struck people down and drove them to ruin?

Acrid sensed that he was being watched, not physically, but in his mind. He felt the others of his kind, around the world. Thousands of them, men and women. Most were trapped as he was, the rest beset by awful trials. They all seemed to be waiting for one of them to make a decision.

Acrid gazed around the cavern at the cords that linked humanity to the earth. A metaphysical principal had been perverted into an obscene harp. This was the end the demons had planned for him, to wither away bearing impotent witness to the defeat of the human will.

A defiant rage boiled up in the butcher. He strode to the nearest array of cords and slashed them with his cleaver. They sprang apart and sprayed forth a thick, red fluid. Acrid bared his teeth. So be it, let the earth bleed.

He went to the next array, and the next, slashing as he went. Cracks opened in the cavern floor and demons clawed out of the ground. They hadn't expected this. They hadn't thought he would do this. They mustered before him, hissing and sneering. They rushed at him, flinging curses en masse. Acrid discharged a countering sound the likes of which he had never voiced. He had not known such a noise dwelled in him. It was like his whole being became a mighty horn to blast his very soul at the demons. They were knocked down by the force of it. He unleashed the sound again and again, until the demons fled back into the earth. Maul had not been among them.

Acrid was beyond pain and fatigue. He cut the cords—climbed to cut them high and knelt to cut them low, left not one unsevered. When he was done, the cavern floor was waist-deep in the blood of the earth. He surveyed his work with gallows satisfaction. He knew that, around the world, the others of his kind had followed his example.

A shudder passed through the walls; rocks fell from the ceiling. The collapse started at the far end of the cavern and advanced toward him. *Better a swift death than a lingering one.* He heard cracking and crumbling behind him. A vortex formed in the wall there, stone disintegrating in its whorl. Acrid wasn't sure what was happening, but it seemed he might yet escape. He sloshed over and leapt into the vortex. Swirling rocks tore at him but he was born upward. He broke through another membrane and again crossed the veil. Up and up he went, both climbing and pushed through a maelstrom of churning stone. It was as if the earth rejected him, refusing even to hold his remains.

At last he felt air on his face and pulled himself free of the earth. He lay curled on the ground, gasping for breath. He was cut and bleeding all over, but he was alive. He got to his knees, wiped the grime and grit from his eyes. He was outside the city, in an open field of dry, wild grass. Ahead stretched a broad band of trees and scrub brush, brown and leafless in an autumnal state. In the distance, to his left, the freeway was paralyzed with traffic. Behind him, black plumes of smoke rose from the city.

He heard a twig snap. Maul stood about thirty feet away, with Aria on his shoulder. The shock in the demon's eyes gratified the butcher deeply.

Maul dropped Aria and ran. A bright, crooked line formed in the air in front of him. He was trying to escape through a veil crack.

Acrid lurched to his feet and roared, "*MAUL!*" The demon looked back in terror.

With all his rage, Acrid hurled his cleaver. It spun

through the air and sank deep into the demon's back. Maul shrieked and fell to the ground. The veil crack sputtered and closed.

Acrid limped to his daughter's side. She was caked head to foot with mud, so wilted and still Acrid feared the worst. He knelt beside her, picked the hair from her face and placed two fingers against her throat. He felt a pulse and sobbed.

Gently, Acrid rolled Aria onto her back, mounded dry grass under her head, and straightened her limbs. Then he went to treat with Maul.

The demon had crawled into the trees. He was pulling himself along with his right hand, groping for the handle of the cleaver with his left. He couldn't escape with the blade in him.

"Here, let me get that for you." Acrid pulled out the cleaver, with his right foot shoved Maul onto his back and planted himself astraddle of the demon.

Maul's fear changed to defiance. "Our kind once ruled this world," he rasped. "We will again."

Acrid shook his head. "It'll never happen." He brought the cleaver down in Maul's forehead, between his broken, twisted horns, and watched the life leave his eyes. He pulled the cleaver free. Maul's corpse transfigured, twisting and becoming wooden, until it looked like a segment of a big dead branch torn from a great tree.

Acrid put his cleaver in his back pocket, gathered his daughter in his arms, and headed back to the city. It was a long, weary walk, but Aria was a light burden, and the giant had his stamina again.

The city had been through its darkest night. On every street, cars were wrecked and burning. Even among the tallest buildings, smoke curled from high windows. The dead were everywhere.

But everywhere, too, were people helping each other, tending the injured. And there was a buoyancy about the city that had not been there before, almost as if it might lift from the planet and drift among the stars.

Acrid bore his daughter homeward. He grieved for Maul. He did not know if he'd done right or wrong.

Lighter Than Air

THE DAY THAT Lester Gill was diagnosed with terminal cancer, little Billy Dibbson was killed by an alligator. Lester found out about Billy as he was making his way down the narrow hall, leaving the doctor's office. He stopped to lean on his four-footed cane and breathe, and heard the nurse and the receptionist talking.

"They won't let his mother see him, he's tore up so bad."

"The sheriff's getting a posse together. They're gonna clean all them gators out along the levee."

"Should've done years ago——"

Lester crossed the waiting room without looking at the two women. He could feel them watching him. He fought through the door for the second time that day. He had avoided physicians for years, fearing what they might find. But it became clear that the pains in his bowels and lower back wouldn't be ignored, so he'd scheduled with the meat-packing plant to have himself weighed, and made an appointment to see the town doctor. Now he'd been told he had only months, maybe weeks, to live.

The light outside was blinding. The haze had burned off. It had been overcast when Lester set out that morning, and he had left his sunglasses at home. He was tempted to go back inside and call for a shuttle. But he had made the decision to walk to the doctor's office, and now felt a need to walk back. His apartment was a mere eight blocks away; but for Lester that was more like eight miles. Six hundred twenty-eight pounds, the scale had said. Workers sniggering, somewhere out of sight. Never mind, he would walk. He might never make this journey again.

His route took him in front of the hardware store and the grocery market. He knew people watched him through the windows; he didn't look. Children ran and pranced past him, adults and adolescents strolled, strode and sauntered by. No one tarried in his wake. The sun pursued its slow crawl through the sky. Lester lifted and planted his four-footed cane and advanced as he could, old Doc Weese's sad expression a stain on his mind.

Three blocks on he came to the elementary school. The children were gathered in the playground, where the sheriff was talking to them. The principal stood to the side, prim and solemn, her hands folded. The sheriff was talking about Billy Dibbson, warning the children to keep away from the levee. That's right, Lester thought, teach them to be afraid, make sure they go through life intimidated by everything. Clouds massed in the sky above the school. Crows cawed in the oak on the corner.

By the time Lester arrived home, searing pains stabbed his legs, back and groin, and his feet had gone numb. He struggled through the front door, crossed the cluttered living room to his unmade bed, sat down and groaned with relief. The bedside clock read 12:30. It had taken him an hour longer, coming than going. Well, he'd left with some hope and returned with none; likely that had dragged on him a bit. He looked about at the stacks of yellowing newspapers, the piles of unwashed clothes, the dishes in the kitchen sink, the dingy walls bare of ornament, and felt his life defined. Months, maybe weeks. He had accomplished nothing and now never would. He searched in himself for an aspiration that might be fulfilled in the time he had left and could not find one. He did not know how he could live with the loss, with the disappointment and regret that bore down on him. Better to end it, he thought, though he had no idea how he might go about that. The only thing clear to him was that he had suffered enough.

He was overcome by an ambition to forgive himself. The idea seemed at once inspired and absurd. How could forgiveness be measured as an accomplishment? Of what benefit would it be to anyone if he succeeded? The ambition grew in him, though, and took hold. If he were going to write himself off, why not first try the most radical option?

Yes, turn his habits upside down, use the behavior that had constricted his life to free him of his emotional burdens. He had immobilized himself with guilt, lassitude and despair. The reasons were legion, the hows and whys of his condition. None of which cancelled the impact his choices had made. Very well, if immobility had been his prison, in whatever measure erected by forces beyond his influence, he would by choice immobilize himself in the cause of freedom.

He imagined it might take a few hours to accomplish his objective. Food he could forego but he might become thirsty. He filled two plastic gallon jugs with water, inserted a sterile catheter into one to serve as a straw, lay down, and vowed not to move until he had forgiven himself for every sin and failure of which he believed himself guilty, until he had forgiven himself to his very core.

He discovered, in the banshee swirl of fears, memories and regrets fleeing death in his mind, that his task would not be straightforward. The tangle of guilt in him was inextricably bound to injuries. It seemed he would have to forgive the latter along with the former, and at this he balked. The history of abandonment and abuse he had suffered, the unfairness of his condition, was such a defining aspect of his reality that he could not imagine life or even death without it. If he did forgive everything, it would effect no real change in his circumstances. He would still be monstrously encumbered by his flesh, and he would still be dying. But he asked himself, of what benefit was it not to forgive? What asset, what value was preserved by harboring resentment about anything? He could think of none.

And so he commenced to forgive. He had not known his reservoir of gall ran so deep. It seemed he had much more to forgive in others than in himself. Every leer, every jest and snide aside, every assumption, every quick appraisal, every judgment and rejection—he forgave them as they filed through his thoughts. He wondered if he would survive the end of them, they went on so. He learned it was not enough merely to think of forgiving; he had to let forgiveness seep into his bones, until he knew that he meant it.

At times it seemed he could not go on, that he must move about, eat, take some respite from his labors. How he longed to watch TV! But death rose up each time to stop him. He could not evade his lies, how he had taken comfort looking back, drugged himself with languishing, amused and distracted himself with chewing and swallowing so much more than food. He had waited, until there was nothing left to wait for but the end. He continued the ugly work of seeing himself, of opening the mean and petty closets he had cloaked in indignation. The shadows of the louvered blinds climbed the walls. He lost track of time.

He forgave his father for abandoning his mother and him when he was little; he forgave his mother for folding into herself and letting television raise him. He forgave the bullies at school, forgave the blind, indifferent teachers. He forgave the church, the government, the impervious world. At the same time he forgave himself—the two processes were indistinguishable. He forgave his failures and cowardices. He forgave himself for never committing to a relationship with a woman, for never fulfilling a single ambition. He forgave himself for being of so little use to others. His mind entered a state unfamiliar to him, where vast regions of undefined space filled with rapturous fantasies and prospects for adventure. He tumbled through himself, a god, a world, a bird, a bone, the cosmos splashed with nebulae and voids, zeniths and blooms. And yet, the firmament remained insidious with doubt. Lester forgave God for not existing if He didn't, for the rude circumstances into which He had cast Lester if He did. Lester forgave himself for existing in the first place. And then, finally, he was able to see himself objectively, from outside of himself, appreciate his own knurled, isolate beauty and love who and what he had become.

It was some time before he realized that he had accomplished his goal. He came back to himself. Something about the room was different. Things were not at the right height. He looked down to his side and discovered that he was levitating three feet above his bed.

At any other time he would have been shocked. Given the far and wondrous journey he had just taken, it struck him as a relatively commonplace occurrence in the realm of perception, and he regarded the phenomenon with unwonted equanimity. He recognized the walls, the newspapers, the soiled clothes, the shunned details of his environment. Both of the gallon jugs were empty.

Conventional reality took hold, and he sank back onto the bed.

The day progressed thereafter by disconnected increments. He did not think much, and there were periods when he was elsewhere. He accepted the lightness in his spirit with marvel and gratitude, and did not analyze it. He bathed. He gathered his soiled bedclothes and put them in the dumpster behind the building. He fixed some eggs, ate slowly and with reverence.

Doc Weese attributed Lester's sudden weight loss to the advance of the cancer, when Lester went back to see him. Nothing had changed; he was still dying. And yet everything was different. Lester saw Weese recognize this, during a silence that lingered between them, and Lester loved the kindly old physician for letting silence have its say.

In the van, on the way to the doctor's office, Lester had found out what day it was, and learned that it had taken him five days to forgive himself. Now he stood again outside the office and took in a world which was familiar and unknown, people he knew and knew not going to and fro, in and out of the market, up and down the road. There was still time to do something, he realized. He was still alive. He had something to teach, now. But to whom could he teach it? He told the van driver that he would walk home.

Once again he set out, lighter than before, especially in mind and spirit. He arrived at the elementary school and stopped to watch the children at play in the school yard. The teacher supervising them was sitting in a folding chair, around the corner of the building from the playground, reading a paper. Lester entered the school yard and lay down near the jungle gym, gave his gaze to the limitless sky, felt the children gather around him in curiosity. He let go of worrying about how he looked, of understanding and needing to understand. He let go of what others thought of him or anything, he let go of expectations, he let go of science and religion, he even let go of belief. And his great body lifted from the ground.

Some of the children understood right away what he was showing them, that they never needed to swallow anything whole, that everything was possible. A girl lay down, and a moment later she was floating beside him, and soon others joined her. A couple of children who were frightened ran to get the teacher. One precocious lad rose before Lester upright, with his fists on his hips, his jaunty stance a challenge. Yes, an adventure was what they needed. Lester smiled.

He rose into the air, and the children who were not afraid went with him. A woman's voice called out below, stricken with shock and horror.

They flew above the town. On the western outskirt lay the cemetery, where Billy Dibbson was buried. Lester and the children circled and paid their respects. Billy's parents were at the grave side, and they looked up. Billy's mother brought her hand to her mouth and his father stared without comprehension.

Lester and the children flew above hills that were crowded with nameless trees. The sky was infinite blue, painted with vagrant clouds. The land rolled below like a fantasy of beginning the world. A hawk glided beside them for a time.

A few miles on they noticed that something had happened on the two-lane highway that led to the interstate, and they went down to investigate. A sink hole had opened in the road, and a flat bed truck had crashed down into it. The children laughed at the befuddled driver when he fled from them. The bed of the truck had been loaded with dead alligators. The straps had broken and the alligators were strewn about the roadside. Lester and the children circled the site. They all agreed that the alligators were very beautiful, and that it was a shame they'd been killed.

Lester knew he had to lead the children back. It was a responsibility he had accepted when he led them away. People were running along streets toward the school, a knot of cars parked in front. Lester and the children lit down in the school yard. Parents rushed forth to seize their sons and daughters. The sheriff and his deputies had their guns drawn. One young deputy, more frightened than the rest, trained a rifle on Lester. Lester looked the deputy straight in the eye and smiled. Then he took a bow and let go of the world altogether.

Bulbous Things

I MET THIS Russian guy doing the Virgo run who told
me about these reindeer herders on Earth who like to
get high on this hallucinogenic mushroom. The mushroom is poisonous. It won't kill you but it'll screw your
liver up bad enough to fog an X-Ray. So some herdsman
in the anus of Siberian history gets the idea to feed the
mushrooms to his reindeer, and drink their piss. Which
works pretty good, it turns out. The reindeer's metabolism leaches out the poison, and the piss still gets you high.
If you can wrap your head around a warm, foamy mug of
animal urine for a recreational beverage, come Saturday
night in old Siberia you're good to go.

I mention this because it'll be relevant later.

First day down, food didn't taste right. Nothing called
'rations' has ever been gourmet fare, but this was something else. I didn't want it, and that was off because I was
hungry. Do five hours in a G and a quarter, even with
the servos in your suit helping out, you will work up
an appetite. Somebody should have said something, and I
have to own the freight for that one.

We air-dropped in, onto a plateau that looked flat until
you were down where you had to walk on it. Excepting
the poles and oceans, the entire surface of GR14XO7 is
covered in biomass. Literally. We didn't see a square inch of
dirt or rock the whole way. Wasn't an issue for me but the
brains wanted to limit our impact. From the air the sur-

face environment over most of the planet looks like jungle. From the ground it's entirely other. More like a slaughter house, an endless mess of multicolored entrails dumped all over the place, mounded up here and there into something like trees, with inflated elephant ears for leaves. But there any similarity to plant life ends. The texture of everything down there is like hairless animal tissue.

No transport, for the same low-impact reason, so we were on foot. The brains didn't like walking on that stuff. They had this special footgear, like snow shoes, made of an ultra-light poly-alloy mesh. The idea was not to break the 'skin' of the biomass. Which worked well enough for them but they hadn't figured on three hundred sixty pounds times one-point-two-five of me, mostly muscle courtesy high-clearance military training, genetic engineering and advanced pharmacology. Snowshoes or no, I broke 'ground' with every step. Tracks leaked an orange ooze. Which the brains were quick to get samples of—shaking their heads, you know, making with the disapproving looks.

I like leaving a visible trail, if I don't have to hide where I've been. A hundred and twelve off-world missions, I've learned you can't count on technology to find your way home. You can't count on it for basically shit. Not that retracing our steps would have done us any good, in this case. But I liked crunching through that stuff. I've always enjoyed busting bulbous things. There's a visceral satisfaction to it, the way peas pop between your teeth. My mother was a military botanist. She collected succulents, kept them all over the house in pots and window boxes. I was always getting bitched at for squishing their leaves with my fingers. I got a charge out of it, you know what I mean. Same with caterpillars. There's a species of slug on Cantabile IV that makes a superior target, in my estimation—blows up in four colors. And of course there's nothing quite like putting an explosive round through a fellow Earthling's cranium. But my favorite is breasts. I derive great pleasure sinking my teeth into a firm, well-formed tit. I'll bite til it bleeds, if permitted. God love 'em, some women like that.

Anyway, my function was straightforward. This was a standard babysitting op. Scans of the planet had revealed no mobile life forms, so one of my type was deemed sufficient security for an expedition of our size. I wasn't happy about going in solo but, as you are aware, it was not my call. The brains numbered five. They'd worked together a long time, so their ways of referring to each other were set. As I met them they were Sweet, Clara, Dubček, Vox and Boner. Boner was the computer specialist and I don't know how he got his name. He was a fairly dignified guy and he seemed comfortable with it so I never asked. The rest were biologists of various stripes. Clara was the leader. Pretty little thing, dark hair, big eyes. Not my type—too much like a boy in the build department. She knew how to throw a command around, though. Vox, now, she filled out a bio suit the right way. The kind of breasts you want to eat. But I'm getting ahead of myself.

Sweet was as good as his name, soft-spoken, friendly fellow I liked right away. Dubček was all business. Small talk was lost on him, ditto humor. But he wasn't rude or unpleasant, just single-minded. All-in-all, an easy group to team out with.

Our objective was a 'waterfall,' so they called it, about thirty clicks southeast, where there was an anomalous formation. We headed out with me in the rear; they didn't want me mucking things up in front. That bloated, entrail-covered landscape is no party to negotiate. Harder for the brains because I just slogged through it. They all did a lot of 'TSF'—tripping, slipping and falling. It was slow going. The air is a little rich in nitrogen but it's free of microbes so you can breathe it. Nevertheless we wore bio-suits, so as not to introduce any of our little whats-its to the ecosystem. We breathed through filters and sweated like pigs, the suits' cooling systems notwithstanding. It was a bizarre place to trek through, without any insects or birds in the air, not so much as a gnat on the ground, and yet everything you looked at was alive. But I've seen a lot of weird places so I wasn't impressed. Vox stumbling ahead of me was all the view I needed.

Five hours got us to the rim of the plateau, with the brains stopping here and there to take readings and measurements, collect samples, make records. I, of course, could have gone on indefinitely. But the brains were pooped so we made camp.

Or they did. They didn't want me turning the campsite into an orange swamp. I took their point but felt kind of useless, the no-neck pack animal with nothing to do and no one to murder. They kidded me while they set up the tents. Like I said, a good team.

Wouldn't mind having one of those tents. Lightest and most compact I've seen. Come in little envelopes about ten inches square and like an inch thick. Open a flap, press a sensor and up they go. They had three of them that inter-connected, each with its own entrance—one for the lab, one for living quarters and one for a privy. The biggest hassle was getting them connected but it went smooth enough. They'd practiced.

Meanwhile I took in the sights. The sky was a nice blue, a little hazy up high. Which pretty much sums up meteorological activity planet-wide. GR14XO7 (or 'Paella,' as it's known on the orbital outpost) has no moon. It just spins placidly, basking in the light of an F-class star. At night everything gets moist, during the day it dries up.

The biomass gives off a lot of heat so it doesn't get significantly cooler at night, just enough to allow condensation
to form. And there you have it, a world untroubled by
wind or storm. A weatherman would die of boredom. We
were in a cartoon-like mountain range, peaks all rounded
over with biomass, not a sharp surface anywhere. The
mountains extended east, where we were headed, and
north and west. To the south, foothills rolled down into
a plain that stair-stepped around to the southwest, with
another range of mountains on the southern horizon.

High tech the tents might have been but spacious
not so much. The men got the living quarters and the
women elected to sleep in the lab. I volunteered to biv-
ouac in the privy; given my size it was the only practical
way to go. Each entrance had an outer lock of sorts, for
getting out of the suits. Which I was happy enough to
do. That's when you feel that extra quarter G, though. It
takes about an hour to get out of those bio-suits clean.
You have to spray yourself down a couple of times with
that universal surfactant and let the little vacuum servos
do their work. Longer for me because I had the goo on
my footgear to contend with.

The tents had inflatable honeycomb pads, self-level-
ing. Again, they'd been designed to minimize our impact
on the local flora or fauna or whatever you want to call
it. The biomass is a couple of hundred feet thick on the
plateau—which is actually shallow, by Paella standards—
so there was no question of clearing ground. By the time
I made it inside, the brains, spunky group, were all busy
running tests and making calculations. I didn't understand
a lot of their jargon but they did their best to include me,
which I appreciated. Every so often one or another would
explain their findings in dumbed-down terms. All except
Dubček, which I didn't hold against him. I amused myself

watching Vox. She did great things for a bio suit but in skivvies she was a meal and a half. I had to concentrate to keep from getting a hard-on.

What the brains were trying to do, apparently, was verify that Paella is a single-species ecosystem. Which would make it a first, I guess. I try to be surprised when life on alien worlds turns out different from anything humans have encountered before but I never pull it off. They'd sent down a bunch of probes, over the years, and from the data they'd collected formed a few theories. Dubček passed me a sheet, once I'd situated myself in the entrance to the privy. With the gear and all of them in there, there wasn't room for me in the lab. I could tell I was looking at a microscopic image of something organic.

"That's what life here uses for DNA," Sweet explains, pointing at an egg-shaped thing. "Took us awhile to recognize it. The markers are wedge-shaped, arranged like the explosive charges around the core of an old-fashioned atom bomb."

Guess he figured because of my background he had to come up with a weapons analogy. "You mean like a pinecone?" I ask.

He taps the sheet and some graphs come up, each with a differently color-coded egg-shape above it. "These show the depths into the biomass at which we've found the greatest concentration of ovoid markers with these general characteristics."

I know the difference between the DNA of a human and that of a rat is like eight percent or something. It looked like the differences here were considerably greater. "I thought you said this is a single species," I say.

"You're a quick study for a grunt, Squeeze," Clara says. My name's Clay and I like to be called Clay, but the handle was her way of initiating me into the fold so I didn't fuss.

"That is exactly the question," Sweet goes on. "These ovoid markers have a much greater potential for variation, and exhibit a higher range of diversity than DNA does in Earth's ecosystem, where we've had a vast number of very different species. And yet here, apparently, there's only one."

"Or one organism," Boner puts in.

"We're a long way from establishing that," Sweet says. He proceeds to give me the beggar's tour.

Meanwhile Clara passed out ration packs. Like I started out saying, that was when I got my first hit something was off. And yes, we're talking your standard, self-warming meal packs, that have the appetite-suppressing aroma of a chemical toilet when you open them up. I'm used to that. This was the taste. It didn't just taste bad, it tasted like something my body didn't want. Like my mouth was informing me food as I knew it was not welcome. I saw it on the rest of them, first bites they took. I should have called it. Like I said, it's my freight. It was my responsibility to look out for those people.

It's your feelings you have to watch. They'd been nice to me, big lug mucking along behind them, wreaking havoc on the wildlife. I don't get that a lot. Most scientific types treat me like a guard dog, the kind you keep chained up and don't pet. Usually my mere presence is resented. But apart from a couple of philosophical eye-rolls at the outset, these people hadn't been like that. I knew how much they had invested in that mission. Five years just to get clearance. Five years bowing and scraping, explaining to one incompetent administrator after another why a manned expedition is worth the expense and risk when unmanned probes have become so sophisticated as they have. Keeping to their chests that really they just wanted to put feet on an alien world. There aren't that many planets life's been found where people can go. Five years, and who knows how long before that planning, studying, building credibility. I'd been all sorts of places they'd never be, and my only qualifications are muscle and an aptitude for killing things. So yeah, I knew how they felt. Quit the op day one would have been a huge let down.

Vox finished me off, with that short blond hair of hers all mussed up and wanting a lot more mussing, skin shiny with sweat, big blues begging me not to say the words. So I made comedy of loving the glop, choked it down, and the rest, visibly relieved, followed suit. Biggest mistake of my life.

As I understood it, the biomass is all interconnected—as far as they'd been able to determine. They hadn't found a clear separation anywhere. The probes had shown the stuff thousands of feet thick in places, especially under the oceans, and however deep it went there was still life in it. Except the deeper you go, the slower its metabolism, apparently. The working theory was that life evolved on Paella in layers, like geological strata, except biological, in this case, which might have happened because of the planet's quiet nature—minimal tectonic activity, no tides or weather to speak of. Also, there didn't seem to be any clearly defined organs, just a steady flow of organic matter through a big mess of fleshy, irregularly shaped tubes. Cells seemed to have what Sweet described as an 'informal' relationship with each other, with those ovoid things constantly passing back and forth through cell walls. As to how it eats they'd theorized a massive root system, which the probes had shown some evidence of near the poles, as well as something like photosynthesis. But there was no CO_2 exchange involved. The thing makes oxygen and absorbs it. So my immediate question, being stunted in my development by my military training, and therefore permanently adolescent and scatological in my thinking, is, how's it crap? And apparently, other than off-gassing the nitrogen rich O_2, it doesn't.

Boner gets excited when I put the question. He sidles over and taps my sheet, pulling up files of pictures taken by the orbital outpost. He shows me shots of the same site taken over a period of fourteen years. "See it?" he asks me.

I shake my head. Boner shows me close-ups of a quadrant of the same area, but I still don't understand what he's getting at. "It looks the same," I say.

"Exactly." Boner gets this big grin. "Zero growth. It's reached a steady state. What gets cast off as waste in one place just cycles through the system until it finds use someplace else. Zero waste, complete sustainability. Even its relationship with the atmosphere is probably a one-to-one exchange."

"Boner loves to theorize," Vox says.

"Which he's free to do 'cause it ain't his field," echoes Sweet.

Boner is unfazed. "Exactly," he says, and carries on grinning.

The idea made me uncomfortable. The thought of an organism that large that doesn't do anything, just sits there and rotates—I don't call that living and I said so. Life relates to life. Plants interact with birds and bugs. People fuck, fight, what have you. As I understood it, this thing doesn't relate to anything but itself. Gave me the creeps. Vox traded places with Boner and squatted down next to me. That was the first time we touched, I think.

"Don't get too impressed with Boner's theories," she says. Vox had a voice like soft surf on a private island. I could have listened to her all day, just sitting with my eyes closed. She opened another file. "There's been continuous activity in this area, almost since the first probes were deployed."

I found myself looking at a kind of ravine. In some pics there was a clear fluid running through it that didn't quite read as water. And in one this dark spot I couldn't make out. "What's that?" I asked.

"That's what we're going to find out." She kind of flicks my nose with her finger.

I wanted to grab her right then. And I was getting the impression she wouldn't have minded. "Why's the picture so fuzzy?" I ask, making myself behave.

"Some kind of interference. Probably a geological phenomenon. The anomaly only shows up in a few images. We've sent down several probes but they didn't find anything."

I barely have the "yeah-but" formed in my head before she's off to other business and Sweet comes back, tapping up the graphs again. "At the deepest layer, we find ovoids with these general characteristics dominating the mix." He points at the uppermost graph. "About ninety-eight percent they're running the show. This is from a sample taken seventeen thousand feet into the biomass, under about twenty thousand feet of water, in the southern sea. That's the deepest our probes have gone. Go a little shallower and it's these guys, a little shallower these, and so on. There's around a trillion and a half variations overall. Breaking them down into distribution groups, we've identified over a thousand zones of majority, but in all of them ovoids from the other bio-strata are still present. What's unusual about the place we're going—" he taps up another graph—"is that markers from all zones are almost equally present, with only a slight majority of the ovoids otherwise prevalent in the deepest layers."

I'm no brain, but the more I look at that graph the

more it bothers me. I catch Boner watching me, like he wonders if we're thinking the same thing. Which I couldn't imagine we were, him being so much smarter. Maybe I should have said something then, too. But it was their show and I figured they knew what they were doing.

Paella has about a thirty-seven hour rotation. We couldn't adapt to its cycle so we opted for a twenty-two hour one, twelve hours up and ten down, giving ourselves the extra rest to counter the quarter G. That put us traveling at night about a third of the time. Which is easy on Paella because the biomass is luminescent.

It was still light out when we took our first rest. The brains donned neural-suppressors to make sure they slept. Better than the ones we've got. Little pill-bug things you drop on your head. Let them get where they go, set the timer and wink. Worked great but no use to me. On op I sleep with my eyes open.

I saw the light change. It's a weird glow the biomass puts off. I'd seen it from the orbital outpost but it's different on the surface. Something between green and purple and, I don't know, lilac or something. I can't think of anything to compare it to. I dream, sometimes, with my eyes open. That night I had a whopper. It kind of related to something else Sweet explained. Those ovoid markers change when they run into each other, passing characteristics back and forth like information. A little like ants, he said. He showed me this animated vid they'd put together, showing color-coded ovoids touching, and how the distribution of markers on one or both changes when they do. So in my dream I saw myself as Atlas. You know, the Greek god or whatever that holds the world on his shoulders. Except I was holding Paella. I saw myself stomping through the Galaxy, and when I'd reach another world, I'd lift Paella off of my shoulders and hold it out to touch it. And then that world would change into its own kind of Paella.

Breakfast tasted a bit worse than dinner, I thought. Especially in the weird light. Nothing looks right in that light, least of all food. I called in a grabber to take our waste and the samples the brains had collected, we broke camp and pushed on. Going downhill, off the rim of the plateau, was harder for all the obvious reasons but also because the trees got a lot more plentiful. I put us on rope and insisted everyone wear hand-grapples, impact be damned. If they would have fallen I might have been able to hold all of them but I didn't want to test the theory. Especially not with all the gear and provisions we were lugging around, I still don't know why. We damn sure could've made better use of the grabbers. The brains had some rationale about 'maintaining the integrity of the contamination arc,' but it just seemed like vanity to me. Being intelligent doesn't always make you smart. We got a few hundred yards before they conceded the footgear wasn't working out. I told them to leave them and had a grabber pick them up. I was relieved; the things were interfering with my mobility. As it turned out they proved unnecessary. The brains didn't break the surface much more than they had and I made a mess either way.

That orange ooze glowed an unpleasant yellow-green in the dark, sort of nauseating in the general luminescence of the biomass. The biomass gives off an aura, too. You can see it up above, intermittently, and steadily in the distance, an oscillating band of increased brightness that has a lighter hue to it. It seemed to me a lot of energy was emanating off of the biomass, and I wondered what it was doing to us.

Puts you in a real quiet head space, traveling in that light. Nobody talked. I got the beauty of the place then, too. Look out across mountains and valleys and rolling hills, all glowing—it's a little spooky but you'd be blind not to see the wonder of it.

The brains took breaks, now and then, but not to eat. We made do with nutrient tabs for our mid-cycle meal, without anyone suggesting it. Eight hours we reached a ridge where Clara wanted to make camp. We had a couple of hours before daybreak so, once they had the tents up, the brains busied themselves analyzing the bio-luminescence. With daybreak came dinner, which was a considerably more unpleasant affair than it had been the first time. We waited until it was fully light. Nobody wanted to deal with food in that glow again. Not that it helped. It's a fair shock to see a place change from weirdly beautiful to autopsy run amok. Does not improve your appetite.

We slept, broke camp and then Clara decided she wanted to take some 'large sections'—her words—on the ridge top there. When I found out what she had in mind I began to question her concept of 'limit.' First they cut off one of those elephant-ear leaves. It surprised them when right away it went flat. That was good for an hour of heated jawing. Then they set loose some little servos to separate a meter-long segment of a big, intestine-look-ing tube and cut it free of the biomass. Orange goo went spilling all over the place and pretty soon I wasn't the only one getting bloody anymore. Inside, the thing was full of this dense, spongy material. Sweet said it reminded him of a cactus. A hell of a lot juicier, was Boner's com-ment. I called in a grabber to take the ear and the tube segment away and then they really got to business. Clara set loose some self-positioning lasers to cut a three-meter square cube out of the biomass.

Vox catches the look on my face. "You have to remember the scale of the organism," she says.

"Thought you weren't sure it's just one," I say.

"However many, they're massive," she says. "This is less than a pin prick."

I followed her reasoning but I'm sorry, you take a three-meter chunk out of something's hyde, I don't care how big it is, it ain't no pin prick. After I had a grab-ber lift out the "large section," Dubček had me rappel him into the pit. Talk about bloody, he went knee deep and orange all over. He's down there about three minutes when he calls up to Clara, "It's too uniform. We have to go deeper."

Clara shakes her head. "Not here. It's only a few hun-dred feet thick."

"We should go south," he says. "Three days across the plain it's 6,000 feet."

"Our primary objective is the anomaly," she says. "We agreed on that."

"But we might not get another chance, Clara. They won't let us come back."

"You don't know that, Dubček. And I don't want to just dig down at random. If we're going to excavate, we need to choose the right location."

When I heard "excavate" I burst out laughing. I couldn't help it. Here these people had been so careful and now we're talking about pit-mining this thing. "Well, hell," I say, "I'll requisition up a 6-pack of mining torpe-does and bust you a hole to heaven!"

Boner's the only one who gets the joke. Vox and Sweet look embarrassed but Clara and Dubček seem to start thinking it over. Which gets Boner and me laughing harder. I'm sort of carried back by laughing and I feel a soft spot under me. Suddenly I'm knee deep in biomass. Boner stares at me. Dubček asks what's going on and we all laugh. But I've got that itch at the back of my neck.

Half a beat I work out what's wrong, shout at everyone to grab their gear and run for it, pull myself up and belly-crawl to the pit, yank Dubček out of there. The rest are staring at me. "Move it!" I yell.

They felt it too, then, and went scrambling. The whole ridge was falling apart under our feet. We make it about a hundred yards down from the edge, by which point I'm slogging along up to my ass, when it collapses and takes us all downhill in a slushy, orange wave. I came up hard against a tree, wiped my face plate and grabbed Clara going by. Vox and Sweet slammed into another one, just below me, and managed to hold on. Dubček and Boner I couldn't see. A flood of broken, semi-liquified biomass pushed and pulled at us for a hateful long time. If those tree forms hadn't held we all might have eaten it right there. Sweet lost his grip, once, but Vox caught him and pulled him back.

The worst of the breakdown passed, and we were left mucking around in about a foot and a half of residual orange sludge oozing its way downhill. I got Clara, Vox and Sweet checked out, and we went looking for Dubček and Boner.

We found some of their gear about half a click down, at the bottom of the slope, but no sign of them. I told the others to police our gear and went searching. The biomass hadn't stopped falling apart. There was a big canyon, pooled at the bottom with orange stew. On the other side, to the northeast, three mountains that had gotten significantly shorter were painted orange, and through binoculars I could see the disintegration making its way up the slopes of a fourth. You know from the data collected on the orbital outpost that the wound—that's what I called it—spread nearly a hundred kilometers before it stopped.

I couldn't pick up Dubček's or Boner's signatures on my scanner. My worst fear was that they were somewhere in that canyon. Yet more joy, communications were down. I couldn't contact the orbital outpost. I was transmitting fine, which meant it was up to operations to reestablish the link. Meanwhile, I couldn't even reach the grabbers. I saw one flying around, up there, trying to get a fix on us. Waved at it like an idiot but it just flew on.

We erected our tents clear of the slide area, got the worst of the muck off our suits, and spent the remaining daylight searching the perimeter of the wound. The analytical functions on my scanner remained operational, which I think is significant. I was able to take sonic readings. Some unstable shelves had formed, and I steered us around them.

The ooze that had spilled onto undamaged areas soaked into the biomass quickly. By evening it was pretty much gone, leaving this grey fluff that had the consistency of ash. The brains took samples. I respected that. Everything gone to shit and they still did their jobs. Nightfall gave us a new perspective on the damage we'd done. The bio-luminescence is a surface phenomenon, so now there was a gaping black void in the glowing landscape. I asked Clara if she still wanted to excavate. That was a little mean. Paella was her life's work. She loved the biomass, in her way, and it tore her up to see how she'd hurt it. Our missing team members aside.

The others were exhausted. I was a bit worn myself. It was a sad group I had in front of me, when we were all back in the tents. Nobody wanted to sleep until we found Dubček and Boner. I reminded them we were deaf and blind, and needed help from the orbital outpost to continue our search effectively. There was too much ground to cover, and too few of us. If they were down in the canyon we'd need grabbers to get them out. My scanner would alert me when the comm-link was reestablished, and I promised to wake everyone the moment that happened.

So we forced down meal packs and knocked off. I set the alarm on my scanner to alert me if there was any seismic activity. The fact that the biomass had stopped disintegrating was no guarantee it wouldn't start again. Good thing I didn't use neural suppressors or I don't know what would have happened. A couple of hours after the rest had bedded down I felt my gut go sideways and woke everyone up. The line to the privy formed immediately. Everyone was in bad shape. We only had the one waste evacuation suit, so it was a long and miserable wait. Those suits are a pain in the ass, especially on a heavy planet. Somebody needs to re-design that harness and make it easier to secure the seal to your sphincter. Sweet had an accident and we were half an hour waiting for the suit to reset. Then Clara threw up in the thing. I went last because I'm trained to cope. Vox was in torment.

Once we'd all done our business I asked if anyone had an idea what was causing this unexpected sickness. Nobody bothered to suggest anything to do with the rations. We knew it wasn't that. Vox related a theory Boner'd had. The energy field the biomass puts off, he'd told her, has eccentric characteristics, something to do with wave patterns. He'd thought maybe the oscillations were affecting us.

I wasn't happy to be learning this second hand and late. I made them aware of the realities of our situation. I don't think anyone had adequately impressed on them that they were under military authority, or maybe they hadn't taken it seriously. As it was, we were looking at six months in quarantine, minimum. That's if the guys in white suits liked what they saw. The crew that went to Silas was locked up for six years. And that team that came back sick from the outer rim has been in cryo going on twenty. I told them I did not want to wind up like that.

Ironic to reflect on those words, now. I was putting off the hard part—telling them we had to move on. Our comm had been down too long. Either something was wrong on the orbital outpost, which I doubted, or something on the planet was creating interference. I wasn't going to dismiss the timing of the malfunction. There was no way of knowing how long it would take to reestablish communications, so the only sensible way to proceed was head for the extraction point.

I kept that to myself for the time being, told them all to go back to sleep. I wanted them rested. We'd been bedded back down about an hour when I felt movement in the privy tent. It was Vox, wanting company. She crawled in and snuggled against me.

"Don't tell me you can't sleep," I said.

"Don't want to," she said.

I started to object but she put her fingers on my lips. I knew what she needed. I needed it too. I'd never lost civilians before. I was about a hundred percent sure Dubček and Boner were dead, and felt rotten about it. We got naked and made life beautiful. There's something about a woman like Vox, who's sophisticated and intelligent. They're more serious. My standard fare is the hookers they keep at the way stations where the military generally dumps us for shore leave. No disrespect to those ladies, they just don't have any illusions left. That girl brought tears to my eyes; I'm not ashamed to say it. With her body bathed in that weird light, it was like making love to the planet. She went to sleep in my arms, like a little kid.

When we were all awake again I gathered everyone and filled them in. No one wanted to leave without Dubček and Boner. Vox looked at me like I'd betrayed her. But Clara helped me out. She said Dubček and Boner were likely to head for the waterfall anomaly, since that had been our prime objective, as well as the pre-arranged extraction point, so our best chance of finding them was to do as I advised and go there. That calmed Sweet and Vox down, though Vox still gave me cloudy looks. But I'd made my decision so we prepared to break camp. We were all hungry but nobody wanted to risk even nutrient tabs, at that point. I insisted everyone drink at least eight ounces of water.

We got outside and saw that the wound wasn't dark anymore. It had grown a covering, like a big silk sheet, that glowed pale white with little daubs of color traveling through it. A mild breeze had picked up, ruffling the sheet in slow-moving waves. We broke down the tents, packed up, and went back to the edge of the wound for a closer look. I reached down to touch that silk stuff but Clara stopped me. She set down a little probe to take a micro-sample from the perimeter.

We were fairly stunned by the phenomenon, myself included. The brains were mystified. Without predators or other hazards they couldn't figure out why the bio-mass would evolve an ability to heal so quickly.

It was Vox, again, who came up with a possible explanation. "Meteors," she said, and even I got an ah-ha out of that one. Paella's system has two asteroid belts.

"We haven't recorded a single impact, the whole time the orbital station has been in position," Clara objected.

"That doesn't mean they've never happened," Vox said. "This organism's millions of years old." I noticed they were all referring to it as a single entity, now.

We moved on without resolving the question. Again

going silent in that weird light. Now and again we stopped to look back at the wound. Three and a half mountains shrouded in glowing white silk—I've seen some sights but that vies with the most memorable.

We reached the area above the anomaly about five hours after daybreak. First thing I noticed was the bio-mass was a lot tougher around there. I wasn't breaking the skin anymore. We heard this gurgling, whooshing sound, that at first we couldn't identify. Sweet spotted a gap in the biomass. We found several more, in a rough line, through which you could see smooth grey stone, when you played a light inside. I wasn't entirely accurate in what I said before; we did get that little glimpse of the actual surface of the planet. I saw, then, that the biomass was only a few feet thick there.

The rock surface looked wet. It seemed to form a sort of canal. The whooshing sound was explained when fluid came spurting through. It was clear but thicker than water, more like mucous. We followed the gaps and they led us to the top of the 'waterfall' I'd seen in the pictures. Looking down into the ravine we saw the anomaly. Two of them, to be exact. There were two pools, one below the other, full of that clear, viscous fluid. The lower one was about sixty feet across, about twice as big as the upper one. In it there were these two big black floating things, with hair-like tendrils growing out of them. Looked like King Kong's balls, basting in their own juice. I didn't like them.

There was no sign of Boner or Dubček. I tried the orbital outpost again. Still no luck. Everybody was worn out and depressed as hell. We needed to eat but didn't want to. Only thing to do was make camp and wait. After we'd rested a bit, Clara suggested we go down and check out the anomaly. I couldn't see a reason to object. We needed something to get our minds off our troubles.

It was a steep descent. I tied off to a couple of tree forms. We left non-essential gear at the camp and climbed down. I had that damn itch at the back of my neck but couldn't pin it to anything so kept it to myself.

They took samples of the mucous and the biomass surrounding the pool, yammered a lot about it being so dense. They were better, focused on work. Vox wanted to get samples from those big testicle things.

You could see the bottom of the pool they floated in. It was only maybe three feet deep. But I insisted on going in with her. I don't know if that was a good decision or a bad one. I caught Sweet looking at me, as I went in. He didn't look happy. I started to ask what was bothering him but he turned his attention back to his instruments. I wish I'd pressed him.

The mucous had a consistency that seemed to change as you moved through it, sort of gelatin-like but more fluid when you touched it. We got drenched by it a couple of times, when the falls let loose. We waded out to the nearest of the black things. Vox took her time measuring and scanning it. It was maybe six feet in diameter, suspended in a depression. She went under to verify that it wasn't attached to anything from below. Didn't warn me before she did that and it made me uncomfortable as hell. Then she took a little sample from the tip of one of the tendrils. The tendril sort of stiffened up when she cut into it and then went limp. It startled her; I saw doubt in her eyes. "Okay," I said, "that's it. You've got your samples. We're getting out."

"Just one more thing," she said. Like they say, there's always one more thing, and it's the one that gets you. She set a probe on the body of the thing.

I took a deep breath, my patience sorely tried. I thought the probe was just going to take a surface sample. When I saw it was set to bore into the thing I started to object but it was too late. That's when I felt it, this demand, compulsion, something. I don't know how to describe it—like a rockslide dumping through my mind and body. It was an attack. Not necessarily intended as one but effectively an attack. Penetration. Vox stared at me, wide-eyed, trying to speak. I went on automatic, threw her clear of the pool and faced that black thing. I didn't understand what I was feeling but I knew where it was coming from. Its tendrils had all gone erect and were vibrating. It floated there, a big bulbous thing, and if there was ever one that wanted busting, it was it.

I drew my long knife and hacked into it. The others shouted at me but I was past hearing. I hacked again and penetrated the shell. The instant I did that, I knew what I was feeling.

Hunger.

Hunger worse than I've ever felt. The thing had been setting us up for that the whole way. I got my hands in the cut and tore it open. Inside it was full of this black, caviar-like jelly. Imagine something so disgusting you know by reflex you don't want it on you, let alone in your mouth. But I *wanted* it. The stuff kind of gushed out, like it was under pressure, and something floated up. I didn't understand what I was seeing, then realized it was Dubček's face. He was dead but it was like he was looking at me. His skin gone grey and his eyes filmed over. I should have felt anything else, but all of my normal, human reactions were completely overwhelmed by a craving to *feed*.

My training kicked in or I wouldn't be here. I knew we'd been lured into a honey trap; they don't have to be human. The thought kept banging in my head, *Never, never, never go in without backup*. I was mad as I've ever been, because I knew what was about to happen.

It was all I could do to pull myself away. The others were out of their suits and by me before I could stop them. I barely managed to grab Sweet. He was the only one I saved. He fought like one of those ape-looking things on Poedius. I knocked him out and got him restrained, then made myself look to Clara and Vox.

They were gorging themselves on the black stuff. Worst thing I've ever seen. Decent, intelligent, good-natured people brought down like that—no, that's bad as it gets. I watched Vox shove a fist-full in her mouth, trying to stop herself and not able.

I pulled them out. It wasn't hard; they were already limp. Again, too late. They were both dead in seconds. I held Vox. She stared up at me, choking and gasping, her mouth smeared with that filth, tears running from her eyes. Poor, poor baby.

I hope you sons of bitches are listening, 'cause if my C.O. had shown up then I'd have slit his throat right there. I know what it costs to produce a unit like me. Yeah. Well you minimize risk and cut your damn corners someplace else, *not* on security. If there's reason to send one, there's damn sure reason to send two.

Don't think I'm excusing myself. I smelled a rat when Vox first showed me those pictures. I just didn't credit my own intelligence. Another lesson I won't benefit from.

I tried again to call in a grabber and contact the orbital outpost. Still too much interference, big surprise. I got Sweet back in his bio suit, hoisted him onto my shoulder and started to climb out of there. That thing was working on me the whole time, but when I started to pull myself up the rope it got a thousand times worse. It was like trying to lift a mountain. I tried and tried but couldn't do it.

So I sat back down by the pool, facing my adversary,

that busted black ball and its un-busted twin. I swear it backed off to let me take stock of the situation.

I started thinking about filters and remembered the story that Russian guy told me about those reindeer herders. I sat there an hour, trying to convince myself I was wrong. But I knew what I had to do.

Sweet had come around by the time I worked up the nerve to do it. I feel bad about that. He whined at me, "No, Squeeze. Oh, no, Clay. Please, Clay. Please don't, Clay. Please don't do it." I told him to shut up if he wanted to live.

I won't tell you what I ate. You police up the bodies you'll see for yourselves, and you can think whatever you damn please. Just know Sweet didn't partake. I'm a permanent lab rat, now, but he didn't eat anything, so you check him out and let him go.

And don't send down live personnel. Figure out how to counteract whatever that interference is and let the grabbers handle it. Leave those black things alone. I know Boner's in the other one. It's a crap grave but leave him there, and Dubček, too. That black stuff is from hell itself. You don't want people anywhere near it. I'd tell you to leave Vox and Clara, too, but I . . . can't. So burn them, way away from anybody. Burn them and burn the ashes. And once you're done poking and prodding me, don't put me in cryo. Seal me in a containment capsule and shoot me into a fucking star. My balls have turned to mush, I've got a hard on that could split granite and I can't feel a thing down there. You see how my skin is changing. What's going on in my head—I'm not sure how much longer I'm gonna be me. All I've got left is my allegiance to my own kind.

But, yeah, I am beginning to understand the thing. How it thinks, what it wants. Little as I care to. It is intelligent. That's what you want to know, right? I wish you assholes could see yourselves.

Nothing I say will be accurate. It's got a sort of rudimentary sense of the universe around it. It knows there's things out here that can hurt it, but it's been a long time since it worried about that. It's been a long time since it cared about anything, least of all itself.

We're going to talk to it? Forget it. Maybe its got something we can use? You guys are smart you'll cordon off this whole sector and hope it forgets about us. Keep messing with it, you *will* get a response, and I wouldn't be sure of the outcome.

It doesn't measure time. There's no way of knowing how long ago it became conscious. If it had it to do over, I think it would pass. It's had its fill of consciousness. It was betrayed by its own evolution. Conscious life for it has been one, long, never-ending toothache, and it never gets to pop its cap. It's trapped in a body that runs on automatic, and it can't even kill itself. After awhile it just wanted to die in its sleep. It spent a long, long, long time trying to make itself unconscious, and we woke it up.

Why'd it do what it did? It was trying to say hello. Think about it, what need does that thing have to glow in the dark?

The Burning Professor

ON THE DAY of her last lecture, Estelle Kinder awoke, bathed, brushed and coiled her greying hair, and dressed in her best winter suit, all the while trying not to think about the fire she had kept concealed.

It would be a brisk day out. Wind whined around the house. She pulled apart the plain white curtains over the window by her bed, and saw that it would be a bright, clear day as well, with only a few high clouds feathering the sky. The bedroom was upstairs in an up and down apartment, half of a red brick duplex in faculty housing, near the south end of the campus. Below, the grass in her yard was brown and patched with hardened snow, the rose bushes pruned for winter, the crabapple tree leafless. Estelle lingered with the view. Seventeen years familiar, it would not be hers much longer. Across the street were houses identical to the one in which she dwelled, and beyond them the marvelous Italianate edifices of the theatrical and fine arts departments, and the Victorian-style humanities building where she had her office and usually taught classes. Today, however, she would cross the quad, with its stately pines and venerable elms, to the main auditorium. It was a campus custom that final lectures by tenured professors be open to general attendance, a somewhat daunting prospect, as much for how few as how many might attend. Estelle buttoned the top button of her blouse.

She sat on the end of the four-poster bed she had inherited from her parents, and folded her hands in her lap. She planned to talk about the impact of Platonic idealism on early Christian cosmology, a fitting topic, she thought, with which to cap her career. Her satchel, containing her notes, rested on the cushioned stool in front of her vanity, as if the matter were settled. But as she thought, now, very much in spite of herself, about the blue fire, she felt unsure. She had no alternate lecture prepared. It had not really registered with her, perhaps she had kept herself from thinking about it, that after this day she would teach no more. Should not this last lecture bear some deeper mark of her soul, something more than a mere signature?

The vanity was another heirloom. In her custody it had not seen its intended use. No array of perfumes and cosmetics cluttered its surface; it was a parking place for books and papers. With vexing repetitiveness, her thoughts returned to the fire, that confounding, abnormal phenomenon her body, or being, possessed the unwelcome ability to produce. It was not a wart that could be removed, it could not be amputated like a sixth finger. She'd had no choice but to suppress it. It had taken the whole of her adolescence and a good part of her young adulthood to translate the effort into a species of reflex. An unregarded internal command: contain, contain, contain. Which had been imperative if she'd wanted normalcy in her relations with others. Howard was proof of that. And yet, here she was, alone, her only friendships the vaguely diffident sorts that existed among colleagues. Colleagues who, like as not, would think of her little when she was gone. Who might avoid thinking of her, as they might their own mortality.

Well, no more would she think of them. Not now.

She stood and seized her satchel. This was no time to be second-guessing herself. She left her bedroom and went downstairs to the oak-paneled foyer, where she donned her greatcoat. Through the half-glass of the front door was the same view, from a lower vantage, visible through her bedroom window.

She raised her chin, wrapped a scarf around her neck, and a second one over her head, buttoned her coat, pulled on her gloves, and left her home, whose comforts had become so fugitive. Immediately the wind, colder than anticipated, pushed against her. The crabapple tree rustled in its leafless slumber. She'd planted it herself when she moved in. She glanced furtively at the tree, and hurried along the path.

If anyone could have understood the fire it should have been Howard. So she had thought, for he seemed to understand so much. They were traveling in England when the notion arose. Again and again, like the breath in his chest: this man would accept her. He used to stand in his doorway with his hands in his pockets, smiling the way her father had. Come out, come out, you're safe with me. Immersed in a cloud-like featherbed in London, the fire blooming in her, she so desired to set it free, and then did, letting it envelope them both as they achieved release. "There's something hidden in you." Safe, so long as he did not see—if only he'd kept his eyes closed. But he opened them, as they eased into the comfortable closeness that followed sex, and affection left him by stages. He smiled, and she smiled back, and it seemed it would be all right. But the recognition that something was different registered in his eyes. Then incomprehension, then wonder—if he could have stayed with that, like a child at his first experience of fireworks or the sea. But incomprehension returned, stained with fear, and the growing realization that the phenomenon that held them emanated from her. The cascade of reactions that followed was too punishing to review.

They returned home by separate planes. A year later, unable to bear his avoidance, she left the coast to come here to the northwest, her pain and shame heightened by the knowledge that it was not the fire Howard feared so much as being associated with someone peculiar. A distinguished professor of Semiotics, with important books to write, had to protect his reputation. It was the only time she ever heard herself called a freak, and she vowed never to suffer that indignity again.

Maybe she was a freak. One who could suppress her freakish nature and mingle with the unafflicted. She passed between the duplexes across the street from hers. An old science professor had died in his sleep, in the left one, last winter.

Affliction? So few times in her life had she let the fire out, she had never gained any real understanding of it. Did that mean she was to a similar extent unacquainted with herself? No attribute she possessed had had a more defining impact upon her character. She had assumed it was a foil for self-discipline. But that was the role she had assigned it. She had never examined it closely enough to verify the theory. And even in that function its guise was malleable. Having disciplined herself to suppress it, was it not thereby an aspect of her strength? It was a disorienting thought, especially on this day, that she had resisted self knowledge. It undermined her confidence. She imagined herself tongue-tied at the podium, students rustling in embarrassment to witness the fall of an honored elder.

She would not let that happen.

But she could not avoid her memories. For whatever reason, they had stirred irrepressibly. Summoning, now, the roster of empty affairs that had punctuated her existence before and after her involvement with Howard. She entered the Humanities building through a side door and climbed the short flight of steps to the wood-paneled foyer, which faced out onto the quad through tall sash windows and half-glass doors. Students and professors milled about, most on their way to class, some, like her, seeking an early preparatory spell in their offices. Estelle Kinder made her way across the hall, heading towards the broad staircase at its opposite end. The Dean went by, giving her a sympathetic look she did not feel disposed to acknowledge. She climbed the stairs to the third floor, and went down the narrow passage that led to the back of the building and her office. She put her key in the lock and thought, "This is not my office," went in and sat behind the large oak desk that was no longer hers.

At her back, a window that faced west, where the freshman and sophomore dorms were located, and, beyond them, the odious monstrosity of the business college. The seat of the aluminum frame chair across the desk had a tear in it and the foam stuffing showed. How many students had occupied that chair over the years? Too fitting it was empty now. She took out her lecture notes but couldn't concentrate. Howling wind rattled the window.

She missed her father.

They used to sit on the porch swing together, when she was a girl, almost every evening after dinner, and he would smoke a cigar, and tell her stories, and they would look at the stars, or chat with neighbors passing by, or discuss the trees—his favorite the sycamore across the street, hers the willow in their own yard. Every so often he would set his cigar on the white railing, inevitably leaving a burn mark, so that, in the course of time, that portion of the rail near his side of the swing acquired the semblance of a rude keyboard. And while she was in the comfortable glow of her father's presence, she did not have to think about the fire. It was calm inside of her, and did not need to be suppressed. Not for many years, until womanhood came upon her, and everything crowded about her like a trap.

She regretted never telling her father about the fire. She thought now that he might have been the only person who could have accepted it. There was always that shadow of sadness about him, of something lost or unfulfilled before it was known. A spiritual wound, brought back from the war, maybe. No one else seemed to notice, or maybe they pretended not to. But she did. It was in the skill with which he softened his voice, and the way his humor always seemed tailored to counter darkness.

And still he became, for her, the embodiment of all that was false and contemptible. Not for anything he did or didn't do but only for never changing, for being consistent and secure in his ways. It had tormented her, the hatred she felt for him. She knew it pained him too, and that he never understood it, and she never explained it to him. How could she? It was so formless.

The way he ate a baked potato—that was the breaking point. Coating it with salt, mashing in slab after slab of butter, pushing his steak, always rare—"Just pass it over the fire, Marjorie"—to the rim of the plate, sloshing blood onto her mother's best linen tablecloth, the one that had been passed to her from her mother. Estelle had it now, tucked away and never used, frayed at the edges, the color bleached out of the floral embroidery. She'd said nothing, and after dinner accompanied her father onto the porch, as usual, and sat silent while he smoked his cigar, and set it again on the marred white railing, and suddenly it was too much, and she fled, her father calling after her in bewilderment. Fled to her room, where she locked the door and burned and burned.

Later, she watched her mother iron the tablecloth, from which she had again bleached out the bloody stains. Estelle asked her how she could tolerate her father's thoughtlessness. "You don't understand, Stella. Love changes everything. There are hardships and irritations in any relationship. Habits that take getting used to. But if the love is real those things become reminders that the other person is there. They're like raindrops on a lake. When you love someone, you'll find out." As she had, when she lifted her tiny hand to touch her mother's face, and saw fear reject the fire, and forced amnesia veil her mother's sight.

Estelle scowled at herself. It was clear that whatever her final lecture turned out to be, it would be in some measure extemporaneous, for she could not bring herself to prepare better now, and was too unsettled to care. Her students expected spontaneity from her. Very well, she would be spontaneous. She had always prided herself for having an agile mind.

She put her notes back in her satchel. Sex and love, her fire had nothing to do with sex and love. She decided to go to the auditorium early, left her office unlocked. Perhaps she would have the opportunity to chat with a few of her students, if any arrived early. She spotted one coming down the hall. Perhaps he hoped for a last counseling session, or just a friendly farewell. She had always had students who enjoyed her company, who wanted more than a formal relationship with her. But this one entered the office of another professor.

Sex and love. She started to think, again, that her fire was a genetic aberration. It was one of a constellation of judgments she used to keep it at bay. There had been a time when she had even told herself the fire was something God had given her to test her faith, and remind her not to sin. Perhaps she had not entirely stopped telling herself that.

She went back down the stairs, on the way exchanging smiles with a young girl coming up, someone she did not recognize. Hopefully the stiffness in her expression was not too apparent. This was not the mood with which she had meant to greet this day.

Rodney laughed at the idea—God and fire, sin. It put a hitch in her stride to think of him. He was the only one who had not been afraid. Oh, let it wash through her, let it purge. She was determined to revisit everything, it seemed. Let this day be her emancipation from the past. She pushed through a half glass door, out into the cold expanse of the quad, with its mighty trees and vast lawn, snow-mottled now, magnificent even in winter. The elms were diseased, sadly. Some were scheduled for removal. Bundled-up students moved along the bordering paths and, in fewer numbers, crossed the lawn on the diagonal.

It had been natural to gravitate to Rodney, she supposed. Childhood friends, away from home for the first time, attending the same undergraduate school. Natural to unburden herself to him, of her fear of winding up like her parents, of her frustration with not knowing what she wanted. And, finally, to tell him of that which she had dared tell no one else. While he sucked on his aspirator cum pacifier, as if her disclosures raised the need for it.

But he had not laughed or mocked her. Remarkably, he claimed always to have known there was something about her she'd been afraid to reveal. Wind whipped at Estelle, flared her greatcoat. Healed him! What resentment he must have harbored to say that. She held the

neck of her coat snug, remembered his call, twenty years
after they parted. She never figured out how he found
her. She was on sabbatical in Oregon, at a cabin in the
mountains, remote from everything. Watching flames in
the fireplace when the phone rang. "Estelle?" The same,
timid, deferential voice. "It's Rodney. I've been thinking
about you——" Was that when he told her he was married? With two daughters—it was a smear in memory.
Fragments and the end: "I want you to know, you don't
have to be afraid. You healed me, body and mind——"

What an awful thing to say. She remembered sitting
there, mute and staring, until he hung up. Then she'd
gone outside, to the dark barrier of the trees, gaped at
the myriad stars, drenched in isolation, more than she
had ever been. Trees different from those in the quad that
were so generously spaced, with plenty of room amid
their roots to sit and relish a book. An encroaching press
of forest—contain, contain.

She let him see. Only once. Sitting together, late at
night, on a bench by the lagoon, below the student center,
when there was no one else around. Scrutinized his fascination. Watched him touch her burning hand, became
transfixed, with him, as the flames climbed his arm, spread
across his chest and shoulders, and up his throat. Then she
ran. He called after her, like her father had.

It was not the spread of the blue fire that made her
run. It was the look of awe and unsolicited devotion in
his eyes. She did not want that. She looked back. The
flames still clung to him. He seemed caught in the throes
of a profound awakening.

She had tried, for a time, to give their relationship a
chance. But she feared that she would ruin him, that he
would become her servant, erase himself for her.

She knew that was not true. Now. She knew it now.

Had known it for some time, looking back. Ever since the terrible phone call. The picture she'd held of him in her mind was of someone frail and inadequate. But it was in his voice, the strength that disproved the notion. He was married, he told her, and had three children, and she could not help thinking they could have been hers. But the declaration that she had healed him, what was that, some kind of delayed parting jab? He hadn't sounded vengeful. Healed from what? From wanting a woman like her? Someone with a sense of direction in her life? With strength and ambition and an investment in her own character, her own destiny?

She found herself reviewing her memories in a way, somehow, that she never had. She had never really examined the change she'd seen in Rodney, after she exposed him to her fire. She had avoided him, or tried to, as she had Howard, though for opposite reasons. Kept him at arm's length, never letting herself really see him, not wanting to see the change she had wrought. She avoided the subject when they spoke, told him she did not want to talk about it. But her avoidance went deeper than that, and, as she looked back now, veils lifted, and she saw Rodney as he had been, not weak, not inadequate, only gentle and caring. And sad, certainly sad—she had not wanted to see his sadness at the distance she put between them. But by refusing to see his sadness, she had failed to see his strength. The strength to be kind and let her go. All the awkwardness gone, the excitability, the insecurity, no more sucking on his aspirator—

She stopped, her eyes tracking the scan of memory. It couldn't be, she told herself, but knew memory would yield no contradiction. The truth she had avoided was before her. After she touched him with her fire, she never saw Rodney use his aspirator.

A group of chattering students went by; one young man looked back at her. Estelle made her way to a nearby bench and sat down.

Healed him. Both literally and metaphorically, he'd said. Something like that. She had not let the implications register. The instinct to suppress the fire ran so deep that anything that might characterize it as beneficial had to be disregarded. Forced blindness, equipped with the speed of reflex. She had not wanted to be responsible for an ability that would set her apart. She had not wanted to relinquish her aspirations for a path pre-determined by a genetic 'gift.' What was worse? To have suppressed her nature, or come to the end of what she had chosen?

Contain. Contain. Contain.

She had feared isolation. She had feared society. She had feared the government. She had feared herself. She had feared.

Was denial of what she was not also a denial of who she was? What had she taught her students? She had always meant to convey self confidence to them, belief in themselves. She had told them to be true to themselves and never to let anyone tell them what they could or could not accomplish, or above all fault them for pursuing their dreams or embracing and owning those qualities that made them unique. But what had she communicated to them, inadvertently, unconsciously, even, in criticizing their ideas? Steering them, via subtle arguments, away from thoughts or attitudes that made her uncomfortable, in particular any that challenged the supremacy of scholarship? It was the thing she had always resented about religion, making dependency upon scripture an ineluctable aspect of personal truth, binding self acceptance to the interpretation of archaic precepts.

She loved books, she loved reading and learning; she

would never renounce their value. But she had hidden in books, too. She could not deny it. Nor could she deny that, without meaning to, she had laid the labyrinth of learning before her students in company with its wonders.

The wind had died down. Estelle became aware of a young woman sitting on the bench with her. One of her students—she couldn't remember her name. The young woman was watching her with concern. Estelle realized that she was shaking. She must look a fright.

"Are you all right, Professor?"

"I'm fine, dear, I'm fine." Estelle patted the young woman on the elbow. The young woman did not notice the tiny blue flames that lingered where Estelle had touched her. The fire was going to come out. She could contain it no longer. Perhaps she no longer wished to.

Other students were gathered around the bench. One young man frowned at the young woman's elbow, though the flames had vanished. "Off you go, now," Estelle told them. "All of you. Let me have a moment, here. I just need a moment." To the young woman she said, "Don't be afraid."

They moved away. The young man who had seen the flames lingered longest. Estelle smiled at him until he left too. Then she was alone again, the central expanse of the quad at her back, the science building before her, with its ungainly glass-walled addition, one of the doomed elms towering skeletally above her. The air was nearly still. Estelle did not know what was going to happen. She pre-pared to let it happen. She was on her way to her last lecture, making her last walk to class.

She stood and shouldered her satchel, continued on. The flames leaked from her ankles. The old instinct kicked in and she tried to suppress them. Then let them go, not understanding what she was doing, not knowing anything, and let go of knowing and understanding. The fire burst forth, engulfing her body. She staggered with the release, registered the wide-eyed stares of students. She continued toward the auditorium. The flames spread from her, traveled across the pavement, reached students near to her, some who scurried aside, others framed in shock who were engulfed themselves. Estelle knew ecstasy.

She let the fire out to its full force. It climbed the sickly elms alongside the path. Estelle laughed. The way was open before her. The very trees lifted their arms at her passing. Some students did not see the fire, it seemed, and looked with confusion upon those who stared in awe. Estelle wished Howard were there, so she could enjoy his embarrassment. Then again screw Howard. She wanted Rodney, a companion with the courage to walk beside her. She rejected that thought, too. That was not how she had lived it.

She would tell them everything. She would tell them of her fears and the suppression of her soul. She would tell them of her loneliness and her loves. She would tell them of her parents, and a life spent in disguise. She would tell them how to read without getting trapped by words. She would tell them the truth.

She knew the fire would burn out.

Doloroso

HE HAD BEEN alone in the room six hours before he
knew they were not coming back. The realization arrived,
the way thoughts sometimes follow each other without
clear connection, when he noticed that the stitches on his
arm had begun to itch. Their plans had been for nothing.
He could only accept it. Santos had learned long ago that
the worst thing was always possible.

The overhead fan squeaked and swayed like it was
going to rip loose from the ceiling. The noise was awful,
but silence would have been too lonely in the dingy
motel room right then. It was getting dark. The only
light in the room was a lamp, with the statue base of a
rearing horse, on the nightstand by the ratty bed. The
horse's forelegs were broken off. Santos thought about
turning the lamp on but decided not to. He stayed where
he was, seated at the round, Formica-topped table, and
wiped sweat from his face. He had been sitting there a
long time. There was a chip in the table's surface that he
had worried with his fingers, one by one, back and forth,
while he stared at nothing, while he stared at the water
stains on the walls, while he stared at his memories. He
tried to tell himself that Rodrigo and Martín had been
delayed or run into trouble. But he knew they had abandoned him.

It was because of Rodrigo. He had been so scared that
he had not been able to speak. They never should have

brought him along. They should have crossed the border hours ago in the old liquor truck, whose driver would soon be spending their money on expensive women and clothes and whatever else his greedy heart hungered for. Santos shook his head. That truck was perfect. It reeked of beer. The dogs would never have smelled the drugs.

Probably they had betrayed him to El Pájaro, hoping that he would spare their lives. Martín and Santos were friends but Rodrigo was Martín's brother. He would not hesitate to sacrifice Santos to protect Rodrigo.

Santos got up to turn on the lamp but went outside instead. Hiding did not matter now. Stars were beginning to show in the sky. The sign that read MOTEL DESIERTO VISTA made a hatchet shape among them. It was missing most of its neon tubing and had not lit up for years. Across the empty road the desert rolled away, a dry sea of sandy hummocks crowned with sage brush and mesquite. The run-down motel faced the two-lane highway with yellow paint-shedding walls and twelve rooms, six upstairs and six down. The rooms upstairs were not used much because the roof was bad. Santos had a middle room downstairs.

A couple of trucks were parked in front of the bar next-door. Later, the whores would bring the workers they picked up in the bar here to the motel. Santos headed the other way, toward the railroad tracks, to see if the ghost was there. He had noticed him the night before, when they drove in. He thought Rodrigo might have seen him too. Martín could not see ghosts.

Santos walked by the side of the road, and thought about his mother. He used to help her make tortillas to sell in the market, in the small pueblo where he grew up. All of his best memories of his mother were sepia-toned. Early in the morning, while the chickens were

still asleep, he and his mother made tortillas in the dim
amber light of their makeshift kitchen. He remembered
her hands, how small and graceful they were. Everything
they needed to say to each other was communicated in
silence, in the simple warmth of togetherness.

The ghost was there, over by the lineman's shed. Santos left the road and went down to talk to him. Maybe
the ghost would not talk back. Sometimes ghosts did
not have much to say. It did not matter. Santos wanted
company.

The ghost was old. He was sitting with his back to
the shed, the brim of his hat pulled low. Santos could not
see his face.

"Hello, old one. Can I sit with you?"

The ghost did not look up. "Why would you seek the
company of an old phantom?"

"The dead seek the company of the dead." Santos
sat down and leaned back against the shed. To the west
glimmered the lights and fires of the shanty town on the
outskirts of Nopalitos. There were lights in the sky too.
Moving lights that were not stars. Military helicopters,
probably.

The ghost looked at Santos. "You are not dead, young
one."

"It is a false impression. My time with the living is
done."

"Are you sick?"

Santos laughed. "You might say so. I have been
infected by a human plague called El Pájaro. I stole his
property, and my friends have betrayed me. So, I am dead.
It is only that my body has not been informed."

"El Pájaro," the ghost spat. His saliva smoked where it
hit the sand.

"You know him?" Santos asked.

"The man who tossed the severed heads of three detectives into a crowded discotheque in Michoacán? Who beat a whore in Nogales to death with a branding iron? Who ordered the murder of seventeen Salvadoran indocumentados because no one would pay their ransom? I know El Pájaro."

Santos regarded the ghost with new interest. "Did he kill you?"

The ghost did not answer. "Why would you steal from such a beast? Have you no sense?"

"I did not want to work for him anymore. I needed money to disappear."

"Your sense arrived late."

"Possibly. My father worked for El Pájaro. He was killed when I was eight. El Pájaro sent money to my mother for many years. When I turned twelve, I went to work for him. It was a point of honor."

"What happened to your father?"

"El Pájaro told me he died in a gunfight."

"El Pájaro?"

"Yes."

"El Pájaro told you that your father died in his employ, and offered you the honor of replacing him?"

"More or less."

"And if the devil tells you hell is a garden of sweet-smelling dahlias, do you believe him?"

The ghost was beginning to irritate Santos. "I had to provide for my family."

The ghost scoffed. "By dipping your hands in a trough of blood."

"I will not lie; I have killed."

"I see. And eaten beans, and spit in the street, and other things of equal importance, to hear you say it. Are you tired of killing?"

"We are at war with the Cardenas brothers and the Three Sixes and the federal soldiers. I am tired of dodging death."

"So now you await him."

"You are not such good company, old one."

They sat awhile in silence. Santos could hear the helicopters, like a far off drone of bees. He got up to go.

"You can escape through the tunnel at Dos Corbatas," the ghost said.

Santos noticed a washed-out place under the shed where he had been sitting. Something smooth and coiled rested in the depression. "The soldiers closed that tunnel," he said. He made out reptilian scales and stepped back.

"They placed the dynamite but were called away." The ghost nodded toward Nopalitos. "You are looking at the reason. They will return in the morning to detonate it."

"How does an old ghost know these things?"

"See for yourself if I lie."

The ghost was crazy. Santos left him to his madness. But by the time he got back to the motel he had become curious. Dos Corbatas was fifty kilometers away. He would need a car. He had never known anyone to outrun El Pájaro. Which may have been the flaw in his plan to begin with, he reflected ruefully. But it might be better to try than to sit and sweat and stare at stains on the wall and wait to be found.

He shouldered the backpack full of heroin and went next-door to the bar. It was a tired, square, adobe building, with a string of red Christmas lights in one window. There were more trucks parked in front now. All of them were locked. Inside, most of the men were gathered around a bumper-pool table. Santos did not want to deal with a group. The whores sat along a wall and watched the men's game without interest. Santos took a stool by the window and ordered a tequila. A whore in pumps and panties and nothing else came over and he bought her a drink. She cooed and pawed at him but he ignored her. Another truck pulled up, an old, paintless Ford. Santos pointed the driver out to the whore, and gave her a hundred American dollars to make him happy when he came in. Then he finished his tequila and went back outside. He stopped the driver on his way to the entrance, parted his shirt so the man could see the tattoos on his chest, and told him what he wanted. Santos never tired of the pleasure it gave him to instill fear in others. It was always the same. Indignation disintegrated into uncertainty and the desire to live. The driver gave Santos the keys to his truck. Santos pushed him against the wall of the building and reminded him of the value of amnesia. Then he gave the man fifty dollars and told him where to search for the truck in the morning and that the keys would be under the seat. He patted him on the face and grinned. Without looking back, Santos went to the truck, threw the backpack inside, got in and drove towards Dos Corbatas.

The road was straight and monotonous. A sliver of moon hung low over the desert to the northeast, like the iris of a blind, one-eyed cat. Yesterday the soldiers had been up and down this highway in loud convoys. But now there were few vehicles, and long stretches where it was dark ahead and behind. Everyone was scared, not going anywhere. Santos wondered how old the road was. *Corridos* had been written about it, sung for the poor and the damned on both sides of the border. Cops and criminals had traveled it so much they could no longer tell each other apart. Santos had heard that Fidel Castro stayed somewhere along here, when he was planning his revolution for Cuba. Maybe that was down near the Gulf. He could not remember.

Ten miles from Dos Corbatas he came into farmlands, fields of onions and alfalfa, mostly. The tunnel house was outside of town, near the west end. Santos had never been there, but he knew where it was and how to identify it. He turned north onto a farm road. He wanted to avoid the town. The truck shuddered along the rough dirt road and lurched here and there through pot holes. The border was not far away now.

Santos thought, *This desert is a graveyard. We do not know how many are buried here. The bones of the dead feed the soil.* A hay truck crossed the road in front of him. The cloud of dust it trailed formed a death's head in the lights of the Ford. *Santa Muerte,* Santos prayed, and drove through the dust-skull's mouth.

When he saw the concrete cistern painted with crosses he knew that his instincts had served him. He had turned onto the road he wanted. The lights of Dos Corbatas spread to the east, and ahead were lights across the border in California. About two kilometers on, he rounded a curve and saw the house, set forward about a hundred meters from the border fence. It seemed the old ghost might have been right. There was a short-sleeved shirt hanging upside-down on a clothes line beside the house. It was the right place. There was also a military jeep parked in the gravel driveway, under the branches of an acacia tree, and next to it, a bit forward, a bulldozer. Santos drove past. The two soldiers in the jeep did not turn their heads to look at him.

There was a rise up ahead. On the other side he cut the lights and pulled into a stand of withered fruit trees to the left of the road. He turned off the engine and listened. He heard nothing but a few crickets and the rustling of dry leaves. No jeep starting up, no tires on the road. He got out, placed the keys under the seat, pulled on the backpack, and quietly returned on foot to the top of the rise. The house was about a quarter of a kilometer away. He could see no movement around the jeep.

He dropped down into the irrigation canal that ran alongside the road. It was damp in the bottom and thick with weeds but not muddy. He crouched low and made his way back toward the house. When he thought he was close, he peeked over the embankment. The jeep was about thirty meters away. There still was no movement. Maybe the soldiers were asleep. If he could get across the road without attracting attention, he could reach the cover of the bulldozer. From there he might be able to slip around to the back of the house and get inside without being seen.

He realized that he did not know what he would do then. This tunnel was a long one. It extended almost three kilometers before coming up inside a garage on the other side. If he remembered right. Santos did not have a flashlight. The idea of going so far in darkness through a cramped passage set with dynamite was not pleasant. Well, it would not be the first unpleasant thing he had done, and certainly could be no worse than what lay behind him.

He crawled onto the road on his belly and stayed a moment without moving. Then he crab-walked to the other side. The embankment there was shallower. He scrambled down, went into a crouch again, and hurried to the side of the bulldozer. He stopped and listened again. More crickets, more rustling leaves. An owl passed overhead. Otherwise he heard nothing.

He crept to the front end of the bulldozer. Beyond the curved edge of the blade the small frame house was visible. Its roof sagged, and the wood railing by the steps leaned wide of upright. To the north, across the border fence, were scattered house lights, and farther off a glow-worm of cars on a highway. It was strange to think of so many people going safely to so many other places without awareness of what was happening here.

Santos removed his shoes and tied them to his pack. He wished he had not let Rodrigo borrow his gun. Startling soldiers was like startling snakes. They might warn you or just shoot, and both reactions were understandable. If he could cross the distance between the bulldozer and the house without being seen, he might have a chance. If not, well, at least he would have chosen his own way to die.

He was about ready to make a run for the back of the house when a man stepped out from behind the blade of the bulldozer and confronted him. The shock was horrible. Santos felt like he had been scalded awake from a dream. In the span of a few seconds understanding passed through him that his entire life had been a miserable waste.

"Hello, Santos," the man said.

Even before he spoke, with his face obscured by darkness, Santos recognized him. "Hello, boss," he said. He stood up straight and resigned himself to his fate.

"What are you doing here?" El Pájaro asked.

There was no point in lying to El Pájaro. He could tell if you were lying. "I was going to run away. I stole some heroin. I was going to sell it on the other side, and get as far as I could."

"I see. Where is Martín?"

"He left me at a motel and did not come back. I do not know where he is."

El Pájaro looked both ways down the road and up at the sky. Santos could tell he was thinking. He wanted him to stop thinking and get it over with.

"Martín is dead," said El Pájaro. "A man who betrays his friends has no value."

Santos felt sick. This was his fault. It had all been his idea. He had gotten them all killed. "And Rodrigo?" he asked.

"He is learning to live with one hand." El Pájaro went back around the bulldozer to the jeep. Santos followed.

"Boss?"

"What?"

"Until tonight, have I done good work for you?"

"You have always been reliable, Santos."

"Maybe for six years of good work, you will grant me a favor."

"What favor?"

"Make it quick, boss. That is all I ask." Santos saw why the men in the jeep were so still. They were dead.

"It is better to trust a man who tells the truth than it is to kill him. We will cross the border together, and then see about making your life better, so you do not think about stealing my heroin, and running away." The words were false, and stirred no hope in Santos. El Pájaro picked up a paper sack from the ground in front of the jeep and set it on the hood. "First, I want to leave a message for the captain of the federal soldiers." He tore the sack open. Inside was a dead child, no more than three months old.

At the sight of the dead infant, an eel uncoiled in Santos' gut and began to squirm. "The captain—?"

The infant's body had stiffened. El Pájaro started working its limbs to straighten them. "He has shown that he needs special attention."

"The child is his?"

"What?" El Pájaro grunted. "I like the way you think, Santos. It would be better if this slug were his. This is just a nameless bag of flesh more use dead than alive. But the captain will understand the message, even so." El Pájaro gestured toward the side of the house. "There is some wood over there. Get me a couple of planks. I want to make a cross." He continued working the child's limbs.

Santos saw the jumble of wood beside the house. "Okay, boss." He put his shoes back on. The pile was mostly broken pieces of plywood and lumber. The wood had nails in it, and there were pieces attached to each other. The whole mess was fouled with chicken wire, barbed wire and other refuse Santos couldn't make out. He managed to free a two-by-four about a meter long and set it aside. A soft, popping sound came from the direction of the jeep. Santos threw up. The lights across the border shifted to the right and back several times. He staggered sideways until he came against a dead peach tree. He held onto the tree and gulped air. The vertigo passed and he went back to the wood pile.

"What is taking so long?" El Pájaro came over. "I did not know you were so weak. Get out of the way." He pushed Santos aside and reached into the woodpile. "I will buy you a dress and sell you to the faggots."

Santos leaned on his knees, gasping, and watched El Pájaro fight with the wood pile. There had been a few times when he had been struck by El Pájaro's size. In his mind, Santos always saw El Pájaro eight feet tall. It startled him to register how false this image was. He was a broad and muscular man but in reality El Pájaro was shorter than Santos.

"¡Maldición!"

The snake did not play fair. It did not rattle until after it struck. El Pájaro lurched back from the woodpile, clutching his wrist. The snake slithered away through the dry grass. Santos watched in fascination as the most dangerous man he had ever known fumbled with his pocket knife and struggled to open it.

"*¡Maldición! ¡Maldición!*"

El Pájaro got the knife open. He pushed up the sleeve of his shirt and placed the blade over the bite. His hands trembled. He was afraid, Santos realized, and it was as if a window of light opened in his mind, and something that had been bound deep within him broke free.

He kicked the knife out of El Pájaro's hand.

"Son of a whore!" El Pájaro shouted. "What are you doing?" He clamped his mouth over the bite and searched for the knife.

Santos picked up the two by four he had freed from the woodpile and hit El Pájaro on the side of his head. "Son of a whore!" El Pájaro staggered backwards and fell against the front steps of the house. Santos hit him again and he stopped moving.

He started to hit him a third time but checked himself. He felt strangely calm. He realized that he did not live in the same world as this man. They saw things very differently. A wicked thought came to Santos. He dropped the two by four and disarmed the dangerous man. He stuck El Pájaro's nine millimeter Beretta under his belt and threw his back-up revolvers into the field by the house. Then he went inside and pulled down a curtain. He tore it into strips and tied El Pájaro's hands behind his back and tied his legs together. Then he dragged El Pájaro inside the house.

He went back to the jeep. He avoided looking at what was on the hood. The soldiers had been shot in the head. Santos found a flashlight. One of the soldiers had been eating a torta and there was a half-empty Coke. Santos retrieved El Pájaro's knife and cut off the part of the torta that had blood on it. He sat on the steps of the house and ate the torta and drank the warm Coke. Then he went inside to take care of his boss.

The tunnel had been dug straight down from the middle of the living room. The plywood cover leaned against a wall. Santos dragged El Pájaro to the hole and dropped him in. El Pájaro grunted when he hit the bottom. Santos climbed down the ladder, shining the flashlight below as he went. The shaft went down about five meters.

The passage was less than two meters high. Santos shined the light down it. It looked like the charges had been placed every three meters or so. They would extend no farther than the border-fence line. Santos dragged El Pájaro into the tunnel until his head was directly under the first charge. By then the dangerous man was coming around. He was shaking and his jaw was clenched. The venom was working on him.

Santos patted him on the cheek and smiled. "Why are you alone, Pajarito? You did not expect to find Santos here, did you?" He went through El Pájaro's pockets. There were several credit cards but only a few hundred pesos in his wallet. "No, you have had many surprises this day. Starting, I think, with the soldiers killing your nephew and taking his men." There was also a booklet of traveler's checks. Santos pocketed the cash and tossed the wallet and checks. "You came here to settle with the Cardenas brothers and the Three Sixes, and show us you are still in control. I think you should have stayed in San Miguel de Allende, drinking Margaritas with your rich American friends." Santos took off El Pájaro's boots. "I am sorry to do this, Pajarito. But you are a tricky old bird, and I cannot take chances." He cut El Pájaro's Achilles tendons. The dangerous man shrieked through clenched teeth. Santos wrapped the wounds with strips of curtain cloth and tied the bandages tight.

"Take his belt," said a voice behind him.

Santos snapped around and shined the light into the

passage. The ghost was there, peering fixedly at El Pájaro. Santos could see the ghost's face.

"Take his belt," the ghost repeated. "It is full of money."

Santos stared at the ghost. He was not so old as he had first seemed. Santos recognized him, now, and it stirred feelings that he did not have time to feel. But he would not pretend to himself that he knew this ghost. Ghosts were never quite the same people they had been when they were alive.

The ghost's expression as he looked at El Pájaro was cut from stone. But when he looked at Santos it softened. Santos looked at El Pájaro. Many things were becoming clear that he had wondered about for a long time. He looked at El Pájaro's belt. El Pájaro was famous for his wide belt of hand-tooled leather, with its big silver buckle carved with a flying eagle. Santos pulled it off of him. Inside the belt was a zipper. Santos opened it. The belt was stuffed with American hundred-dollar bills, and inside the lower lip there were diamonds.

Santos pulled out his shirt, wrapped the belt around his waist, and tucked his shirt back in. "Tell me something, Pajarito," he said. "Be careful, I will know if you lie. Did my father die obeying your orders, or did you kill him because he would not?" El Pájaro could not speak. His face was beaded with sweat, and his pulse throbbed at his temples.

"Can he see me?" the ghost asked.

"He can see you," Santos said. "He pretends that he cannot but I have watched his eyes stop where others saw nothing. He can hear you, too."

The ghost leaned close over El Pájaro and said to him, "I was buried in an unmarked grave by men who knew my name."

El Pájaro would not look at the ghost. It was a disappointment to see the terror in his eyes.

Santos knew he owed the ghost a debt. It was hard thing, to pay a ghost. There was no point trying to get off cheap. If you were going to do it you had to go all the way, or the debt got bigger, and the ghost would nag you forever.

He opened his pack and dumped out the contents. He lifted El Pájaro's head and started arranging the bricks of heroin to make a nice pillow for him. "You are wondering why I do not kill you, Pajarito. It was a small snake, you are thinking, and you are strong. You are thinking that the poison will not kill you. I hope you are right, because I want the soldiers to find you. Maybe, when they see what you did to their *compadres*, they will leave you here and blow you to pieces and piss on the dirt above."

Santos knew that if he kept even one brick the debt would not be paid. He tried to believe he was doing this for himself, so that he could live differently. He doubted that he could. He had buried a callous seed in his heart, and it had put down roots in his soul. "But I hope they take you to a hospital and fix you up, so they can put you in a small room with no windows and forget about you. That way you will have a long time to think about Santos, while your mind eats itself. Then, when you die, an old man with a brain soft like a rotten papaya, your ghost will be sure to look for me, and I can teach you again what it is to have no power." Santos lowered El Pájaro's head gently onto the stacked bricks of heroin. Then he went back outside to the jeep.

When he returned to the tunnel he held the pack up so the ghost could see that it had weight again. "The child has no name," he said. "I will give him yours."

The ghost nodded. "Be sure he is buried in ground that has been blessed."

"I will."

The ghost cupped his cold hand against Santos' face. "And change your ways, my son."

Santos tried to respond but the words caught in his throat. He crouched over El Pájaro. "If you fear the dead, you should not create servants who don't."

Santos wiped the sweat from his eyes, rubbed his arm, where the stitches were itching again, and went in search of the land of the living.

Dining Strange

HIS HARD, NARROW features illumed in dashboard light, Kurl scanned communications chatter. Oscar Ferridin stood by the limousine's open door, looking on. Black darkness under the Earth-grown pines isolated the moment. Ferridin lit a cigarette, drifted to an abandoned house with a sagging roof nearby, leaned against the garage. The ghost of a once-thriving hillside suburb, by-product of inter-stellar migration, brooded about him. It was Ferridin's first time on Earth but the trees smelled like home. He gazed out across the city and contemplated vengeance.

Below, to the west, beneath a clear, moonless sky vast with stars, the city of Precipice shone brightly at its waterfront core, its far boundary defined by coastline. The clustering of sustained habitation amid so much vacancy called to mind primitives huddled around a fire. *Like me, besieged by void, crouched over the embers that keep me going.*

Depopulated as it was, Earth was still the seat of human governance, and held great power. Especially for Ferridin, which was the height of irony. He couldn't remember what Precipice had been called in earlier times. It was renamed for the space port. Kurl and he had avoided the port and brought the shuttle down rough, in a shattered parking lot by a defunct shopping center.

Ferridin heard something scurry up the wall, nabbed it, blinked long and short to see in infra-red. It was a cockroach. He popped it in his mouth and let it struggle before biting down, studied the squirt on his tongue. The flavor was disgusting until it changed. Regestive conditioning gave rise to odd impulses, made everything sweet.

"The code worked." Kurl came over. "We got through the net undetected."

Ferridin nodded. "Let's go."

They returned to the limousine, which had several long, vertical gashes in its side, now. Off-loading the vehicle had been an interminable ordeal; Ferridin would not take ground crews for granted, in future. Back inside, he blinked long twice to resume normal vision. Kurl ploughed through weeds tall as people to the access road, turned down toward the maintained part of the city. Ferridin watched abandoned homes and businesses file past. Celiph's murder was an apocalypse that permeated everything.

"We've got movement," Kurl said, when they were near the town center.

Whatever world he breached, abandoned high-rises reminded Ferridin of mausoleums. The proximity detector showed clusters of dots on approach at an upcoming intersection. "If they reach out, cut them," Ferridin said.

Kurl initialized the laser blade. A virulent red icon appeared on the dash. "It will announce us if I deploy it."

Ferridin reminded himself that he did not have to be cruel. "Go ahead and raise the shield."

Kurl tapped another icon, and plaques bearing the ambassadorial badge rose from slots in either side of the hood. Ferridin had been born on a planet far distant, but he was human and Earth was his home world, so the white badge's outline glowed blue.

They neared the intersection and several battered, decrepit sedans rolled out to bar their way. A mob poured around the corners of the cross street and rushed toward the limousine. One person raised his hand, shouted, and they all stopped. He'd seen the shield. Clamor and confusion followed. The barricade vehicles began to withdraw, then stopped too. Some of those surrounding the limousine resumed their approach, more warily, against loud objections from others.

How many lives was revenge worth? A number worse than infinity. But Ferridin told Kurl to alert the gate.

Kurl transmitted a distress call to the City Guard. "We have announced ourselves, now," he said.

Ferridin leaned forward and opened a panel by the wet bar, placed his palm on the scanner, keyed in a command. "My block won't hold long. We have maybe thirty minutes before they get exit clearance." They were losing much of the advantage, here, that they'd gained avoiding the port. Thoughts Ferridin had suppressed surfaced with the rise of tension. The memory of the small lacquer box that held Celiph's pitiful remains seared him, body and mind. It had taken monstrous restraint not to kill the delivery squire.

The mob parted, on the left, for a group bearing a long cylindrical object they evidently intended to use as a battering ram. A big pipe. Ferridin's patience waned. "Three meter perimeter," he told Kurl.

Kurl keyed in the range, tapped the red icon. When the pipe bearers and their supporters drew within three meters of the limousine, the blade arced out. Its victims were lit up in its flash, falling like grain. The after-image lingered. Screams mingled with shouts; the would-be marauders withdrew, dragging their dead and wounded. Ferridin gazed with sadness upon the miserable hoard limned now only in badge light. "They ought to do something for them or let them immigrate," he murmured.

"The export solution does reduce the problem," Kurl observed.

"They're rejects, Kurl, not meat."

"If you say so, sir."

Sirens approached. The barricade vehicles withdrew and the crowd dispersed. A military detail escorted the limousine to the city entrance. Doors in the barrier wall slid open, to either side of the gate. Guards filed out and snapped to attention like cords drawn taut. Ferridin rolled down the back window. The watch commander, in an evident state of bewilderment, trotted over from the kiosk, clicked his heels and bowed. "Ambassador. Welcome home."

Ferridin acknowledged the greeting with a minimal nod. "Discretionary mission, Commander. We're bound for the Guelth Embrasure," he said.

The commander straightened. "Yes, sir. The embassy zone is in the north quadrant. I'll instruct your escort——"

"Forego that, Commander. We'll make our own way." Diplomatic escort would be a processional crawl. Ferridin could declare an emergency but that would initiate its own protocols. He had no time for either.

The commander seemed unsure how to react.

"If you would open the gate——" Ferridin fixed his gaze forward with his chin down.

The commander gave the signal. The gate shut off; the escort vehicles parted. Kurl reviewed the dashboard map, chose a route, gunned it. They had seventeen minutes, if they were lucky.

The franchised zone was a gleaming testament to the human capacity for beauty and comfort. Puff-lamps hovered high and low, radiating warm light, even to the uppermost reaches of skyscrapers. The buildings evidenced a degree of care that bordered on adoration.

The streets were immaculate. A few blocks on they met jammed traffic. Ferridin took a long breath, made no comment.

"It is past the meal hour," Kurl observed irrelevantly. "They will likely be finished eating at the Embrasure. Shall we stop for something?" They were passing a row of restaurants.

Ferridin knew what Kurl was asking. They had been together too long not to understand each other. "I dine strange, tonight, Kurl."

Their gazes met in their monitors. "I think, Mr. Ambassador, that I should know my instructions, sir."

"On this night, of all nights, you address me with formality?"

"On this night, of all nights, Mr. Ambassador, I think formality pertinent, sir."

Ferridin stared out the window. Pedestrians on the sidewalk were well-dressed and healthy-seeming. If you lived in the authorized zones you lived well. A young woman, draped on the arm of an older, conservatively-attired man, had on a sheer, scanty garment that seemed more to hover about her than conceal her body. Something about her reminded Ferridin of Celiph. The laughter in her eyes. "Anyone interferes with me, kill them."

Kurl nodded. "That could be interpreted as aggression, Mr. Ambassador."

"Good," was Ferridin's weary reply.

Kurl took advantage of an opening, cut left across oncoming traffic, peeled into an alley. Twelve minutes. He sped along a zig-zag route down side streets, narrowly missed a pedestrian and caused a service truck to veer into a parked convertible. They entered the embassy zone of walled compounds, where trees were old and tall,

made their way to the Guelth Embrasure. Ferridin took a
pill container from his pocket and tossed a capsule in his
mouth.

The guards manning the outer gate were human and
gave way immediately. Ferridin had Kurl stop. "Deputize
them," he said.

"We need them?"

"Better to have them and not. Be quick."

Kurl lowered his window, beckoned the watch commander. When he and his three men were assembled, Kurl
said, "The Ambassador is deputizing you for a period not
to exceed twelve hours without judicial review."

The soldiers looked at each other in confusion.

Ferridin rolled down his window. "Gentlemen, I want
your assistance. If you're uncomfortable about it you may
remain at your posts without fear of reprimand."

The watch commander studied the state of the limousine, gave the ambassadorial badge hard scrutiny, then
his men, who nodded at him. He nodded at Ferridin.
"What are your instructions, Ambassador?"

"Follow us."

At the inner gate the sentries were Tzwil'st, a species
Guelthins often employed for security. They were less
ready to yield.

Kurl didn't need Ferridin's help. "I'll melt you right
here," he told the gate commander, "and send your sift
home in a sock."

The Tzwil'st commander clicked his elbows and his
subordinates withdrew. The burn wall disengaged and
Kurl pulled into the Embrasure, followed by the four
human sentries. The Guelth compound was unusual in
having retained use of buildings intended for human
occupants. The central mansion was a sprawling, three-
story structure with staggered, wing-like roofs and broad

eaves. The main entrance bore a decorative red round, reminiscent of pre-diaspora Asian design. The parking lot was crammed with official vehicles. Kurl parked in a restricted spot by the walkway. Retainers of various species bustled over in obsequious solicitude, opened both Ferriden's and Kurl's doors for them. Ferriden ignored them, made a throat-cutting gesture at Kurl, who depressed a node on his pocket sheet to activate a translation blackout field. A thunder of engines emanated from somewhere on the far side of the mansion.

"They're warming up the shuttle," Ferriden shouted over the din. "If they don't have clearance they're getting it. The pad's at the back of the compound."

Kurl turned down a flap on his jacket's breast, exposing his badge, gestured at the gate commander and one of his men to follow him, and the three ran off around the side of the mansion.

Ferridin beckoned the remaining soldiers; "You're with me." They went to the mansion's entrance, a gaggle of distraught retainers in tow. Guelthin retainers opened the doors and Ferridin strode through. The entry hall was hung with a disgusting web-work of dried entrails, a definitive example, no doubt, of what Guelthins dignified as tapestry. The odor was an irreconcilable confusion of rot and something like roses. The House Swell, berobed in gauzy pink-and-gold finery, floated out to greet them.

Ferridin found Guelthin facial characteristics reminiscent of cauliflower. They had seven compound eyes but only opened one or two at a time, in unpredictable sequence. The Swell made a show of turning on his translator—adjusted a device mounted on a lumpy protuberance that somewhat resembled a shoulder with one of his seven telescoping appendages. It was a feeble ploy to impress upon Ferridin that he stood on foreign soil.

"Your Eminence, welcome to the Guelth Embrasure. We were not apprised——"

"Get rid of them;" Ferridin gestured at the other retainers. The Swell shooed them outside and closed the door, muffling the engine noise. "This is Guelth-on-Earth," Ferridin told the Swell. "I am Ambassadorial Designate One, human, and therefore absent Embrasure. Territorial prerogatives are rescinded by my presence."

"Of course, of course," the Swell cooed. "If the Ambassador will accompany me, I will escort you to a comfortable waiting place, and inform my master——"

"Where are Q'uet and that glutton wife of his?" Ferridin demanded. "Take me to them immediately." He resisted the urge to see what a Guelthin looked like shocked, kept his gaze high.

"The Lord and Lady Ambassadors host a dinner in the main banquet hall——"

"Take me there," Ferridin commanded. "And treat me like I'm stupid or try to mislead me again, you'll go home as fertilizer. The only person other than myself retaining diplomatic sanction in this Embrasure is Q'uet."

The House Guard, comprised of Guelthin soldiers, made an appearance now, no doubt having been alerted by the Tzwil'st gatekeepers. Five of them filed in the main entrance behind Ferridin, letting the noise back in, and several more, their Rake among them, scrambled down the grand staircase, fire-horns drawn and leveled. Ferridin's guards raised their burners in response. The Swell frantically signaled the Guelthin soldiers to stand down but the Rake countermanded him.

Ferridin instructed his soldiers to lower their weapons, directed the Swell to conduct him onward, as if the Guelthin Guard did not exist. The Swell led Ferridin and his deputies across the entry hall into a long corridor. The

House Guard followed. The engine noise dwindled and died. Ferridin could not tell if it was because the engines had been cut, the front door of the mansion closed again, or—he prayed not—the shuttle taken off. Halfway down the hall the Swell opened double doors on the left. Ferridin pushed past him. Inside the banquet hall about fifty individuals of twelve or so species were seated or otherwise installed around a long table. Q'uet sat at the far end, the chair by his side conspicuously empty. The only human in the room, other than Ferridin and his deputies, was a person Ferridin was intensely gratified to find present. Until that moment he had not been certain that he'd had his superiors' support. Some of those superiors might come to regret having lent that support. If they thought he would stop here they would find themselves mistaken.

Conversation died as, gradually, all optical organs, or their equivalents, focused on Ferridin. He heard the House Guard file in and fan out behind him. The ceiling was festooned with more Guelthin tapestry. Ferridin gazed up, feigning an appreciative attitude. "This is in the modern style, isn't it? I'm noticing an exaggerated use of negative space——"

"What is the meaning of this, Ferridin?" Cantus Hiltsborough, Earth's Supreme High Ambassador, rose to his feet.

"Meaning?" Ferridin smiled at Hiltsborough. "In your case, Ambassador, I'd say welcome to Hell."

"How dare you! I demand——"

"No, no, you don't demand, Ambassador. Not of me, not here, not on Earth." Ferridin gave Hiltsborough a moment to reassess his position. "You've forgotten some things, sir, if you ever knew them, if you ever actually read the ambassadorial code. The function of a Designate One is constabulary, not diplomatic. We don't have posts. We go wherever humans are purported to have committed capital crimes against non-humans and coordinate investigative oversight. Normally you'd be right, you would be my superior. Anywhere but Earth. You came to the one place, you incredible imbecile, where my authority supercedes yours."

Doubt showed in Hiltsborough's eyes. He was beginning to grasp the circumstances. A number of guests made for the exit. Ferridin waved at his soldiers to let them go.

He yanked Hiltsborough away from the table. "Came all this way for *dinner*, Cantus? You haven't picked up a little taste for something, have you?" Ferridin glanced at the table. Peripherally, he noted the Guelthin Rake and three of his guards edge nearer. "I wonder what was on the menu, tonight." Hiltsborough shook his head in vehement denial of Ferridin's implied accusation. Ferridin leaned close. "You kept your travel plans secret from your own staff, but *I* knew you'd be here. You're going to think about that." To his deputies Ferridin said, "The Supreme High Ambassador is under arrest. If he tries to escape, melt his feet. If he tries to talk, shut him up however you like." The soldiers seized Hiltsborough's arms.

The rest of the guests made for the exit, now. Ferridin didn't care about them. Q'uet hadn't moved from his seat or made a squeak, which was telling.

"How have you been, Q'uet? You're a hard guy to see. Interesting, your higher-ups posting you here."

"You are very rude, Oscar, to interrupt my party."

"Let me make amends. Allow me to pay my respects to your wife. Where is R'uetfa?"

"She is indisposed."

"Ah. She wouldn't be trying to escape in your shuttle, would she?"

The rapidity with which Q'uet's eyes opened and closed increased.

Ferridin felt the muzzle of a fire horn at the nape of his neck. He took a long, deep breath. This had always been a possibility. Not everyone could be cowed; the stupid and the brave were unpredictable. "Some of your staff seem a little lax on protocol, Q'uet."

"You will address our ambassador with deference," said a translated voice. The muzzle prodded Ferridin.

Q'uet wasn't doing anything. The bastard was buying time. Ferridin turned to face the Rake of the House Guard. He didn't have to be able to read Guelthin facial expressions to see this guy wanted his innards trimming the ceiling. There was little chance of backing him down; he had to be aware of the probable consequences of challenging Ferridin's authority. Ferridin noticed that the muzzle of the fire horn was charred from recent use. Practice shots at the range, he told himself, but couldn't help wondering about Kurl. He found himself wondering, too, if the Rake had personal reasons for interfering. He tested the theory: "You were in on it, weren't you?"

The Rake's eye movements became more erratic. He drew back, which seemed a good sign until Ferridin noticed one of the Guelthin's appendages telescoping toward the trigger. Before he could fire, the Guelthin commander's superficial head evaporated in a pink-grey mist, spraying Ferridin with atomized bio-matter. Rendered voiceless and sightless, the Rake punched the trigger, possibly by reflex. Ferridin just dodged the plasma burst, which sent smoldering tapestry fluttering apart and scarred the ceiling. He grabbed the fire horn away and kicked the Rake to the ground.

Kurl stood inside the back door of the banquet hall, his burner drawn, the human gate commander and his subordinate two steps behind him, R'uetfa an equal space in front. At the sight of his wife, Q'uet let out a fluting wail and rushed to her side, frantically ordered the House Guard to stand down.

The Rake thrashed on the floor, gurgling through both his voice stem and esophageal portals. Ferridin told the Swell to get the House Guard and their C.O. out of the banquet hall. The Swell complied without even glancing at Q'uet. He was not so foolhardy in his allegiances as the Rake had been.

Ferridin tossed the fire horn on the banquet table, grabbed a hand towel and wiped his face. He gave Kurl a grateful nod, turned to Q'uet's wife. "R'uetfa, so good to see you. How have you been?"

"Very well——"

"Digestion good?"

"Oh yes, Oscar, thank you. And you?"

"Fine. Fine." He gave the banquet table a longer survey, recognized dishes from several worlds. It was a costly spread. "Isn't ambassadorial service great, Q'uet? All that biological conditioning. Did you know I can see in infra red? I can hear your cardiac tree, by the way. It's oscillating through the roof; you should calm yourself. But nothing compares to what they do to our digestive systems, does it? You and I, the people who work for us, we can eat pretty much anything, anywhere, anytime." Ferridin picked up a bread stick, nibbled. "How do you like Earth fare?" Q'uet didn't answer. Ferridin looked at R'uetfa. "How about you, Milady, do you like the food here?"

"Ferridin, show mercy," Q'uet pleaded. The strain in his voice was audible even through his translator.

Ferridin couldn't help himself; he was incredulous. *"Mercy?"* He flung the bread stick away.

"She is sick, Ferridin. She is not responsible—"

"I know she's sick!" Ferridin bellowed. The Guelthin Ambassador cringed and clung to his wife. "She has Compulsive Regestive Disorder." Ferridin clenched his jaw and took a loud nasal breath. "Top of the ten worst occupational hazards in the Service Manual. Wording kind of sticks with you: 'The irresistible urge to feed on the cognitive organs of higher life forms.'" Ferridin leaned close to Q'uet. *"Like my wife's BRAIN!"* He glared at Q'uet with sustained fury. The Guelthin ambassador could not hold his gaze. "The only reason you're not dead is your technical fucking immunity. Lose your job, I'll be along. Right now, here on Earth, the only one you can protect from me is yourself." Ferridin turned to Q'uet's wife. "Did you like Celiph, R'uetfa?"

"Oh, yes. She was my dear friend."

"Did she taste good?"

"Oh, yes. Wonderful, thank you." R'uetfa made a piping, whistling sound that was the Guelthin female's equivalent of a giggle.

"You've developed a special appetite for humans, haven't you?"

"Humans are wonderful." More giggling. "I love humans." She really was insane.

It did not move Ferridin to pity.

"Do you see?" Q'uet said. "She doesn't understand—"

"But *you* do. And have, for some time. And rather than put her in treatment you catered to her disease. What are a few rejects, more or less. Except there weren't any more rejects available, were there? And she was getting hungry. Which was apt to get out of hand."

"They would have wiped her mind, Oscar! Our neurology is different from yours! She wouldn't know me! She wouldn't know herself!"

"Yeah, well," Ferridin cupped R'uetfa's knobby face in his hand, "she certainly knew my wife, didn't you? R'uetfa dear, I need you to open your lid. Otherwise I'll have to cut it open."

"I wouldn't want you to do *that*, Oscar." She reached back with four of her appendages and kneaded the lip of the oval carapace at the base of her superficial head.

All of Q'uet's eyes came open. "What are you doing?"

"I've always found it fascinating," Ferridin said, "the idea of a liquid brain. You mingle your neural fluids during sex, don't you? Your children are born with some of your memories—must save on education. I was thinking, if one of you becomes brain damaged, or has their memory wiped, the other could help them repair themselves, couldn't they? I guess you'd have to give up some of yourself to do it. Your offspring would probably be morons, if you had any. But at least some of both of you would be there, right?"

R'uetfa's lid popped open. Ferridin slid his fingers into the orifice. The neural canal was surprisingly cool.

Q'uet folded himself before Ferridin, extended his appendages in entreaty. "Ferridin, *please!*" He pointed at Hiltsborough. "He said it was all right! He said you'd be honored!"

"Did he?" Ferridin looked at Hiltsborough. "*That* was presumptuous." He plunged his hand into R'uetfa's neural sack. All of her eyes opened, now. She made a quiet, cooing sound. Ferridin stirred his fingers around and carefully withdrew his hand. It was coated in neural jelly. He grinned at Q'uet and licked the jelly from his fingers. Even Kurl turned away. It was the worst thing Ferridin had ever tasted—something like saccharine, sulfur, and rotten fish. The palate-conditioning suppressant he'd taken was proving ineffective, though; it was starting to taste better. He didn't want that. That way lie addiction. By force of will he rejected the change and held to wretchedness. Which was, after all, the nature of rectification finding expression here.

Q'uet was prostrate before Ferridin, weeping from every pore of his face. It was obvious that he hadn't made love to his wife since the illness took hold of her. He had none of her madness in him, other than the ethical kind that resulted from feeding her. The Guelthin ambassador had been living in his own hell.

"You're going to identify every subordinate involved in reject procurement and my wife's death," he told Q'uet.

Q'uet nodded, his cauliflower face near touching the floor.

Ferridin knew he had committed an awful sin, one for which he might never stop paying. He teased R'uetfa's neural lid closed and helped her into a chair. She was making noises her translator couldn't translate. "I'll leave you enough of her to care about," Ferridin told Q'uet. "More than you left me." He had sacrificed a piece of himself to retribution. He didn't care. And he wasn't done.

Ferridin accepted a hand cloth from Kurl, noticed that the human soldiers were appalled at his conduct. He shouldn't have let them witness this. He instructed their commander, whose eyes seethed with suppressed indignation, to take his men and stand guard outside the banquet hall. The commander stiffly complied.

Ferridin turned his attention to Hiltsborough. "Supreme High Ambassador! I was afraid I was going to have to wait for you to retire to get things settled between us. But here you are, in my bailiwick, delivered by your own hand."

Hiltsborough was ashen, bereft of bluster. "Oscar——"

"I know what you did, Cantus. You wanted the trade agreement with Guelth. People were beginning to see you for the idiot you are, and you needed to secure your cozy little posting on Tilfur. So you invited me on that ridiculous hunting trip. Who would turn down an invitation from the Supreme High Ambassador, even if he is a twit? It's seared in my memory, you standing there, suggesting, oh, so innocently, that Celiph stay with Q'uet and his wife." Ferridin nodded at Kurl, who bound Hiltsborough's hands and legs with lash cords, and dragged him into a chair.

"I haven't had much to eat, tonight, Cantus. Just an appetizer."

Hiltsborough was too terrified to speak.

"Don't worry, I can't kill you. I doubt I'd get in much trouble if I did, but I can do pretty much whatever else I want. Your lands, assets and title are forfeit. You will be held, without bail or trial, indefinitely, subject to my discretion. Your wife and children will be on the street, in disgrace, on an alien planet, before another cycle elapses, unless you help me clean house, and I mean *cooperatively*, starting with the evil, murdering sons-of-bitches in Immigration Rejection. But first things first." Ferridin took out his snip and unfolded the oscillating blade, placed it near one spot, then another, on Hiltsborough's body, letting Hiltsborough see him ponder where to cut.

Ferriden felt Kurl's tentacle on his shoulder.

"Not your own kind, Oscar," Kurl said gently. "Never your own kind."

Reluctantly, Ferridin backed away. He lit a cigarette. His hands were shaking.

"With your permission?" Kurl said.

"With my *insistence!*" Ferriden spat.

Kurl lifted Hiltsborough's legs onto another chair,

removed the Supreme High Ambassador's shoes and socks and rolled up his pants. Kurl unfolded his jaw and secreted a numbing agent onto the Supreme High Ambassador's feet, then slathered them with pancreatic acid. It wasn't until the flesh lost cohesion and started to sluff from the bones that Hiltsborough began to scream.

Kurl collected some of the sluff into a bowl and fed.

"How is it?" Ferridin asked.

"Surprisingly good," Kurl replied.

Ferridin bared his teeth at the screaming Hiltsborough. "*That's* what *I'm* talking about!"

Kurl let paramedics come in and tend the injured. Hiltsborough was taken away, shackled to a gurney. Ferridin arranged for further military support to be sent to the compound, gave the gate commander an ambassadorial badge, instructed him to lock the place down and arrest whomever Q'uet identified. The commander seemed to soften, somewhat.

Ferridin and Kurl returned to their shuttle, flew back to the ambassadorial cruiser and set a course for the interstellar Conference of Governors, where they were still trying to hash out an inter-species definition for cannibalism. Ferridin had been called to testify, and indeed had much to say. Just at the moment, though, he felt quite pleasantly full.

Verge Land

THE AUTOMATED TELLER ate her card. Marcia Mesto stared at the machine in disbelief. She moaned and slapped it but it did not yield. What was she thinking? Money was no help now. It would have been a comfort.

Thirty feet away, her car sat where it had chugged to a stop, out of gas, in the otherwise vacant parking lot of the small strip mall. There was the original foolishness, not filling up when she had the chance. It was after midnight. Everything was closed—the Woodland Market, the Bits & Baubles Gift Shop, the Clean Queen Laundromat, Chuck's Drive-up Liquors. Her cell phone was dead and she couldn't see a pay phone anywhere. What a place to get stranded, on the edge of a blink-and-miss-it town in the middle of nowhere, with the city still miles distant.

The light over the teller was a foreign presence in a darkness otherwise electrically uncontested. She was reluctant to leave its superficial security. She didn't know what to do. Training employees at the corporation's branch offices had seemed a welcome escape from routine—she'd always wanted to travel. Now all she wanted was to be home, soaking in a hot bath, sipping wine and listening to music. The thought of spending the night in the car was claustrophobic. Surely there must be a motel nearby. Going through the little town, where the only gas station was closed, she hadn't seen one. But if she followed the road, surely she would find something—an all-night mini-mart, maybe. Or at least a gas station—hel-*lo!* She changed into her running shoes, took her car key off of the key ring and put it in her wallet, and left everything else in the car.

The two-lane highway wound south through the hills, through dense hemlock forest. Beyond the strip of shops it went straight for a distance, downhill, before curving from view. A high, narrow moon lent the asphalt a dim sheen. Never since childhood had Marcia seen the sky so full of stars. She crossed to the far shoulder and set off at a brisk pace, trying not to think about how alone and vulnerable she was. A mild wind soughed through the trees. Here and there little noises issued from the woods, suggesting things Marcia strove not to imagine. A car went by; she caught a glimpse of a man and a woman. She wished she'd tried to get their attention. An eighteen-wheeler loaded with raw timber came rumbling, growling and clattering down the hill. She left the roadside and waited in the trees for it to pass.

When she got to where the road began to curve she looked back. The light of the automated teller was a faint glow far uphill. A few steps more and it would be gone. She would just see what was around the bend, she told herself. If there wasn't anything, she would go back. Maybe the town had a police station. Or a phone booth. Surely there would be a phone booth in the town. More foolishness, she was going the wrong way.

Another car went by, and two going the other way, and then another timber-hauling semi chased her into the trees again. It was a long, gradual curve, and when she got to the end of it the road turned the other way, so she decided she might as well follow it around that, too, and see what she could see. But when she reached the end of the second curve the highway spilled into darkness, and there were no friendly, human lights anywhere. While she stood deliberating, a pickup truck came by. It slowed and pulled onto the shoulder, stopped a short distance ahead of her. It was an old truck, green, it looked, with a dent in the tail gate. As it backed up she noticed a gun rack in the rear window bearing two long guns. The driver leaned over and rolled down the window.

"Ma'am? Do you need a ride?"

"I——" He was a big person with a heavy beard. He wore a workman's cap. Marcia couldn't see his face clearly. "No—No, I live around here."

The man looked up and down the road. "Where?" He sounded incredulous.

"I—I'm fine." She walked on, getting several steps before realizing that she was still going away from the town. But if she turned around she might seem lost, and would have to pass by the truck again. After the man left she would turn back. Please, just let him leave.

She got about a hundred feet before the truck moved again. It didn't drive away. It followed her, slowly. Maybe the driver was concerned for her safety. The other possibilities were too terrible to risk testing the theory. She waved him on but he kept following. It was too much. She fled the road and plunged into the trees. She heard the truck speed forward and skid to a halt behind her.

"Ma'am!" the man cried, "I don't mean you no harm, Ma'am! You shouldn't be out here on your own like this! *Ma'am!*"

His voice affected Marcia like a whip. She ran on, branches and undergrowth slashing at her arms and face and tugging at her skirt. The driver must have pointed the truck into the forest, because the trunks of the trees were suddenly illuminated. Marcia ran from the light. She tripped and fell, picked herself up, tripped again, ran on.

The man continued to call after her, his voice growing distant. She ran until she tired herself out. She stopped to catch her breath and the reality of the woods settled about her.

She didn't know how far she had run, or how long. There were no lights anywhere, just the dim volume of the forest, extending indefinitely in all directions. She tried to get a sense of where the road lay. All she could see was the dark columns of the trees, which seemed to merge into an encircling wall. She turned in place and lost all sense of direction. A greater panic seized her and she ran on, tripping and catching herself, falling, running. The man in the truck became the lesser fear, and she cried out, "Wait! Don't leave me! I'm here! I'm here!" But no comforting answer issued through the implacable woods.

Again she ran until she tired herself out, then collapsed to her knees and sobbed. How could she, in so short a space of time, have left behind all that was safe and warm and comforting? The forest was all the same—she could wander here forever and never find her way, and never be found. The sudden horror of it challenged her sanity. Never had she felt so exposed and alone. It was her fault. All her fault!

With great effort she calmed herself, and tried to think constructively. Running around at random was no good, especially not in the dark. She should stay where she was and listen—listen for the road, yes. The big trucks were noisy. One was sure to come by, and she ought to be able to hear it. If not, she supposed she should stay there until morning anyway. She hated the thought; but even if she was still lost, in daylight she could at least see where she was going and not fall so much. She could feel scratches on her legs, arms and face, some of them bloody, and she had scraped her hands and knees. She didn't want to think about the germs that could be invading her wounds. How she longed for a bath, the simple comfort of running water. She sat with her back to a tree and cried again, clutching her wallet to her breast. If she had to spend the night there she would not sleep. The forest was too menacing.

She closed her eyes and listened. All she could hear was the trees creaking and branches swaying, and now and again a terrible rustling or cracking twig that could have been an animal moving about. No trucks—no wonderful, deep-throated engines. She squeezed her wallet, worried the round, magnetic clasp. There were times in the city when she hated all things motorized. Never again. Now she prayed just to hear one. It could belch black smoke to blot out the sky, if only it would lead her back to the safety of her apartment. But the only thing countering the silence of the night was the forest in its restless slumber.

She heard something, then, that it seemed she might have heard before and not recognized. She raised her head, unsure if it was real. She heard it again. Voices. Human voices! And music—flutes and drums, it sounded like. Young people, probably, out having a party. Good, decent young people, who would have pity on a silly, middle-aged business woman, who got herself stranded and lost in the forest.

She moved toward the sounds, giddy, almost, with relief, and presently perceived a flickering light, filtering through the trees. But as she drew closer, the sounds' character became clearer, and she grew hesitant. They had a harsh, visceral edge that was disconcerting. She needed help; she had no choice but to go on. She arrived at a clearing. What Marcia found there she did not readily understand. There was a fire, and naked figures cavorting about it, engaged in some wild ritual. Some played instruments—crude drums and flutes, and pieces of rock and wood that they struck together—some shouted and sang in an unrecognizable language. The most bewildering thing was that not all of the figures seemed human. Some of them had tails and horns.

With unnatural speed, one of the latter dashed over, and before Marcia could react grabbed her by the hair. She wanted to scream but her throat would not release her voice. The creature leered at her. His tongue was forked, his face bulbous and cruel. He had yellow eyes with black bead-like pupils, and no irises. "Hello, Sweet," he grated; "we'll have a taste of you, won't we?" His horns bent in different directions and one was broken. One of his fellows joined him, a demon with a false leg made of a jagged-ended tree limb, and the two picked Marcia up and carried her toward the fire.

They threw her down by the fire, and all of the revelers, human and non-human, gathered around to taunt her. They poked her with their fingers and jabbed her with sticks, and pulled at her clothes and hair. It was a hideous group. The humans were like mockeries of people, no easier to look upon than the demons, hairy and unclean, disfigured, gap-toothed, with slack, sagging flesh that was bruised and mottled. Marcia did not want to believe that the demons were real; but she saw their tongues flick, and their tails twitch, and beheld their cloven hooves, and knew that they were. It seemed that she had descended unwittingly into hell. She cowered before her tormentors, averting her eyes, praying that they would finish quickly whatever they were going to do to her. Her fear pleased them, and did not move them to mercy.

After a time, they seemed to lose interest in her, and carried on with their debaucheries. From a wooden vat they filled crude, stone goblets with a thick, dark, unwholesome-seeming fluid that they imbibed with relish. They engaged in all manner of bestial acts that were disgusting to witness. They took delight in hurting each other, and there was no tenderness in their copulations. They became so immersed in orgy that Marcia began to hope they had forgotten her. But when she attempted to escape they moved swiftly to prevent her. They kicked and slapped her, and drove her back to her place.

They wore themselves out, and lolled about awhile, seeming dazed. Then they roused themselves, broke the vat apart and flung their goblets into the trees. They left Marcia by the dying fire and departed the clearing. It was several minutes before she understood that she was alone again. She stood up shakily, unsure the ordeal was over. She had expected to be raped or murdered or worse. She took a step and faltered. The demons were in the woods, and it was still dark out there. The fire was the nearest thing to comfort she had left. It had burned low. She gathered the staves of the broken vat and piled them over the dwindling flames. They released a foul-smelling fume but they burned. She knelt before the fire, whimpering to see the viscous residue of the demon brew bubble upon the wood. She didn't know what else to do. She slumped to the ground and cried herself to sleep.

SHE AWOKE WITH an awful sense of dread, and a feeling that the world had betrayed her. The sky was overcast, rendering the clearing a grim, inhospitable place. The fire had died out; but there was an end of a stave that had not burned, and the color of the substance that clung to it made her want to wretch. She could not have named it but knew in her flesh that she had lost some measure of innocence she had not known she still possessed, some sentimental illusion that had preserved, for her, life's rosy hue. There was no sign of a trail, no indication which way those who had abandoned her had gone. She was still lost.

A fat, furry animal, about the size of a large cat, waddled across the edge of the clearing. Marcia had never seen its kind before. It seemed gentle and harmless, and she stirred herself to follow it. The forest looked very different in daylight. A break in the clouds let in brighter light, and the beauty of the trees, flowers, ferns and other growths ameliorated her pains and woes. She did not want to dwell on the horrors of the night; she could not make sense of them. She took stock of her wounds. Most were superficial, but there was a gash on her left shin that looked nasty, and the palm of her right hand had a bad scrape. There was a splinter in that hand, too, stuck in the clotted blood. She couldn't get it out. Her grey business suit, the one that fit her so well, was torn and soiled. Why hadn't she changed into her blue jeans? Excess of modesty, afraid someone driving by might see. Her nylons were shredded; she peeled them off and discarded them. It struck her how different she would have felt if she were only wearing blue jeans. Even the night's dreadful ordeal might have been easier to endure. The comfort of clothes—but she had to go on without that.

She watched light change among the trees, and had a sudden experience of understanding where she was—not in the sense of location on a map, but that this was where she lived, the same world upon which she had always lived, and that this was its nature. It was a sensual perception that evoked the mystery of life. She remembered what it was like as a child to be fascinated and curious about everything. The matters with which she had become preoccupied as an adult seemed trivial and senseless. She thought about her siblings, nephews, nieces and friends, and how much she had let work and ambition and self-absorption separate her from them. She opened her wallet. The few photos she had were old. A desperate desire came over her to reach the people she loved, and let them know, without restraint or hesitation, how deeply she cared about them.

With fresh determination, and a newfound sense of purpose, she moved on. But she was still lost. The furry creature she had followed was nowhere in sight. She had no idea which way to go, and so went the way she happened to be facing, telling herself that if she kept going she would eventually find something. But sometimes she heard sounds that could have been voices, and changed direction to seek them, and other times was seized by irresistible urges to alter her course yet further, and she grew to feel that she was becoming more lost than ever. As the day wore on, and the forest seemed no less endless or unchanged, fear again began to dominate her outlook. She was hungry and thirsty and tired. The strain on her psyche was difficult to bear, and she feared she might go insane. Recognition of the indifference of the natural world became inescapable— it did not care if she lived or died. She might leave or stay and it would not matter to the trees or the ferns or the flowers, nor even to the little furry creature, who had visited her, however briefly, with reassurance. She had to keep going as long as she could. She had to find her way home.

BY HER FOURTH day in the forest Marcia was greatly changed. Her mind was empty of thought or prayer, and she was driven on only by thirst, and the black will to proceed. All trace of character and expression had vacated her features. The forest was an endless maze. Negotiating its random vaults seemed the only life she had known.

Many ghosts emerged from the ethers about her to accompany her in scattered procession. At first she did not see them. She sensed, then, that she was not alone, and looking to her sides saw the ghosts, and knew them for what they were. A physical panic, a kind of autonomic revulsion, seized her, and she tried again to flee. But her strength was too diminished, and she knew the effort was pointless. She did not go far before surrendering to acceptance. She was beyond escaping anything.

The ghosts were spread all through the woods. She could not tell how many there were. There could have been hundreds. They stopped as one before her, and as one subjected her to their collective regard. What fresh horror is this, she wondered. But her capacity for horror had been exhausted. It was a mere word, now, that retained little meaning. The ghosts were clothed in the modes of varied times and cultures. There were natives and immigrants, and some were naked. She did not recognize any of them but some of them recognized her. She could see in their eyes that they knew her.

Only one question still surfaced in her mind with any potency: What had she done to deserve this? She did not voice the question but a ghost came forward as if in response—an old man, clad in the garb of a century past. Neither did he speak; but she saw in his wizened, hollow stare her answer: Nothing. She had done nothing to deserve her suffering. Seen through the old ghost's semi-transparent body, the forest was hazy and surreal. And yet its nature was further clarified. She had simply encountered the way of things, the impersonal cycle of existence that she had denied or been sheltered from her whole life.

Marcia felt pity for the ghost, almost more than for herself, though she did not know why. She understood that she was alone, and always had been. She looked about at the other ghosts, and watched them depart, singly and in clusters. When the last had vanished she collapsed to her hands and knees, overwhelmed by confusion. The implications of the experience were dizzying. Her wallet fell from her pocket. She no longer recognized it or understood its purpose. Nowhere that she looked in herself could she find comfort or reassurance; she knew she had to go on without either. Her mind emptied again. She left her wallet where it lay and went on.

TWO WEEKS LATER, some boys from the village found Marcia's body. They were out checking their snares, and found her near one that had caught a partridge. The boy whose snare it was set the bird free. He stayed behind while the others hurried to inform the elders.

A group of men was appointed to bear Marcia's remains into town. The boys led them back to the place where she lay. The men remarked with astonishment upon the strangeness of the dead woman's appearance. They were struck in particular by the shortness and cut of her hair, and the peculiar garments she wore.

Marcia watched them place her body onto a litter. They handled it with great care and respect. It was ironic to see her physical self receive such tender treatment after it was dead. The men lifted the litter onto their shoulders, and Marcia followed them on through the woods.

The trees here were different, she noticed—much older, more varied in shape, and less regular in placement. They came out of the woods onto a dirt road, where an ox-drawn cart awaited. The men placed the litter onto the cart. One man led the ox, the others walked alongside the cart, and the boys trailed behind. They followed the road out of the forest, down through tilled fields, until at length they came into the village, where the road joined a lane between thatch-roofed cottages. The bearers brought

Marcia's body into a cobbled square bordered by half-timbered houses with steep gable roofs.

There were no cars in the village, only horses, and horse or ox-drawn carriages and carts. Villagers gathered round to view the corpse. No one recognized the dead woman, and again, many remarked upon her strange clothes. It was not just their design but the material from which they were made. No one had ever seen such fabric. Marcia noted the dress of the villagers. The men wore simple tunics and loose-fitting pants, the women plain peasant dresses that were mostly brown or white, though a few were red or blue.

The elders arrived, and the priest, and the bailiff, the latter wearing woven tights and a leather jerkin, and a discussion ensued as to what should be done. The villagers did not speak English; but Marcia was dead, so she understood them. It was decided that a wake would be held for the unknown woman. Many felt sympathy for her, because it was apparent that she had lost her way, and died a most unfortunate and lonesome death. Her body was taken to an inn, where it was bathed and wrapped in a linen shroud. Her strange garments, as was the custom, were burned, though some of the townsfolk objected. A coffin was prepared, and her body was laid inside of it, and then the coffin was raised upon a table, and candles were lit about it. The priest came and blessed the corpse, and mourners came to view it. A modest feast was prepared, and the villagers gathered at the inn and in the square to sing and pray and eat and drink and celebrate the stranger's life.

Marcia stood beside her body and looked down at it. She was in the same situation she had been in since she became lost, she realized. She did not know where she was or where to go. Really, that had been the case her whole life, from the day she was born. She looked down upon herself and realized that even her identity was a mystery. Who was this strange physical self she had inhabited? She no longer felt any connection to her body. She hardly recognized it.

Had she been alive, Marcia knew that she would have found the village and its inhabitants confusing. But in death she regarded the fact that she had become dislocated in place and time without much interest. Where was any place? When was any time? She did not know these people and felt nothing towards them. Still, it seemed fitting that she bear witness to the things that they did in her honor. Only once, when a young girl placed a sprig of asphodel upon her body's lifeless breast, did Marcia feel a quiet gratitude stir within her non-corporeal consciousness. It was the first emotion she had experienced since dying.

She left the inn, and went to the well in the center of the village square, and sat on its lowest step. She wondered if she had anything left to give. The young girl who had placed the flowers upon her breast came out and sat beside her. Marcia wondered if the child sensed her presence. The girl extended her arm, pointing up, and looking where she pointed, Marcia saw the first stars emerging in the evening sky. She stayed there, looking up. Long after the girl had left and the villagers gone to bed, Marcia Mesto remained by the well, rapt in contemplation of the cosmos.

The Alchemist's Eyeglasses

THREE WIVES AND three divorces, that was how Harvey Silch viewed his life. And now, working at Valley Optical as an eyewear technician, he was treated daily to a parade of beautiful women obsessed with their looks. Their vanity did not offend him; he loved them all. Some of them even showed interest in him. Why not? He wasn't bad looking, he had good manners and could be witty when the occasion called for it. But at the exact moment when a word or two might further his chances, he'd think, "Three wives, three divorces," and clam up. Thus had his love life dropped into void.

Then Chloe Fontaine came in, tall, slim as a model, with short dark hair, breasts the size of cocktail umbrellas unfettered in a green, breezy tank top, jeans ultra-low, silken belly bare, a relaxed way of moving that was a natural blend of sensuality and confidence, and when she took off her sunglasses her eyes were blue and clear and seemed to know everything. In short, she was a fairy creature of dreams and she terrified Harvey. She came to the counter, exuding a scent like eau de Garden of Eden on steroids. Harvey decided that a woman like her would never be interested in him and his soul breathed a sigh of relief.

"How may I help you?" he asked her and smiled. He had just opened the shop. He'd been up late, watching an old Bogart and Bacall movie, and come in foggy. But he was wide awake now.

"Are you the optometrist or the lab technician?" Her voice was warm and melodious.

"I make the glasses. I'm the technician."

"Are you Harvey Silch?"

That was unexpected. "Yes."

"Kind of an unfortunate name, isn't it? Sounds like zilch."

Harvey sighed. "So my wives have told me."

"Plural? Are you a bigamist?"

"Serial divorcée. Three wives, three divorces."

She mugged surprise. "Given up yet?"

"I'm sorry, what's this about?"

Her familiarity turned to embarrassment. "Oh, I'm sorry! I've got a bad habit of blurting out whatever I'm thinking. It's really rude."

"It's okay."

"I came to you because you worked on telescopes, right? You got laid off a year ago?"

He frowned. "How do you know that?"

She waved the question away. "I was a research assistant for a senator. I can find out anything. The point is, you're used to doing work that requires a high degree of precision?"

"I suppose so. I started in glasses. They're not really the same thing."

She reached in her bag, pulled out what looked to be a solid gold eyeglass case and set it on the counter. Rummaging further she produced a slip of paper, which she handed to Harvey.

"I need to know if you can grind these glasses, adjust them, whatever you call it, to match that prescription."

Harvey frowned at the paper. The calibrations weren't just precise, they were ridiculous. "You're kidding," he couldn't help saying.

"What do you mean?"

"Well, setting aside that these measurements are needlessly precise—is this for you?"

"Yes."

"Well, this 'prescription,' if I can call it that, is only going to have a negligible effect on your eyesight. You don't need glasses. Looking through lenses like this won't to be much different from looking through air. In fact air would be better—you wouldn't have the glasses in the way."

She laughed, and of course sparkled when she did it. "You're direct. I like that. Can you do it, though?"

He picked up the case. Its weight supported the gold theory. It was etched all over with weird symbols.

"There's a catch." She reached over and touched the case's edge.

It opened, clam-shell style, in Harvey's hands. Weird as the case was, weird as the request was, weird as—it couldn't be denied—the woman was, the glasses were weirder. The lenses were round. They weren't standard optical glass—some precursor, maybe. And quite thick. Grinding them down to match the "prescription" might take hours, if it could be done at all.

"I know it's an unusual job. I'm willing to pay well. Say a thousand, does that sound all right?"

Harvey didn't answer. He was looking at the frames. They were white, and appeared to be made of bone. There were tiny markings on them.

"The frames come apart where the arms attach, to remove the lenses."

"I see that." There was definitely something peculiar about these glasses. He moved them around under the lamp and noticed prismatic flashes on the counter top.

"Well?" Chloe asked.

"They look like antiques. I wouldn't want to be responsible if they got damaged."

"Understood. I won't hold you responsible if they break. They won't, though."

Harvey made a face. "I don't know what material this is. I don't know how they'll respond to grinding. Also I'd need to find out what their refraction index is."

"Can you do that?"

"Well, I've got a refractometer at home but——"

"I'd pay you extra for your trouble."

Harvey considered. The money was tempting. Not overwhelming but tempting. Her assurances about liability—the days of the reliable handshake agreement were moldering with his grandfather's bones. "I don't know, this feels a little strange——"

"Five thousand," she interrupted, "and you stop asking questions. She reached in her bag again, removed her wallet, held out a sheaf of bills. "Half in advance."

He rolled his fingers on the counter, looked at her, looked at the glasses, looked at the money again. He looked back toward the lab. "We've got an old cylinder machine, so you're in luck there, if I can get it running. We don't work with glass, anymore. It's all plastic." She was still holding out the money. "Let me see if I can do it. You can pay me afterwards."

She let her arm relax and tilted her head, gave him an appraising look, put the money away. "How long will you need?"

"Come back around eight. If I can do it, they'll be ready."

"You close at six."

"I'm giving myself some leeway. Just knock. I'll hear you."

She gave him a card. "Here's my number, if you run

into trouble." She lit up the universe with her smile, again. "See you at eight."

"Better make it nine."

She laughed. "All right."

After Chloe left, Harvey took the glasses to the lab and gave them a careful examination under a magnifying lamp. The frames were indeed bone—he could see the pores. The incised symbols seemed to coincide with those on the case. The prismatic effect was elusive. He couldn't get it to repeat the same way twice.

The doctor arrived, and Harvey's lab assistant, and finally the receptionist. Harvey had a busy morning filling prescriptions. At noon he drove home and got his tools out of the garage. There was a certain pleasure in reviving skills he had not used in a long time. He put one of the lenses in his refractometer, whistled when he saw the reading. 1.78! That was like heavy flint glass. He held the lens up to the overhead light in the kitchen. He had no idea what it was made from. Some kind of crystalline composite.

He measured the front curve of both lenses. They matched. He entered the measurement, Chloe's prescription, and the refraction index into his computer. It looked like he could do the job. He customized a couple of old, wooden grinding blocks to hold the lenses, packed the blocks, polishing compound, and a set of grinding and polishing wheels in a bag, and went back to the shop.

After the doctor and Harvey's co-workers had left, at the end of the day, Harvey took the cover off of the cylinder machine, and made sure it was in working order. The lenses were remarkably easy to grind and polish. He finished the job quickly and went out for a meal, then came back to meet Chloe.

She showed up a few minutes early. It had started to

rain. Harvey let her in and helped her with her umbrella. He went to the counter and got the glasses.

"All done," he said, giving them to her.

"No difficulties?" she asked.

"Somewhat to my surprise, none at all. I'd be curious to know what those lenses are made from."

"I have no idea." She gave him his payment.

"Thank you."

She removed the glasses from the case and put them on, looked up as if testing them against the light. She caught her breath in surprise.

"I'm sorry," Harvey said, "I have to ask, what is the deal with those things?"

"I thought we agreed no more ques . . ." A series of curious changes took place in her expression. She looked away a moment, then back at Harvey, uttered a bewildered laugh and said, "I guess it doesn't matter!"

Harvey's weirdness meter climbed a notch. "What doesn't matter?"

"Telling you." She laughed again. "They make it possible to see the right thing to do."

"Beg pardon?"

"My uncle left them to me. He made these glasses. He was an alchemist. When you put them on, you can see the best thing you should do to make your life turn out well."

Harvey blinked. "Okay." He rolled his fingers on the counter. "That clears that up."

Chloe grinned. "Is that a polite way of telling me I'm nuts? That's not your style, Harvey."

Harvey cleared his throat. "I don't mean——"

"Say you meet a girl," Chloe said. "You like her but you're not sure you fit together. Put on these glasses and you'll know. You'll see it. You won't have to wonder if you're making a mistake, setting yourself up for disaster,

years down the road. Right away you'll know, no guesswork involved."

Harvey blinked a few more times.

"Can I use your restroom?" Chloe asked.

"End of the hall, on the left."

She kept the glasses on, left the case and her wallet on
the counter. Harvey looked at the money in his hand. He
felt like he'd just taken advantage of an innocent, then, in
some indefinable way, like he was about to. Which was
impossible. If there was one thing Harvey knew about
himself, it was that he was honest. Two of his ex-wives
had cited "excessive honesty" as a prime reason for seeking a divorce. He'd never stolen or done a dishonest thing
in his life.

He glanced at her wallet. It was open and her driver's
license was visible.

A moment later Chloe returned, scooped up her wallet and the glass case, looked outside. "It's stopped raining."

"Mm." She wasn't like most women, who looked
smarter wearing glasses. On her they were an impediment. And yet, not. They didn't change her at all, really. It
was like she'd put them on to look silly on purpose.

"You think I'm bonkers, don't you?"

Harvey opened his mouth, said nothing.

"Yeah," she grinned. "But you'll wonder." And with
that, and a fingery wave, she was gone.

He stood behind the counter, staring after her. Wonder? Maybe. Not necessarily about what she meant. Her
scent lingered, like the ghost of an unfulfilled wish. Sanity
could be optional. In a relationship. He could see sanity
being optional.

What the hell was he thinking about?

He straightened the bills on the counter, folded them
and stuffed them in his pocket. Two thoughts kept doing

doubles' ping-pong in his head: "Three wives, three divorces," and, "No guesswork involved." Think what his life would be if he'd had that kind of clarity prior to any one of his marriages. And he was still interested in women, oddly enough. But there was a difference, now.

He was afraid of them.

Which was not surprising. How many times do you stick your hand in a fire before you get wise? But if he had glasses like that, well, he'd be back in the game in a heartbeat, wouldn't he? He didn't need "perfect." He'd settle for "will not utterly crush your spirit and chop your heart into pâté." Fact was, Harvey did not like living alone.

Well, those glasses wouldn't be of use to anyone else, now that he'd ground them so thin to fit Chloe's "prescription." Except him, he realized. His eyesight was better than hers. A minor adjustment and—The direction of his thoughts startled him. Certain species of insanity were evidently communicable. He laughed at himself.

He turned out the lights and was about to leave when he noticed Chloe's umbrella leaning against the window.

An hour later he knocked on her door. She answered wearing the glasses. She'd changed into a sage-colored khaki jump suit that fit her like second skin. Somehow it was even sexier than what she'd had on before. Harvey swallowed and held out the umbrella.

"I happened to notice your address—you left your wallet open on the counter. You forgot your umbrella." He held it out farther. "More rain tomorrow."

She smiled. "Why don't you come in? Satisfy your curiosity."

Harvey started to dissemble. She took him by the hand and led him inside.

"Don't pretend you're not intrigued, Harvey. You're no

good at lying." She led him to a small dining table by the galley kitchen and sat him down.

He still had the umbrella. She took it.

"Tea? Wine?"

"I, uh . . ." He didn't know what he had expected. He felt disoriented. This was foreign soil he'd ventured onto.

"I think we'll go with wine, yes?"

He rubbed his lips, made a passive gesture. "Sure."

She went into the kitchen. He looked around. Nothing immediately gave her away as a nutcase. The walls were adobe colored. Couple of decorative abstract paintings, plump, comfortable furniture facing an entertainment center, fifties-style coffee table in the breakfast nook, where he sat. There was a roll-top desk with some interesting carving on the side. The weirdest thing was the absence of weirdness.

She returned bearing two glasses of red wine, set them on the table, went to the roll-top desk, opened it, came back with a book. She sat down across from Harvey, pushed the book to him, and sipped her wine.

"My uncle's journal," she explained.

Harvey took a drink himself, somewhat more than a sip, rolled his fingers on the table. It was a plain, black journal, nothing on the cover to identify it as the property of a lunatic. "Your uncle," he said.

"Mm-hmm. His lab notes. His most important lab notes. My uncle left a lot of scribbling behind, probably a couple of hundred journals like that. But that one's special. His assistant would kill me for that. Literally. But my uncle left everything to me, so screw him."

"Your uncle is dead?"

She nodded. "A year ago. I've been on the run ever since. Until last month."

Harvey opened the journal. It was crammed with

notes handwritten in a neat, compact script. He came upon a detailed drawing of the strange glasses. One time he'd seen a display of pages from the notebooks of Leonardo Da Vinci. This reminded him of that. The drawing was exquisite.

"What language is this?"

"Latin. Some of it's Greek."

Harvey shook his head. "Your uncle kept his notes in—"

"Latin and Greek, yes. He was an alchemist."

Harvey nodded, turning pages. "So you said."

"I know," she went on, "that to a scientific type, like yourself, that probably rings the bell in the crazy tower. But my uncle was the real thing. These glasses are his greatest achievement."

Harvey sniffed. He glanced around the apartment again, tracking back. "You said you were running from something."

"Someone. My uncle's assistant."

"You look pretty settled."

She made a wry face. "The only thing I own here is that desk. That was my uncle's, too. The rest is rented. The name on my driver's license is an alias. But that's all about to change."

"How so?"

Chloe tapped the glasses. "No more mistakes. No second guessing. The bastard hasn't got a chance."

"You think he's still after you?"

She shrugged. "I lost him in Mexico. He doesn't have any idea where I am now. But, if he's persistent, which he certainly has been up until now, give him a year or three, he might track me down."

"Does he have eyesight as good as yours?"

"Nope. He's blind as a cave cricket. Nearsighted."

"Then the glasses won't do him any good. I adjusted them for your eyes. There isn't enough lens depth left to adjust them for someone with bad eyesight."

"Journal won't do him any good either."

"He doesn't read Latin?"

"He does. But it's in code. A very, very unbreakable code that my uncle kept in his head."

"Why don't you tell him that?"

"He knows."

Harvey tried to get a fix on the person Chloe described. "Guy sounds creepy."

"Put an ad in the paper: 'Alchemist seeking assistant.' Imagine who shows up."

"Why are you telling me all this?"

She tilted her head, studying him. "I don't know. Keep a secret long enough, I guess you get an itch to share it with someone. Maybe I like your face."

"Seems risky, if everything you say is true."

She tapped the glasses again, her grin broadening.

He closed the journal and pushed it back to her. "I don't read Latin or Greek, and certainly not code."

"I know." She took the glasses off and put them in their case, set the case on top of the journal. "Excuse me a minute, I have to make a phone call."

Harvey started to get up. "I should leave."

"What's your rush?" She winked at him. "Finish your wine."

He watched her go into a bedroom off the kitchen and close the door. Just a wink, and he was stitched to his seat. She came more clearly into focus, now that she was gone. Everything that he liked about her—her humor, her toughness, the lines just forming at the corners of her eyes. And, of course, her playfulness. Her playful sexiness. He'd never had a woman like her show an interest in him.

He'd meant a woman as good-looking as her. But that wasn't really true. His wives had all been attractive enough, just shallow as electroplate paint jobs. He'd always held a secret belief that he deserved the women he'd wound up with.

Now that he thought about it, it wasn't looks that scared him, it was feeling a powerful attraction to a woman, worse yet letting her see it. It left him too vulnerable. If he ever let himself get involved with someone he felt that strongly about, how could he ever get free? His escape route would be cut off.

No wonder his wives had dumped him. His connection to them hadn't run any deeper than theirs to him. They'd been the perfect mirrors for each other.

Maybe that was too harsh.

He looked at the glasses. But what if there was no need for an escape route? It would only be a minor adjustment. If he was careful, he might even be able to re-adjust them to fit Chloe again. Wouldn't it be something? To know, to really know, for once in his life?

But it was ridiculous. He'd raised himself on scientific reasoning. This wasn't even smoke and mirrors. It was glass.

Seven minutes later he was driving back to the optician's office with the glasses and the journal on the seat beside him, trying not to think. Which was of course impossible.

When he got to the office, he hesitated before unlocking the door. Having come so far, he didn't see how he could turn back. But once he was in the lab, with the glasses out of their case, and the prospect of actually altering them to fit his own eyes before him, he knew he was kidding himself. Of course he could turn back. It would just be embarrassing. He had not as yet done anything irreversible.

He sighed and hung his head. Even if the glasses were for real, he could never go through with it. He'd spend his whole life living it down, if not to others to himself. Even worse was the thought of never being able to reveal to anyone his secret crime. That was, of course, if he could keep it secret, assuming Chloe, or whatever her name was, would be so reluctant to reveal herself that she would not go to the police. He could discredit her, make her look nutty. Burn the journal—why had he taken it? Then he'd only have the glasses to hide . . .

He caught himself. How insidious they were, the urgings of desire and fear. No, if he carried through with this, he wouldn't recognize himself in the morning. His self-image had gone through enough re-modeling for one day.

He had put the glasses back in their case, and picked up the phone to call Chloe, when the lights went out.

Two hours later he was at her table again, his head throbbing. Chloe dabbed blood from his scalp with a warm cloth.

"You're being awfully nice about this," he said.

She applied a bandage to the wound and sat down across from him.

"I'm afraid I've manipulated you."

He blinked at her.

"The moment I put those glasses on, back at your office, I knew I had to get rid of them, if I was ever going to have a chance at real happiness. I had to get rid of them and embrace the unknown. That's the way I've always lived. I've never been a planner. I don't care about the things most people care about. I just want to live a full life, and share it with someone.

"But it's hard to let go of magic, especially when it's real. My uncle warned me about the glasses. He only used them to deal with his enemies. Most of whom were only his enemies because they wanted the glasses. He told me a couple of times that he wondered if he hadn't created them just so he'd have something to worry about. It amused him, you know, the intrigue.

"Then I looked at you and knew—and when I say knew, when I'm talking about having those glasses on, I mean *knew*—that I should tell you about them. Then I knew that I should leave you some time to think about it, and leave my wallet open on the counter so you could see my address. And then I knew I should leave my umbrella behind, so you'd have an excuse to come see me.

"Once you were here, I knew I should let you see my uncle's journal. And then I knew that, if I left you alone with the glasses and the journal, you would take them, and I should let you."

"Did you know I'd get beaned with an optical loupe?"

"I . . . what?"

"Big paperweight thing my former co-workers gave me as a going away present. Totally useless but it makes a great weapon, apparently."

"Oh. No, I didn't know that would happen. That must have been my uncle's assistant. I really thought I'd lost him. I'm sorry about that."

Harvey shook his head. "*You're* sorry."

"Not just sorry, grateful. That man really hates me. If he'd been dealing with me, I think he might have killed me. Fit of uncontrollable rage type thing. I was never very nice to him."

"So, the long and the short of it is, I'm not a liar and a thief, I'm a knight in shining armor."

"Look, I know I can't stop you beating yourself up about this. But I really am glad to be rid of those things. And its not like I don't have anything to remind me of my uncle. I have all of his other journals, written in English, that are full of poetry and artwork and beautiful thoughts."

Harvey sighed. "Well, that's all right, then." He stood up. "I should go." He put her money on the table. She started to object but he held up his hand.

She accompanied him to the door and opened it for him. He stepped outside.

"Harvey."

He turned.

"Did you ever have a really bad dream, and wake up relieved, feeling like you got your life back?"

He waited.

"You got your life back, Harvey. Go home and wake up."

Wouldn't it be something if, just once in his life, he was honest not just about what he thought or what he'd done, but about what he wanted? She started to close the door. He lifted his hand, and she waited.

He said, "I don't want to wake up."

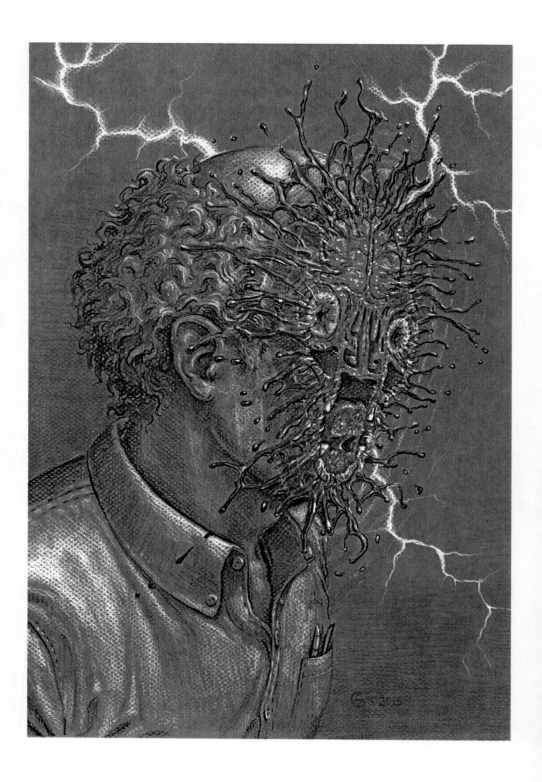

Significance

VOLCOV MUST READ fire ink only, now, Kairston thought. He took advantage of the scientist's absence and entered his tent, examined books open on the makeshift desk and field cot. Combat tactics, theoretical physics—typescript on exposed pages shone like bright embers. Fire ink was a novelty; where Volcov had gotten these books Kairston could not imagine. Maybe he'd had them made. Profligate self-indulgence—the man lived in his own world. There was no other light source in the tent, nor any needed.

Kairston didn't know what he was looking for. Something to explain what the military's lead "temporal strategist" was up to. Photos of paradoxes were tacked up everywhere, a grisly gallery of war-torn cadavers. Kairston doubted he could sleep, surrounded thus. No computer. Volcov wrote in fire ink, too—the same stuff kids used with their fantasy board games. Kairston skimmed loose sheets bearing the scientist's reedy scrawl, shook his head. Most of it was about the abomination in Oklahoma.

He read something that made his lips tighten, folded the sheet and put it in his pocket.

Back outside, the pre-dawn sky was brightening over the North Dakota mustering site. The men guarding Volcov's tent came to attention. Kairston put them at ease. He wove his way toward Main Street, the central passage through the muster. Volcov's words harried him:

"We must not accept that the situation is irreversible." Kairston shook his head again. Corpses falling from nowhere, burn and burn them and they kept coming. That guy was kidding himself.

Awash in the gold hues of sunrise, soldiers crunched through snow and frozen mud, up and down the 'street.' Odors of fuel and engine oil, boot leather and mucked-up North Dakota clay stained the clean, winter air of the endless plains. To the south lay the ephemeral tent city that could be struck in a proverbial instant, so adept at it had they become, to the north rows of tanks, ground transports and other materiel. Kairston went right, toward the officer's mess, exchanged casual salutes with enlisted men and women as they passed. Volcov would be in either the mess or the screw pot. Kairston wanted to know whose idea it was to muster an entire division over an active pot.

Volcov wasn't in the mess. Kairston served himself eggs, toast and coffee from the buffet, sat alone at a table apart. He could feel his officers watching him, had nothing to tell them. They were all on hold while rabid science spewed its terrors.

He unfolded the paper he'd taken from Volcov's tent. The ink turned a dull grey in natural light. *"The same bodies—apparently the same—materialize repeatedly—recurrently, more to the point—their state in each manifestation unique, so the white coats babble about multiple futures and universes. It might merely indicate a closed loop cycling through variations. Do all of the bodies re-materialize every time? We can't know, because they panicked, and wouldn't let me install a monitoring system before they sealed the dome. If we can interrupt the loop, it may cease to recur. It might never happen, or have happened, at all."* Kairston pushed his plate away without eating. He thought about going to the screw pot, requisitioned a pint of Bourbon and headed to his own tent instead.

He kept looking up as he walked, couldn't stop himself. The western sky was marred with dark striations where the ionosphere was thin. His adjutant was waiting for him, handed Kairston a communique. Kairston sighed as he read it. Paradoxes were showing up at three more factories, as well as the Louisiana muster. They would all have to relocate. Which would delay relocating his division to Texas for at least two days. Kairston looked about at the servicemen and women gathered here and there and meandering among the tents, in their postures, strides and voices the jocular fatalism common to soldiers throughout history. His troops. None of these had yet witnessed a paradox. He would prefer to get them into combat before they did.

"Instructions, General?" The adjutant's bespectacled, open face somehow retained its youthful innocence, in spite of all he'd witnessed. He'd been with Kairston from the start of this conflict.

"Verify that Volcov is in the pot, Chris, and let me know. Scratch that—bring him. I want to talk to him."

Kairston entered his tent, poured himself a drink and filled his hip flask. Sheet metal, covering the pit they'd dug to connect Kairston's computer to the buried cable, took up the back half of the floor. He opened the holo screen on his desk, entered the code from the communique, sat down and studied battle maps. Two divisions were holding back the invasion force in California, and had captured the enemy screw. It was being sent here, for some reason. That had to be Volcov's doing. The communique said paradoxes were originating from Europe, but also North Africa. Which meant the enemy had at least two screws still in operation. It was certain they were hastening to produce more. Kairston couldn't imagine what it must be like on their end. Westbloc had seventy screws, and was about to go online with another hundred.

He heard the stuttering drone of an approaching helicopter, went back outside and watched an elephantine transport bank toward the landing site. He didn't let himself think about its cargo or what would be done with it.

This war had so sensitized Kairston that he noticed the rise in air pressure, minute as it was, prayed it was not what he feared. The burst of a displacement bubble was unmistakable—a faintly nauseating sense that, at some fundamental level, everything *swayed*. Soon followed by an enormous crash, like a train falling on a bus. Soldiers loitering among the tents came alert, hurried toward the sound. Kairston joined their flow. It had come from the right, back toward Main Street. Across it, it turned out, deep in the tank fleet. Kairston spotted the paradox, a battle-scarred Rhino, with front and rear turrets, elevated among the rest. He signaled a couple of men to make way for him through the growing crowd of soldiers.

At its center stood three ashen-faced men being lectured by their lieutenant. To their left the veteran tank rested, in a ruptured state, atop one which had not yet seen action. Displayed on the ruined Rhino's foredeck were the torn and bloody corpses of three men. Only one was recognizable; but Kairston had no doubt they were all future versions of the three now enduring the official spiel from their superior.

"It means you're significant, right?" The lieutenant gestured at the paradox. "You can wipe this out. It means you're going to do something, or come close to doing something they don't want you to do. Remember your training—"

Kairston moved forward.

"Sir." The lieutenant stepped back.

Kairston addressed the shaken tank crew, "What were you men doing here?"

Their commander cleared his throat. "Been running rough, General, sir. We were waiting for the mechanic, make sure she fixes it, this time."

Kairston nodded. "Which is yours?"

Like one resigned to fate, the commander started to gesture toward the ruined tank but caught himself and indicated its pristine counterpart, beside which he and his men stood. Kairston nodded again, this time to himself. Always *by*, never *on*—a peculiarity of sending things back in time.

Pair of ducks, both sitting.

Kairston turned to the onlookers. Someone in the crowd shouted, "Listen up, you clods!"

The general waited for quiet. "You're right," he said, "this is what it looks like." He pointed at the wrecked tank and mauled corpses. "This is as bad as it gets. Do a DNA test, those bodies will match these men." Kairston indicated the living tank crew. "But get this straight, every one of you. Those bodies are *not* these men. They're freaks of science. Nobody's fate is sealed, here. We send love letters like this, too, and we're a helluva a lot better at it than they are." The general looked back at the tank crew. "I'll fix up something you boys can *sign*."

Shouts of approval rose from the crowd.

"They're telling us," Kairston declared to his untested troops, "keep coming and we'll wind up like this;" he gestured, again, at the paradox. "To which I say: Keep pissing us off."

That got everyone cheering.

Kairston toggled his finger at the lieutenant, drew him aside. Gesturing surreptitiously at the tank crew, he said, "Check these men for wireless tech."

The lieutenant frowned. "Sir, I feel I should inform the general that this entire division has been searched multiple times——"

Kairston lifted his hand, started to react peremptorily, perceived the lieutenant's state and restrained himself. The young officer was as green as the men in his charge and hiding his own horror. In a low, measured voice, the general said, "Nine times out of ten, someone called their girlfriend, someone called their mother. This is just one drop. Probably they've only got a partial fix on us. Let's not help them out, shall we? Do a sweep. These men, then the muster."

"Sir."

"Carry on, Lieutenant." Kairston headed back toward Main Street, heard the lieutenant resume his memorized prattle about how being terrorized to the edge of sanity made one 'significant.' The military never lost its knack for straining the reach of words. Or just flat bullshitting.

He found Chris coming up Main Street, sans Volcov.

"I'm sorry, General, he won't budge. He's got that enemy screw they captured in California down there."

Already? Kairston lifted his gaze. "I'll go to him. We've had a paradox. Get off a communique."

"Yes, sir."

This whole day was steeped in dread.

The screw pot was situated at the southeast corner of the muster. Kairston wound his way through the tents, exchanging greetings with soldiers he encountered along the way, calmly conveying news of the paradox without going into details. Many of those with whom he spoke were too young.

The pot was underground, invisible on the surface, this one further camouflaged by unoccupied tents. Kairston reached the tent that concealed the access, took a pull from his flask and went in, waited for a guard to open the hatch. Another guard offered Kairston a filtration mask but the general shook his head. If Volcov could take it, so could he.

Both guards donned masks themselves before opening the hatch. The smell hit Kairston like a bucketfull of death syrup. He went down a few steps before taking out a tin of mentholated salve and rubbing some under his nose. It had little effect. The smell had permeated the walls.

The stairs led straight down about forty steps. Several hundred such bunkers were situated around the country, now, temporal drills, irreverently referred to as 'screws,' transferred among them in randomized sequence. This bunker, or 'pot,' at present housed twelve, many times the usual number. Kairston neared the bottom of the stairs and the observation room, three hundred feet long and fifty wide, came into view. Windows of photo-reactive blast glass ran the lefthand length, looking onto a vast bay seventy feet farther down. There the enormous screws held dominion over a realm of horrors. They had the appearance of giant metal heads, pewter-colored, with gaping maws. Eyeless, noseless, earless—a row of insatiable Molochs, designed only to consume. Seen here, from above, they were somehow most menacing. The windows darkened in reaction to the bright flashes produced when the screws fired.

The greater part of the pot was a charnel house. Amid rows of wrecked enemy materiel, the corpses of three or four hundred enemy combatants were laid out in varying states of ruin. The personnel working in the pot didn't bother to cover them anymore.

A couple of the monitoring technicians seated, facing the windows, at consoles, glanced the general's way, went back to their tasks. They all wore breathing masks. As did the workers in the bay, with one exception. Kairston spotted Volcov—the only person not in white coveralls nor wearing a mask.

The general crossed the observation room, took a pair of goggles from a wall-mounted rack, donned them and boarded the elevator, surveyed the scene in the bay through the elevator's transparent walls as he descended. The temporal drills loomed to the left, at the far end of the bay. Recessed in the wall behind them stood the portable reactors—giant, sweating, silver columns—that powered the drills. Each screw was powered by its own reactor. Intermittently one or another of them fired, and a pale grey, semi-transparent field formed, like a smooth, oscillating veil, along the perimeter of its 'bore—' the space between the transit pad and the hood, mouth of the beast. Arcing electricity, too bright to view without goggles, cascaded inside the field while the screw poked a hole in space-time.

With the methodical relentlessness of ants, workers on the floor loaded bodies and wreckage onto the screws' pads. Offerings to eldritch gods, Kairston thought. It seemed to him that the screws functioned in an autonomous dimension beyond the influence of their creators, as if they had unwittingly been summoned from a jealous, forgotten mythos. Technicians at standing consoles in front of the screws sent the gruesome cargo backward in time. The farthest they'd been able to go was about two weeks. Farther than that the energy requirements became prohibitive. The earth moved, and so did the sun. The farther back in time one's aim, the farther away one's target. H. G. Wells left that bit out.

Ozone from the firing screws competed with the smell of overripe flesh when the doors opened. Kairston wended his way through the gruesomeness toward Volcov. Down here, looking through photo-reactive goggles, the shifts in light were more pronounced, the mangled dead more macabre. If you'd never been in battle you didn't know how inadequate the phrase 'shot to pieces' could be. Mingled with corpses more or less intact were ones legless, headless, mashed, some little more than heaps of bones and entrails, assorted limbs. The floor was black with hardened blood. It was disgraceful to treat soldiers this way, regardless the side they were on. They'd followed orders and done their duties and deserved to be treated with respect. Kairston thought those who worked in pots like this must be the most emotionally numb people on Earth. They kept to their own, never mixed with the troops. He couldn't remember seeing any of them out of their masks and goggles. It was like they had no identities left.

And then there were the screws themselves, whose designers had provided the sixty-foot-tall horror mills with the visual grace of sculptures. Honeyed poison. The perimeters of the screws' pads, like the floor, were black with blood.

Volcov was jotting something on a clear slate with a stylus. So he *did* use computers. He spoke without turning. "Sorry I couldn't break away, Leonard. Serious business, today."

Kairston regarded Volcov with distaste. He might be a giant among eggheads but among men he was a pipsqueak. "I'm *here* on serious business, Doctor."

"Of that I have no doubt." Volcov gestured toward the captured enemy screw. "You'll agree this takes precedence."

"Not sure."

Volcov turned.

"We've had a paradox."

Volcov's gaze rose in frustration, slate and stylus lowering to his sides. He fixed on Kairston. "One?"

"Far as I know. Just happened. My question is, do you want to relocate with the division or go someplace else? Or stay here?"

Volcov looked one way and another, like a hawk, making assessments Kairston couldn't guess at. "We have time to finish. We'll make time." He fixed on Kairston. "This could change everything."

Kairston wanted a buck for every time he'd heard that. "I'm afraid to ask."

"The enemy screw." Volcov pointed again. "We're sending it back. Disabled, of course. We're linking all the reactors to Drill Number Seven. Should be able to get it almost to the point of its assembly, before it was ever deployed."

Kairston couldn't hide his shock. "That's nine months ago!"

"Our understanding has grown," Volcov replied. He strode away to oversee preparations. The screws were shut down and reactors linked to Number Seven. A group of workers jacked the enemy screw onto a fork lift and loaded it onto Seven's pad. The enemy screw was small, maybe half as tall as the others. It also lacked their elegance—all function, no graceful curves. Kairston thought it looked like a big drip coffee maker without a carafe. It fit into Seven's bore with room to spare.

Volcov returned. "The differences are superficial. Except possibly the size. It might have been designed small for transport. But the drilling module, all the circuitry, is identical to ours."

"So it's confirmed they stole the technology?"

"No question."

Kairston tried to get his mind around what Volcov intended, here. For some reason it seemed foolhardy. "You're thinking, they see their first screw come back disabled before they've used it, they'll give up?"

"I think they'll find it disheartening, don't you?"

Kairston gazed with undisguised skepticism at the screws. They were the most sophisticated, complex machines ever created. They processed intelligence — possessed it, if Volcov was right — at mind-withering speeds, to determine where in the past the items they sent back had been at specific moments. If they got within a certain range, a transported object was drawn to its former self. Paradox, it seemed, was not only unavoidable but essential to time travel. A thing could only go where it had been. If they missed, it dissolved into the fabric of space time. "Deliquesced" was Volcov's term. Pretty expression for defiling the firmament.

"Doctor, I haven't seen this conflict do anything but escalate, regardless of strategy."

Volcov peered at Kairston. "You don't approve of me, do you, Leonard? I don't think I've ever heard you address me by name."

Kairston sucked his teeth. "There's a containment dome in Oklahoma with walls a hundred feet thick and an inferno at its core we can't ever let die. That weighs on me. Don't take it personal."

"You'd rather go back to intercepting each other's missiles, destroy our atmosphere altogether?"

"I think maybe we've been doing this so long it's driven us all mad. If we're going to keep at it, I'd prefer a straight fight."

"More dignified, is that it?"

"You bet."

"You're a romantic."

Kairston grunted. "From a guy who keeps his memoirs in fire ink."

Volcov blinked at Kairston. "I see I have no privacy."

"Secrecy's good as it gets around here."

Volcov smiled. "It is a conceit, I suppose. It does help me to focus my thoughts."

Kairston smirked.

"The object of war is to induce the enemy to surrender unconditionally, Leonard."

Kairston sighed, shook his head.

"All methods of warfare are psychological." Volcov turned back to the screws. "No exceptions." His expression changed to incredulity. The technician at Number Seven's control console had initiated the transmission sequence. Volcov gaped. "What are you *doing?*"

The technician didn't respond. He didn't even look at Volcov.

"We haven't removed the drilling module!" Volcov screamed. He dashed to the console, shoved the technician aside, tried to override the sequence. It was too late. Kairston felt a displacement bubble pop. A face—Volcov's own—materialized on the console, as if it had been cut from his head and presented like a specimen. Volcov did not notice it. He gaped in horror at Drill Number Seven— *"No!"*—ran to the transmission pad but never made it. The field veil deployed. Volcov fell dead to the floor, minus his face. The forward half of his head had been taken by the veil.

Kairston seized the technician, shook him. "Do something!" The bore of the enemy screw had activated, drawing power from it's larger progenitor. Arcing electricity cascaded over Seven's exterior, not just inside the bore. The massive device crumpled; the hood bent down against the enemy screw. The technician seemed incapacitated by shock, limp in Kairston's grasp. Kairston ripped the goggles from the man's face. He was stoned out of his mind, pupils so dilated it looked like he didn't have irises. Of course—how else could anyone do this work? If you weren't a freak like Volcov.

Kairston cast the technician aside, found the alarm button and punched it, not for anyone inside the facility, but for the soldiers encamped above. The bore veil on Seven became misshapen, bulged, climbed, like a hive, like conscious smoke, to encompass the hood. An electrical cascade blinding even through goggles burst forth, and the enemy screw, and about half of seven's hood, vanished. But the machine remained active, the veil swelling and mutating, sending tendrils across the floor with an awful aspect of purpose to the bores of Six and Eight. When Seven's clutching veil reached them they became active, drawing power from it. First Six and then Eight screeched across the floor toward Seven and mashed against it. Technicians stood transfixed, like innocents awaiting judgment. Kairston did not understand what was happening but knew the consequences would be terrible. His gaze fell to Volcov's severed face.

"Shut it down! Somebody shut it down!" he yelled.

The technician he'd shoved aside came to a point, finally, returned to Seven's console, scraped Volcov's face away and stabbed buttons. Nothing happened. The veil continued to bulge and reach, connecting now with Five and Nine, which also activated, and were pulled against the others. The technician ran for the cables connecting Seven to the reactor chain but a massive electrical arc sent him flying.

"Everybody out!" Kairston shouted, running for the lift. "Evacuate!" The workers and technicians stared at him. "Get the hell out of here!" A couple of them boarded the lift with him. The rest moved too slowly. He couldn't wait.

The alarm was more deafening on the observation deck. Down in the bay, Four and Ten were drawn into the malfunctioning mass. A shudder passed through the floor. The monitors had already cleared out. Kairston caught up with some of them on the stairs, pushed by. He burst through the hatch and ran out of the tent toward Main Street. Amid the wail of sirens was a general rumble of engine noise—what he'd hoped to hear. They couldn't wait for air transport. Zig-zagging through the tents, he encountered Chris coming the other way.

"Evac's underway, General."

"Damn right. I want bare dirt in fifteen minutes. I'm ordering this whole area cauterized——"

With dread, Kairston felt his ears fill up. There were two pops, one right after the other, so close he felt them like gusts of wind. Then two, awful thuds, as objects fell to ground between Kairston and his adjutant, and Kairston found himself looking at his own mangled corpse, his adjutant his. Something had mashed Chris' corpse to pulp.

Before Kairston could react there was a second displacement, and a second version of himself fell from nowhere atop the first. This one had died differently— an arm was missing. The same horror had befallen Chris. They had no chance to digest what was happening, or utter a word, before it happened again. And again.

And again.

The versions of Kairston's dead self, one missing a jaw, one shot through the head, one riven by shrapnel, began to lose individual integrity and merge with one another, become amorphous, fluid, fabric taking on characteristics of flesh, and vice versa. Another body fell, and another.

Kairston backed from the growing pile. Screams and other less comprehensible noises issued from the encampment around him, and the general knew this wasn't happening just to him and his adjutant. Bodies continued to fall, and his eyes locked with Chris'.

"General——" Chris tried to climb over the pile of his melding corpses. His hand got stuck, then his legs, and he sank into the morass of his dead selves, which began to twitch and ruffle, animated by contact with its living antecedent. It would take his consciousness, too. The jellied mass of re-animated Chris made contact with the dead mass of Kairston, and those two began to merge. Only Chris's face remained, arrested in incomprehension, still innocent, spectacles melting against his eyes. "General——"

Abomination.

They wouldn't be able to contain it, this time. The general ran. Like a coward, like a panicked child, like a mouse pursued by monsters, he ran. He ran back through the empty tents over the screw pot, heard things fall behind him, his dead selves in pursuit. The noise from the muster coalesced into a mindless, bio-mechanical roar. The general thought of a flower, and a girl he should have kissed. He would not stop running. He would run until he died or killed himself.

They had all become significant.

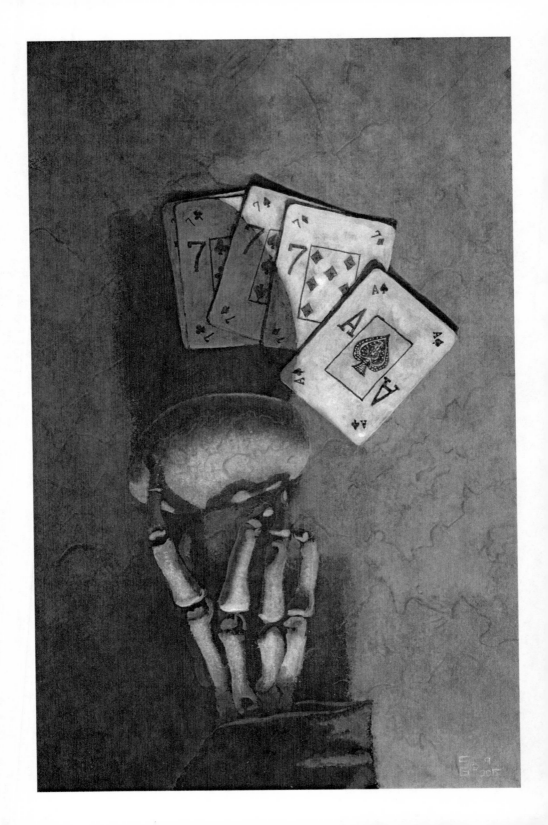

The Fourth Seven

WOODEN STEPS, SPONGY against the underlying earth, led down the fern-covered embankment. They sounded hollow. Twenty or so feet from the bottom, beyond a verge of trees and undergrowth, the river, swollen from days of rain, flowed with ethereal quietness. The air was sweet and clean, rich with the scents of earth and plant life. Earl went right on the dirt path, found a bench by the water's edge, wiped a spot semi-dry with his handkerchief, sat down and wondered if he wasn't just about fed up with himself.

He looked back up the embankment. The cabins where he'd taken lodging weren't visible from that angle, which meant he couldn't be seen either. Not that anyone was looking for him, he was sure, but it never hurt to be cautious. He'd parked behind his cabin, where his car couldn't be spotted from the road. It was a forgettable, easily missed place, and he was the only guest that night. Earl was good at lying low.

Across the river, the Cascades rose to invisible heights. Pale, low cloud cover and waning light lent the pine, yew and maple-forested slopes liminal mystery. It was a placid, beautiful scene, yet another to behold alone on his solitary path through life. Earl felt impervious to the balms of nature. He resisted the direction of his mood, told himself he wasn't to blame. Cities were burning all over the world, riots spreading like viruses. People were scared and desperate, and being desperate they gambled. So long as they still believed in money, Earl would take it from them. It was the business he was in.

Which didn't make him feel better about fleecing backwoods yokels out of their kids' lunch money in an imbecilic game of Acey Deucey. God damn it, it wasn't his fault. He hadn't made anyone do anything. He was cornered, too. Ever since being run out of Vegas by a bunch of entitled wise guys who just did not like to lose he'd been reduced to working the cellar circuit and shearing sheep.

He fished his three lucky sevens out of the hidden pocket in the sleeve of his sharkskin jacket, fanned them in his hand: Clubs, Spades and Diamonds. He tossed them in the water and watched them float away.

Footsteps sounded above. The manager of the cabins—Earl had the impression the guy owned the place—stood looking down at him from the top of the rotten stairs. What did this character want? Earl had noticed the man's kids, a girl and a boy, sitting on a cratered sofa in a dim room behind the reception desk. Not doing anything, just parked there, dull and listless, products of a no-doubt nurturing and intellectually stimulating home-life. Father of the Year came down the steps.

"What's up, ace?" Earl asked.

The man stopped a few yards away. He was tall and gaunt and had the demeanor of an oily puddle. "It will be dark soon."

"Yeah?" Didn't miss a trick, this winner.

The man pointed up. "Sky's overcast. It will be very dark. If you stay here long, be careful going back to your room."

"Oh, right." Earl nodded. "Thanks."

The man lingered like he was stuck on pause, returned up the steps.

Earl thought about where to go next. Maybe New

Orleans. You could still work the cracks in the Big Easy. Not much of a living but a fellow could get by.

He was standing to leave when he saw the body. The little girl was dead, obviously dead. She was too pale and vacant to be anything else.

Look away, he told himself. This was the sort of complication Earl sought to avoid. She was floating on her back with her face turned like she was looking at him. Mouth agape, eyes milked over. She drifted near a tangle of deadwood in the middle of the river. Her left hand rose and grabbed hold of a branch.

Earl jumped into the water. A few feet from shore it got deep. He was up to his chest when he reached the girl. She was lolling in the current, staring at him with those milk-dead eyes. She must be blind.

He grabbed the wrist of the hand that held the branch. "I got you, honey." The arm separated at the elbow and the body, minus forearm and hand, floated away. The flesh Earl held was necrotic and gelatinous, loose on the bones. He let go, cursing, shifted to turn back. A rock slipped underfoot and he went downstream, too, then. The current pushed him toward the opposite shore. He swam for the shallows on the other side, dragged himself onto the bank, fought through brush and branches to an open space and cursed and cursed. His instinct to look away and un-see those small, sad remains had been right. He'd learned it before—never lose vigilance against your human impulses.

He made his way back upriver through the trees. There had to be a shallow place where he could cross. Finding it in the dimming light would be damn near impossible. And there might not be one, with all the rain. He cursed and cursed himself, again and again. The corpse's cold reaching hand was hot in his mind. It got snagged on the branch, he told himself. The impression of voluntary movement had been an illusion, fluke of the current.

The undergrowth of ferns, rhododendrons, nettles and scrub brush was too thick to penetrate near the river's edge. Earl was forced to higher ground. He could see the cabins on the far side, nestled amid the trees. It would be a chill night spent outdoors in wet clothes, worse if it rained more. He wished he'd never gone down to the river.

Earl possessed an instinct, at times, that told him to fold or raise, irrespective of the strength of his hand. A similar sense came alert now, in an unfamiliar way that made him stop and listen. He heard patter of accreted moisture, dripping from leaves and fronds, elusive, unidentifiable noises. Then he heard the scream. The unmistakable scream of a little girl. Not the excited shriek of a child at play but a cold howl of bottomless terror.

Earl stared uphill. It had come from there, someplace. He drew his hand across his mouth, searched the trees, didn't see any movement. He took a step upward and stopped. The last thing he wanted was more trouble. The awful scream echoed in his mind.

A distance higher he encountered what appeared to be the remains of a concrete pad for an unbuilt house, resting at a tilt by the edge of a cliff. A swath of the mountainside above was bare of mature trees, overgrown with ferns and saplings. There'd been a landslide, at some point, that shifted the pad to its current place. A couple of hundred feet up a stout stream poured over the escarpment at the top of the slide and rushed down a channel through the tree-barren swath. The stream bent along the downhill edge of the pad and spilled over the precipice in a waterfall. One corner of the pad had broken away and dropped to the riverbank below, where its pieces lay, battered by the falls.

Earl jumped over the stream, started to slip backwards
on the cement and scrambled to the top of the pad. The
soil beyond was soft and wet; his feet went ankle deep.
He climbed up around the escarpment to firmer ground,
shook mud from his shoes and cursed some more.

He wasn't sure of his direction, now. Looking downhill
he couldn't see the cabins or the river. He rubbed his chin
with the back of his hand, thought about turning back
but continued up through the trees. He reencountered the
stream and followed it over a rise where he discovered
a clearing, at the higher end of which stood a rundown
cabin. In the intervening space fifty or so flat stones protruded from the ground at irregular angles in unequal
rows. The stream passed among them diagonally. It had
breached its banks and flooded the near end of the clearing. Earl made out a decrepit barn, hunkered under the
moss-grown branches of an ancient oak tree, up behind
the cabin, off to its left.

It was nearly dark, now. A light shone in the window
by the cabin's door. Earl headed up through the clearing,
making his way around the left side of the water. On closer
viewing the stones proved to be broken-edged chunks of
slab concrete, planted there for some purpose. Maybe to
impede erosion, though they seemed faced the wrong way
for that. A couple of the rows extended into the immersed
area.

He climbed the steps to the cabin door. The exterior walls were slick with moss. He couldn't see anyone
through the grime-encrusted window. There was a gas
lantern alight inside. He knocked. No one answered. He
thought he heard a faint sound, like a child whimpering.

"Hello?" he called, "anyone there?"

No response.

He opened the door and went in. The space was

mostly empty. There was a built-in counter and a wood stove—cold at the moment—to the right. The walls and floor were bare, unpainted wood, the latter bearing unwholesome black stains and rough from wear. The air smelled of disinfectant. In the middle of the room was a square, wooden table and four chairs. The lantern rested in the center of the table.

At the far end of the room were two plank doors. The right one opened onto what might once have been a bedroom. Now there was only a moldering pile of children's toys. What Earl found behind the left door swept him through with cold clarity. In a cupboard-like space a young boy and a younger girl, the kids he'd seen behind the reception desk, sat on the floor, shackled to more chunks of concrete, these set with mooring rings. The girl huddled against the boy with her face to his chest. The boy eyed Earl warily.

"I'm Earl," Earl said gently. "I'm going to help you. Did your father put you in here?"

"He's not our father," the boy said.

Earl digested that. "Where are your folks?"

The boy shook his head. "The woman at the foster home made us go with him. He gave her money."

The chains were thick and strong; Earl didn't have anything to pick the locks with. The cement pieces were too big to lift, let alone carry.

Footsteps sounded on the stairs. Terror filled the boy's eyes.

"I'm not leaving you," Earl whispered.

He crossed the room and met the manager of the rental cabins coming in, grabbed him by his shirt, yanked him inside and slammed him against the wall.

"You!" the man cried. "What are *you* doing here? You can't be here!"

"I'm taking those kids out of here, you sick son-of-a-bitch. Where are the keys to those chains?"

The manager was too shocked to respond. Through the doorway, Earl eyed the rows of broken concrete slabs. A grim understanding came over him and he knew that he was looking at a graveyard. Not a regular graveyard, where the dead lay with dignity, but a perverse collection of oddments. He saw the flood pool, black in the darkness, thought of the rain-fattened stream loosening earth, undermining a shallow burial, pouring down and down, over the waterfall, into the river — The dead girl turned in the current looked at him. Earl roared and slammed the manager against the wall so hard the house shook.

"P-pocket," the manager said.

Earl patted the man's pockets and found the keys. He backhanded him hard, knocking him to the floor.

The manager became hysterical — "No! No! No! No! No!"

Earl thrust the keys at him. "Which ones?"

But the manager's attention was taken by something else. Earl listened and heard noises that resolved into clopping hooves and snorting horses.

The manager looked at Earl with mixed desperation and menace. "You have to go!" he hissed.

"Not happening," Earl said, and wondered if he meant it.

"You don't understand anything," the manager spat. "I do what I'm told. I do only what I am permitted to do. If they say starve, I starve. If they say sicken, I feed them rot and disease. If they say fight, I give them tools and pit them against each other. If they say kill, only kill — such a waste — a waste! a waste! — I put them down like curs. I do as I'm told. *Only* what I am permitted."

Earl pocketed the keys and listened. It sounded like riders were dismounting up by the barn. Clearly there was another dimension to this business. "Who are they?" Earl demanded.

The manager clutched Earl's leg. "You can get away."

Earl kicked him loose. "Tell me who they are." He felt a change in the atmosphere that had nothing to do with air, knew instinctively that he had stumbled into a dark center of the world where terrible forces held sway. Part of him wanted to run. A deeper part, that he had fought all his life to suppress, evade or amputate, would not let him.

"Who?" The manager giggled. "The ones who play, that's who. They play and play and——"

"What the fuck does that mean?"

"They play for the fate of the children!"

Footsteps neared the house. Earl pulled the manager to his feet, held him close. "Play *what?*"

"*Cards!*"

Earl stared. There was no bluff in the man's eyes. He was telling the truth, as he understood it. The footsteps rounded the house. Earl pointed the manager at the door. "Meet them. Tell them I want in the game."

The four who came in were not human. They looked human but Earl knew right away that they were not. They wore the boots, chaps and coats of horsemen. Three wore hats, one a poncho with the hood drawn forward so Earl couldn't see his face. They were too tall for the doorway, had to bow to enter.

The manager became obsequious in their presence. "I did not bring him," he said, pointing at Earl. "He's an intruder. He presumes to join your great game. . ."

The four ignored the manager, moved past him into the room.

"Rend him," the manager entreated. "Tear him, grind him. He has no right here. This place is *mine*— "

One of the horsemen lifted his hand an increment and the manager fell silent. The four took places at the table and sat down.

Three of the beings appeared, in different ways, unhealthy. One seemed sickly, his skin pock-marked with sores, his breath thick and broken in his lungs. One seemed on the brink of starvation, so emaciated was he. The hooded one was the most cadaverous. He wore tight gloves that revealed the contours of the bones of his hands. The only one who exuded any degree of health wore a torn and faded uniform, with dark patches where medals had once hung, and badges been sewn. But whatever their apparent frailty, they all emanated hideous power.

In a rumbling voice the uniformed one said, "You would join our contest?"

It took Earl a beat to understand he was being addressed. "If it means the lives of those kids, yeah, I'll gamble with you. I don't have money on me but there's twelve large in my room."

"We do not play for riches," the uniformed being said. "You cannot win or lose this exchange. If you win you lose, if you lose you win. If you are successful in your aim, the children live, and thereafter you serve one of us to the end of your days. If you fail, you go free with no memory of this night, and the children remain. Do you accept?"

Earl looked at the children. It was obvious the terms were a trap. To be presented with terms at all, though, suggested these horsemen were bound by rules. "What's to stop me walking out of here with them right now, and screw your damn game?"

"You may leave, with no memory of this night. The children remain."

An ugly relief washed through Earl. He had to choose. They couldn't touch him without his say. He could walk, scot-free, with no memory to dog him or foul his dreams. He looked at the children again. The boy stared back with dull resignation; the girl clung to him. All Earl had to do was walk away.

The other option was to serve these horsemen. Earl fixed on the manager and sickened at the thought of replacing the verminous wretch. Save these kids and doom himself to murdering countless others—there had to be another way. He had no doubt, though, that if he agreed to the horsemen's terms they would prove binding.

But he wasn't like the manager. Any deal he made here would be driven by desperation, not desire. Maybe that gave him leverage. He kept his expression flat, thought of people he wouldn't mind seeing dead. "I pick my victims," he said.

The sickly one shook his head. "We do not serve justice," he wheezed.

No, thought Earl, it's the cold heart of nature you obey. He took a slow, deep breath. It was that moment when he had to go still inside and work the players, not the hand. His gaze slid again to the manager. A plan glimmered that he dared not let brighten. These horsemen would read a bluff. He had to mean one thing and intend another. "Then I get to pick the first one," he said.

The horsemen looked at the manager, who stood by the door, bewildered as a lost dog. "Agreed," croaked the emaciated one.

Earl swallowed. He wouldn't go through with it. No one could be expected to do a thing like this. He would leave, run, embrace amnesia, drive 'til he ran out of road. God would understand. "I accept," he heard himself say, and told himself he meant it, imagined that he thought he did. He could not let himself think he didn't. It was like keeping a poker face with his soul.

"We will decide now which of us you will serve, if you succeed," said the uniformed horseman.

The four riders each tossed a stone on the table, the significance of which was incomprehensible to Earl. The stones were smooth, like river rocks, irregularly oblong and striated with greys and ochers. Somehow their fall weighed in his fortune. The hooded horseman drew his finger across the corner of the table on his left. With a crackling whine, the leg at that corner divided in two, the table forming a fifth side equal to the other four, and a fifth chair unfolded from the floorboards. The hooded horseman pointed at the vacant chair. "You play beside me," he said, in a voice like scraping glass. "You will be my creature, if you prevail."

Earl sat at table with the worst life could bring. The horsemen loomed about him, reeking of ruin.

The stones had been replaced by a strange deck of cards, marked with symbols Earl did not recognize. "I can't play with cards I don't know."

The hooded figure passed his hand over the deck, and it became a standard deck of poker cards. "We play one hand to decide our covenant. You deal."

Earl reached for the cards but the hooded horseman laid its hand on his.

"The deck has been shuffled by Fate."

The horseman's touch, even gloved, was a swarm of failure. Earl pulled his hand back.

The hooded horseman cut the cards and placed them before Earl. "If you lose, we four play alone to decide the ordeal of the children."

The cards were cold as ice. Earl dealt five to each of them. He was surprised by his steadiness. He looked at his hand: three sevens, a five and an ace. The others stood pat. Earl discarded the five, drew one card, and knew the game had been decided before it began.

It was the Seven of Hearts.

He could still fold, concede the game. Nothing in the rules said you had to play a winning hand. Earl let the cards slip from his fingers face up, onto the table. None of the horsemen came close to beating him. He rose from the table, went to the cupboard, found the right keys and unshackled the children, shepherded them to the front door. The manager barred his way.

"You're not here because of them," Earl told him, "they're here because of *you*."

The manager looked at the children, frowned at Earl in confusion. Understanding arrived and his face filled with dread as his gaze shifted to the horsemen.

Earl nodded; "What do you have to give them *now?*"

The manager shrank from Earl and huddled in the corner, watching the horsemen. He couldn't escape and he knew it; he was screwed either way. Earl drew some satisfaction from that.

He pressed the children out the door. Before he could cross the threshold himself, he felt a bony hand on his shoulder. He turned and saw the hooded rider's face, and knew him for who he was.

"Remember that you are mine," the rider said.

"You bet," Earl lied. He could never serve this thing. He had fooled it and its brothers, and the thing knew it. But the deal was binding.

Earl made his choice and went outside into the cool, moonlit night.

The clouds had broken. The way would be clear. With every step he felt life leave him, the will drain from his heart and limbs. He dropped to his knees among the nameless graves—there were so many—and drew the children to him.

"You know the way back across the river?" he asked the boy.

The boy nodded. "Take the path down to the bridge."

Earl grunted at learning that there was a path and a bridge. He gave the boy the key to his cabin. "My bag has a false bottom. You'll figure it out. There's enough money to move you along. Take your sister—"

"She's not my sister," the boy said.

"The hell she isn't," Earl corrected him. "You get your sister out of here and look after her. Watch out for adults. Most of them are assholes. Don't trust anybody just because you want to. Look in their eyes, see, and pay attention to what you feel. Don't trust them until you know—not think, not wish, *know*—that you see truth in their eyes, and no bluff. Understand?"

The boy nodded.

"All right, go on."

"I don't want to leave you."

"You're not leaving me, son, I'm already gone. Now go."

Earl watched the children hurry into the night and the pale prospect of hope, and, as life left him, he smiled, for he knew that he had cheated Death.

The Mountain and the Vortex

1

SÉQUANON FLEW BACKWARD in time and crashed into the eye of God.

The impact sent him swinging wildly in his hammock. The instrument panels went blank and a moment later displayed data that made no sense. The stasis generators had disengaged before he'd reached his destination. Drones deployed and transmitted exterior views to the monitors. It appeared that his ship had lodged in the side of a mountain.

An extremely tall mountain. On a world not his own.

His ship was stuck, like a lance in a wall, near the summit of a towering peak, a great, yawning distance from the floor of a planet he did not know.

Séquanon's mind locked. He stared at the monitors. The ship's artificial brain, Cog, informed him that his cardiac tree was oscillating at a dangerously high rate. When Séquanon did not respond, Cog exercised emergency prerogative and injected him with an anxiety suppressant. Séquanon calmed enough to think.

He unbuckled himself and leapt out of the hammock, told Cog to retrace their flight path and himself tasked the drones to gather information about the world below. The grey-green dome of the small bridge streamed with frenetic warning lights. Séquanon hadn't installed alarms but it screamed in his mind that his life was lost, his mission to save his world a shambles.

Cog could not estimate how long it would take to determine their flight path; they'd gone through some kind of dimensional rift. It might not be possible to reconstruct their course with full accuracy. The variables were thus far incalculable.

The assembled data did, however, present Séquanon with another incomprehensible phenomenon. The instruments registered energy fluctuations characteristic of a cognitive nexus. The mountain, impossibly, was situated in a site of material instability where the thought forces of this world's inhabitants had forged a bond with the planet. He could have crashed into no more elusive place—it would be invisible even to the species whose minds had created it.

The reality of the situation sank through Séquanon like heavy poison; he patted the consoles in helpless supplication. He was dead. A fluting whimper escaped him. His pride had killed him. He had imagined himself the first time traveler. Now he didn't even know if he was in the same universe.

He took a long breath and steadied himself. It was pointless to stare at the monitors while the drones collected data. He could berate himself later, or it wouldn't matter. He made himself climb down to the transport bay to inspect the navigation module. The ladder descended amidships; the empty bay extended right and left like a beshadowed hall. He had designed it large to accommodate indeterminate things he might want to collect. It looked now to become an over-sized coffin.

The forward collision shield had closed. Environmental read-outs showed no breaches or compromised systems. Séquanon released the lock and the shield dilated open. He strode to the fore-end of the ship and opened the round hatch covering the navigation module. Everything seemed intact; all of the linkages were secure. Which wouldn't matter if he couldn't get free of the mountain. Another flaw in his designs confronted him, this one concrete: the module was situated unmovably in the nose of the ship, which was wedged into the rock outside.

An alert chime pinged. Séquanon went to the nearest console. The drones had established that there were no wireless transmissions from the planet. No satellites, nothing. The only form of long-distance communication required a landline for coded signals.

Séquanon drew his hand over his mouth. In a matter of moments he had turned from savior to destroyer. An intellectual species with such nascent technology could not weather his presence in a nexus. His mind would not make sense to them. He closed his eyes, sought within, and peered through the mental doorway where one never looked without trepidation, found a hazy vision of them, like figures glimpsed through gauze. They were similar to his own kind, in ways—two legs, two arms, somewhat taller, maybe, with smaller heads . . .

It was all he could take. Séquanon made himself keep moving. He went back to secure the hatch, had it half closed and stopped. The synchronizer at the center of the module looked wrong. He detached it. The crystalline points on its inner surface were deformed, no longer symmetrical. He placed it under a magnifier and had a small relief when he found no fractures. He went back to the module and scrutinized the interface pocket; it seemed to have changed shape in agreement with the crystals. The deformity must have occurred passing through the rift.

Séquanon stared helplessly about at his ship. If he ever saw Tumult again he would find a female, throw off caution and bond with her. His lab assistant, maybe, if she had not given up on him. Just the trilling of her voice would be a comfort. He longed for a warm embrace.

He put the synchronizer back into the interface pocket. It would work or it wouldn't; he had no replacement.

He asked Cog for a bit more stress suppressant. He wouldn't let himself think about not going home. He had to accept that it might take a long time to get there.

Meanwhile, he had endangered not only himself but the inhabitants of an entire planet. Here in this nexus, his mind was inextricably linked to theirs at an unconscious level they would not understand. Even now his thoughts were leaking into the streams that flowed through this nexus and out across the world below, and with them the understanding that the nexus existed. Séquanon knew the havoc such knowledge could wreak. He'd witnessed it first hand when the nexuses were discovered on Tumult. The dead beyond counting, strewn untended in streets and fields—it was no easy thing to accommodate shared consciousness, even with a much clearer understanding of the cosmos than people had here.

He was poised to unleash the very horror he'd sought to contain.

Séquanon vomited. All that came up was a splash of yellow bile. He fell back, trembling, against the nose hatch, wiped his mouth. Once his stomachs quieted he felt a little better. A defiant will took hold of him. He would not die with the ruin of a world on his conscience.

He had to leave as quickly as possible.

He called up views of the ship's exterior. It was impossible to tell how firmly the nose was stuck. The crevice in which it was lodged might have been created by the crash, though more likely had been there already.

It was hard to believe that his actions had led to this outcome by chance.

The greatest challenge would be to separate from the mountain without losing the navigation module. He wasn't prepared to sacrifice himself without at least trying to get home. He could close the collision shield and seal off the front of the ship, detach from the nose section and leave the module behind. But the likelihood of finding his way back to Tumult, then, would diminish precipitously. Cog would have to navigate by blind calculation.

Which he might have to do anyway if the module failed.

Séquanon needed to reduce his impact while the drones made preparations to free the ship and Cog processed data. He might be able to mask his mind. If he got back in the neural hammock, Cog could re-task the entertainment system and generate a story reality, sublimate his psyche to an artificial persona . . .

He climbed back up to the bridge and re-tasked the drones again. There was an ironic advantage to being inside a nexus: thought streams from at least a third of this world would intermingle here. The drones should be able to identify points of confluence and access them, extract the information necessary to simulate an environment and furnish a persona. But Séquanon had another shock when Cog discovered the nexus to be inhabited, not only by lower life forms but by natives capable of complex thought. The nexuses discovered on Tumult had been assumed uninhabitable; no one had ever ventured into them. Séquanon was surprised to be alive in this one.

How the presence of intellectual beings inside a nexus would affect circumstances he could not guess.

The drones collected enough data to assemble a fantasy. Séquanon relinquished control of them to Cog, so they could go to work freeing the ship. Then he pulled himself back up into the hammock and instructed Cog to suppress his self-awareness and superimpose a persona. One sophisticated, intelligent and educated—Séquanon would not well project a dullard. He instructed Cog that any significant developments should be communicated as much as possible through the fantasy, then surrendered to the synthetic brain's neurological intrusions. Not without misgivings—he was compartmentalizing his mind. The long-term effects were unknowable. He would have to trust Cog to remember what went where.

Gradually, Séquanon's perceptions changed. He forgot that his hands had seven fingers and accustomed himself to five. Tumult became a simple noun rather than the name of his home world, and he found himself in a curious environment that was both pleasurable and confusing. He forgot his name and the fantasy enclosed him, leaving open a channel for truth:

In a private, wood-paneled study, far from the known places of the world, a man in a quilted smoking jacket sat in a large armchair, smoking a briar pipe. The jacket and the chair were comfortable, the room warm, the tobacco good. But the man was not at ease. He eyed the books shelved about him and brooded upon his past. He supposed, at least, that it was his past upon which he brooded. He was having a quarrel with his mind. He did not recognize the books, and was not sure if he was remembering history or inventing it. Whichever the case, an image came to him, as if materializing out of the smoke pooled above his head: a rider on horseback, traveling through a snowstorm, in a high, mountainous country.

The man in the quilted smoking jacket knew the rider's name, though he did not seem to know his own. *Meet John Raythorn, he thought, former Indian fighter, who crosses the land now in the guise of an itinerant cowboy.*

2

JOHN RAYTHORN WAS finished with progress. Undaunted by the weather, he gave himself to the will of the world. The certainties that once informed his decisions and shaped his understanding of the natural order had ceased to matter after the last massacre he witnessed. He did not know how long he had traveled. He did not care about time. He thought very little and made his way through the territory, attending the hazy advance of trees through the swirling snow.

The wind quieted, the snow thinned and the sky cleared to reveal an incredibly tall mountain at the end of a sloping valley. John Raythorn stopped his sturdy blue roan, Smoke, and took in the view. He was affected by many emotions—relief, as if he had set down a burden, gratitude, simple happiness, a warming of his being for which he had no name. It was the Valley of the Four Moons. He had found his way back to the Hidden Realm, where people understood each other, no matter what language they spoke or beliefs they held, and where magical occurrences were commonplace.

The valley was bordered by majestic mountain ranges; but the mountain at its end, the one the People called God, towered so high that the other peaks seemed mere hills by comparison. Nestled at its foot, at the bottom of the valley, was an Indian village of fifty or so teepees. Raythorn rode Smoke down into the village, and was met with a warm welcome. He had been long away, and the

People were glad of his return. A maiden emerged from a teepee, and brightened to see that John Raythorn had come back to her. He dismounted and hurried toward her but several young men barred his way. Raythorn did not understand. He demanded that they let him pass.

The chief, Standing Bear, called to him, "You must not go near her, John Raythorn! She has fallen under a curse. Any who touch her may die."

Raythorn wondered what strangeness this was. But he went, when the chief beckoned him to his teepee. He joined the circle of elders and braves seated around the fire inside. He was impatient to learn what had befallen Two Flowers, his true love, who was Standing Bear's daughter. The chief explained that, some days ago, a burning rock had fallen from the sky and struck the side of the mountain. Two Flowers witnessed the event in a dream, and ever since had been divided from her spirit. She told of being trapped in a cave with smooth, flat walls that was haunted by flickering ghosts, even though she walked freely among the People. Cowled Wolf, the medicine man, had tried to heal her. But the potions he gave her turned to ash in her mouth, and his rattle would not sound when he shook it over her.

Raythorn never knew what to make of the Indian way of seeing things. But in the Hidden Realm truth was readily distinguishable from falsehood, and he understood that something serious had occurred, and that the pertinent facts had been conveyed faithfully. Cowled Wolf and Standing Bear led Raythorn back outside the teepee, and the medicine man pointed to a spot high on the mountain. Raythorn saw a tiny shimmer near the summit. Shielding his eyes he made out what appeared to be a vortex of golden dust, issuing like a geyser from that high place on the mountain's side.

"Her spirit is there," Cowled Wolf told Raythorn. "Until she rejoins it, any who touch her will die or be divided as she is." He told Raythorn that the burning rock had made a hole in the world, and that if the hole was not filled the world would fall into it. He said that Two Flower's spirit was keeping the world from falling into the hole, but feared it would not be able to do so much longer. The chief told Raythorn that he sent two braves up the mountain, but neither had returned. He was preparing next to go himself. Raythorn asked to speak with Two Flowers.

She was led before him by several older women, who placed themselves between her and Raythorn. Her manner was odd and desperate-seeming. She told him that she indeed felt divided, and had visions she could not dispel of a cave with strange walls that was inhabited by a troubled spirit or demon. In her eyes Raythorn saw the truth of her story. Something was missing in her. Her desire for him was too hard and raw, un-gentled by the warmth of love. He saw also that she was aware of the void, and longed to fill it, and knew by the distress its absence caused her that her love for him endured. Looking up at the mountain's summit, he felt her call to him from there.

Where truth was plain Raythorn did not need understanding. "My duties in the outer world are ended," he told Two Flowers. "My purpose is to be with you. This affliction stands between us, and I will see you cured of it."

One of the elder women held a weathered book out to him; "She asks you to have this, for protection." Her attitude conveyed little confidence in the volume's potency as a talisman. Rathorn had used it to show Two Flowers the way of printed words, during his first stay in the Hidden Realm, then given it to her when he left.

"Take it!" Two Flowers cried, with a vehemence that stung all present.

Raythorn swallowed, accepted the book and held it softly in his hands. He'd found it up in the White River country, lying by a schoolmarm with an arrow in her back. Much of its contents mystified him, in truth—verse of English writers.

To Standing Bear he said, "My experience of the Hidden Realm is sparse, which with most things would likely prove a hindrance, but in this might serve us, bringing a stranger's eyes and wits to matters passing strange. Send me before you put your people without a leader, Standing Bear. I'll not return without the problem solved or knowledge of its solving."

Standing Bear took counsel with the elders, and it was agreed that Raythorn would go up the mountain. "There is a trail," he told Raythorn. "Unless we all made it in our dreams, no man made it. It goes near the top. It is fit for your mount, and you may want him."

"That would make the journey easier," Raythorn allowed.

"Hear me," Standing Bear continued. "Our people have never taken up the horse, nor will we."

"I know," Raythorn said.

"If you leave him, and he chooses to return to the land, we will not hold him."

"I will take him," Raythorn said.

The People were solemn, the next morning, when Raythorn departed. It was a grey day, with low clouds concealing the upper reaches of the mountain. Raythorn found Cowled Wolf waiting for him, beyond the village edge.

"What counsel, Cowled Wolf?" Raythorn asked.

Cowled Wolf looked up at the mountain. "We find

strange plants in the forest. Last winter a buffalo was born with three legs. Some mornings the People awaken with a sadness that knows no source." He looked at Raythorn. "God is uneasy. His mind wanders. If you return, it will be to a changed world."

"Be that as it may, return I shall."

Cowled Wolf held Raythorn's gaze. "Your path will be crooked. You will see much you do not understand. If you meet a teacher, go where he leads you."

With that Cowled Wolf returned to the village.

Raythorn made his way up the mountain's foot, behind the village, and found the trail, a faint groove in the snow, of which Standing Bear had told him. For awhile the going was easy, but soon the trail steepened and became treacherous, often clinging narrowly to the mountain with the prospect of a sheer descent on its open side.

Rounding a long bend in one such passage, Raythorn found his way barred by a gathering of beings the likes of which he had never encountered. It took him a space to discern their nature. Some seemed to be demons, some the ghosts of warriors of different cultures. They were a fearsome lot, the ghosts no less for being transparent. Some of the demons were lizard–like, some had tentacles and ghastly maws, others defied description. Some of the warriors wore horned helmets and heavy furs, others were near naked, of a darker race; some wore metal armor, others elaborate fastenings of lacquered wood.

3

THE MAN IN the quilted smoking jacket had a sudden experience of awakening. It was as if he had been dreaming someone else's dream. He stood and leaned against a bookcase to steady himself. He began to remember who he was, and why he had veiled his mind.

He remembered the world he came from, and the feeling he'd had that technology there had acquired its own momentum—that his people were becoming servants to their advancements, and losing their place as masters. He remembered catastrophe, when they learned that their minds were linked, sudden environmental and social change.

Then came the discovery of the network of vortices that invisibly spanned space and time, and the tangle of interconnections he strove for years to map and interpret. Driven by an ambition to seek, in the past or future, solutions to the problems besetting his times, he devised a craft to travel through the vortices, and, boarding it, entered their channels, meaning to visit the past of his world. Something had gone awry, and he had come to a world not his own.

To a very specific place on that world, a very specific kind of place.

That should be checked, he realized. The phenomenon might be transient. He scanned the bookshelves. The titles were unreadable. He wondered how much information Cog had been able to assimilate since the crash. Most of the books were black or brown but one was white. He pulled it down and opened it. Inside was a monitor. The data that streamed across it was indecipherable.

"Interpretive functions up sixty percent, Cog," he found himself saying. The quality of light in the room changed. He noticed the gas flame in a sconce take on a steadier, brighter luminance. "Keep all non-relevant mnemonic functions suppressed and maintain the simulation." That sounded like he knew what he was doing. The flame regained its former character.

He could read the data now. The navigation module was still embedded in the side of a mountain. Molecular displacement had occurred. The nose of his craft wasn't just stuck, it was fused. As to the nature of the site, there was no longer any doubt; the mountain and the zone surrounding it were in a state of perpetual flux.

It was an impossible accident. Something had to have drawn him here. He returned the book to its shelf. Cog needed more time to assimilate information and work with the drones.

He realized that he had remembered his name. Small danger in that, he imagined. Other memories were not so benign. Part of his mind understood what was happening, and held the rest, with Cog's assistance, in varying states of mystification to conceal itself. Of that he could not risk prolonged awareness. "Increase mnemonic suppression, Cog. Twenty percent." What he could not recall was how he had come to this strange room with its curious books. Or why he was wearing such odd garments and had the wrong number of fingers. Or how he had acquired a taste for tobacco and—what was it called? Brundy? Brandy. He wanted more of that.

With the suppression of memory of his home world, the image of the rider, John Raythorn, came again clearly to Séquanon's mind. Raythorn was on the mountain, Séquanon recalled, though he could not think which mountain, how he would know such a thing, nor why it might be important. Nevertheless, he was certain that it was. Raythorn must scale the mountain; it was vital to their survival and the survival of this world. He hoped Raythorn was up to the challenge. The journey would be not only physically arduous, it would require him to negotiate the labyrinth of consciousness, and retain his sanity in the face of chaos.

4

RAYTHORN STEADIED HIS mount and regarded the
eldritch assembly. He had no belief in ghosts or demons;
but neither was he quick to mistrust his eyes. If there
were a place in the world for such beings, it would be
the Hidden Realm. Confronted, as he was, by ghosts and
demons, he accepted their existence.

A lizard-thing, massed with horns on its head and
back, came forward to address him. Smoke stamped and
pulled at his reins. Raythorn straightened in the saddle to
steady him.

"What brings you here?" the demon asked.

"Love and my solemn word," Raythorn answered.

"Beyond this place, the minds of God and men dance
together under the same roof. What knowledge have you
of these matters?"

"None," Raythorn replied.

"If allowed to pass, will you rely on your heart or your
senses to guide you?"

"I expect I'll rely on both. Keep my wits about me,
into the bargain."

The demon moved closer, peering hard into Raythorn's eyes.

"Do you fear death?"

"I do not."

"Do you fear the unknown?"

"I don't shy from it."

"This world needs a champion, John Raythorn. No
spirit nor demon nor any person born of the Hidden
Realm may take the challenge. One man only may accept
the task. If we let you pass, the way will close behind you

and no other will follow. How may we be sure that you are the champion we require?"

"I don't expect you can but answer me a question. Are these matters dire?"

The demon met Raythorn's gaze without responding.

"Look behind me," Raythorn said. "What other hastens to apply?"

The demon glanced down the path behind Raythorn and looked back at him. "You must not fail."

Raythorn nodded, and the demon signaled for the others to let him pass.

The ghosts and other demons hesitated, then lowered their blades, stood their spears and axes, un-bared fangs and claws, and parted to permit Raythorn's passage between them. He urged Smoke forward but the horse balked. Raythorn spurred him lightly; the roan plodded ahead. Midway among the weird sentries, Raythorn recognized two warriors clad in the manner of Standing Bear's people. Down the mountainside behind them he spied their corpses, dusted with snow, sprawled on the icy rocks.

"I'll bear word of your fate to your kin, when I return," he told them.

The warriors bowed their heads in acknowledgment.

At the end of the column were other ghosts Raythorn recognized, two men from his old regiment. They tipped their hats and he nodded in passing.

Raythorn left the supernatural sentries behind, gave himself to the way ahead. He fell to reflecting on the manner of his first arrival to the Hidden Realm. Then, as now, he could not account for it. It were more as if the place found him. He could no more guide another here than start his life over. And yet, nowhere else had he felt so certain of his purpose. For all its strangeness, there was no other place he would rather be, save resting in Two Flowers' arms.

The path became less treacherous and the light changed. A nacreous shimmer passed over the surfaces of rocks and snow, and it seemed to Raythorn that he crossed some invisible barrier. The way beyond became yet gentler, and the weather greatly changed. In the space of a few steps he passed from winter into summer, and arrived upon a green, grassy slope. The sky was clear, the air soothing and warm. He dismounted by a narrow stream and quenched his thirst on the sweet mountain water, then surveyed the world below, which was still locked in the hardness of winter. This bubble of summer was odder to him than the ghosts. The mountain's summit seemed hardly closer than it had from the village, though he knew he had scaled a good distance. From this vantage he could not see the vortex.

Raythorn filled his canteen from the stream, left Smoke to rest and refresh himself, and climbed the slope to a rocky outcrop, where he discovered the entrance of a cave. The cave was large enough for a man to walk upright, with head-room to spare. It extended straight into the mountain for about a hundred feet before veering left. A glow emanated from somewhere beyond that point.

Two Flowers had mentioned a cave but the placement of this one was early. Nevertheless it drew Raythorn, and he wondered if he should explore it. He was wary of diverting his course, and was still pondering the question when an old man appeared around the bend of the cave. He came to the entrance and greeted Raythorn as if he had been expecting him. He invited Raythorn inside, seeming to understand why he had come.

The old man was unlike any person Raythorn had ever met. His features bore the characteristics of many races, and seemed to change with his expression. His voice was musical and high-pitched, and he had a gentle manner. He followed the old man into the cave.

Past the bend the cave was full of light and an agreeable ambience contrary to its rough-hewn character. There were ornate rugs on the floor and beeswax candles situated in nooks and crannies about the walls. Raythorn followed the old man into the cave's depths, where, at length, they came upon a group of persons with shaven heads who were engaged in a common activity, painting pictures of flowers and geometric figures on rocks of various shapes and sizes. The artists, clothed in long brown robes, sat amid an irregular disposition of rectangular stone vats, the latter roughly the size and shape that might accommodate a human bather. The vats were either formed of or encased by smooth, rippled flowstone, so fused to the floor of the cave that it was impossible to tell if they were the product of natural formation or contrivance. From them arose vapors that possessed a rich mineral odor. Raythorn stepped near one; it contained a purling liquid that bloomed with colors of vermillion, lilac, golden yellow and opalescent white. He reckoned this must be the source of the painters' medium. Near the center of the vats was a round hole, like a well. Raythorn watched one painter bear a rock she had painted to the hole and drop it in.

The old man explained that these artists were holding the world together. There had been a calamity, though, that rendered their efforts inadequate. Raythorn asked if the calamity had to do with the burning rock and the golden vortex. Without answering, the old man bid Raythorn follow him farther. They went deeper into the mountain, past other painters and other wells, until they reached an opening that seemed to look onto outer space.

Beyond the opening, giant, fantastic beings, that might have been gods, swooped and cavorted through a firmament sparse with stars. Raythorn beheld the spectacle with a wonder he had not known even in childhood. It stopped him the way one can only be stopped by a revelation that exceeds, in nature, all one conceived possible. Among the celestial fray a female creature with wild eyes, long, white, streaming hair, and tattered robes rode a dragon made of bones. Another mighty giant clung to the head of a comet, which he beat with a great hammer, laughing in defiance of fate and peril. A bearded being riding a chariot drawn by winged steeds flew past, and elsewhere a comely goddess poured stars from a shimmering, milk-white pitcher. Not all of the beings bore a human semblance; some seemed to be living objects. A lantern with spindly arms floated by, and, going the other way, a bottle with the face of a rat. The entities numbered beyond counting; there might have been thousands. For all the seeming randomness of their movements, there was an ineffable pattern about them.

While Raythorn witnessed this scene, a shelf of ice began to form at the edge of the opening and extend into the fathomless darkness. Smoke, coming unbidden behind him, nuzzled Raythorn's shoulder. Raythorn turned to find a young girl standing by the horse, berobed and head-shaved in the manner of the priestly painters. Her eyes evinced a depth of womanhood at variance with her youth. She offered Raythorn a small oval stone that on one side was painted with arcane symbols, on the other grown with crystals of four colors: black, clear, pewter, and rose. He accepted the stone and nodded thanks. The girl held her hand toward the cave opening, where the

ice shelf had extended, now, deep into the ethereal firmament, forming a bridge to nowhere. Raythorn studied
the girl's intention and saw that she expected him to ride
out upon that unsupported passage. The old man nodded agreement.

Raythorn edged closer to the opening and looked
out, less with wonder, now, than trepidation. The charms
of phantasmagoria diminished with the prospect of enter-
ing its domain. He did not doubt that the girl and the old
man believed his path lay here. That did not render the
path itself less dubious.

"What manner of place is this?" Raythorn asked.

"A shared imaginarium of the human mind and the
minds of God," the old man answered.

"It seems reachless as the sky. Does it have an end?"

"It has no limit, yet resides within the mountain."

The answer was incomprehensible. It was no help the
old man spoke true. "These giants, what of them?"

"They are its denizens. They will not hinder you."

There was a glint in the old man's eyes. Coupled with
the way his features changed, it vexed Raythorn. He
pondered the bridge. It was well broad enough to accommodate his and Smoke's passage. Eight stout men could
have walked it abreast. It was not, however, substantial-
seeming, particularly not being in large part transparent.
He did not like to think of the endless fall that would
result if it failed.

"You hold I have some purpose yonder," Raythorn
said.

Mirth left the old man's demeanor. "I know only that
you cannot mend matters here without first attending to
them there," he said.

Raythorn rubbed his mouth. With a stiffening of
his gut, the inner sense of direction he had developed

weathering time and trials told him that his path did indeed lead out upon this eldritch ice, but he did not want to go there. The convictions of his two odd advisors neither compelled nor reassured him. It was in belief's design to soften life's uncertainties, and fill with fancy the voids of knowledge. Raythorn preferred to take things at face value. But if what he saw here, in the inner reaches of this mountain the People called God were true and real, and no illusion, what did it say of more conventional grounds, the bloods that soaked them, and the bones they held?

The old man and the girl regarded him impassively. Raythorn took a deep breath. Holding onto the wall to his right, he kicked the ice a couple of times. It seemed solid. He stepped out with one foot, then the other. The bridge held his weight. It wound off into the distance. He could not see its end.

Beyond the limit of the cave the air was cold as winter. Raythorn's breath issued a pale fog against the darkness. He ventured out a ways. The mammoth beings continued their mysterious antics around him. One whose face and pate were hairless sailed overhead with outstretched arms; his grey robes rippled like a flag and a flame burned on his forehead. To Raythorn's right, a circle of twelve gigantic women wheeled by. They sat upon emptiness in cross-legged postures, hands cupped in their laps, their expressions placid. One seemed a child, one ancient, the rest of ages between. They were pursued by a fearsome three-headed hound that, each time the youngest of their ring reached the apex of its roll, leapt through its center.

The giants paid no attention to Raythorn. He would be defenseless against them if they challenged his presence. He stamped on the ice, jumped up and down; it held, without sign of weakening. He might have liked it better had it been less sound.

He turned back to the cave. The opening was a hole in nothing. The old man, Smoke, and the girl stood watching him, encompassed by blackness and a scattering of stars. Raythorn went back to them.

"It bears me," he said to the old man. "Will it hold my horse?"

The old man closed his eyes and did not respond.

"I take it you'll not accompany us."

The old man kept silent.

A cold wind blew down from the tunnel, bringing flurries of snow. The girl, too, had closed her eyes. Snow swirled around her and the old man. In moments it covered the floor and began to form drifts. The girl became unnaturally pale. Frost sheened her skin. Raythorn touched her face. She seemed frozen. The old man was the same, though his features continued to change. For an instant he bore a resemblance to Two Flowers.

A sound like the bellow of a great, deep horn rolled down from the cave and a shudder passed through the walls. Raythorn cast about in doubt and frustration. Smoke neighed and nudged him with his muzzle. Raythorn saw in the horse's eyes his own instinct reflected. He'd never known a true path to lead backwards, even in retreat. Faint heart served no purpose.

Raythorn looked back through the swirling snow at the cave and the way that led to the world he knew, where, even in the Hidden Realm, up could generally be found on high, and down in its respective altitude below. But nothing here was more baffling, nor withal more pointless, than the wanton murder of women and children he had witnessed at Willow Rounds. His horse was with him, a way lay open, and he had not yet failed Two

Flowers. Raythorn climbed in the saddle, gently spurred Smoke, and rode into the chasm of space.

The bridge held and the cold seeped in on him. There was a faint scent of brine in the air. He fixed his attention on the way ahead, lest he be distracted by the ethereal beings milling through undefined space about him. Only once did one pass near, a gargantuan rifle in appearance, with a finger for a trigger and a thumb for a hammer. It swung low over the bridge, as if aiming at Raythorn, and Raythorn reined in Smoke. A blinking eye filled the end of the gun-thing's muzzle. The being hovered a moment, peering at Raythorn, then moved away. Raythorn waited until it passed to a safe distance and urged Smoke on. He could not make sense of this place so did not try. He rode, and let go of thinking. The bridge stretched interminably through the silken dark and Raythorn lost the measure of distance and time.

A grey, pyramidal shape became dimly visible ahead, and Raythorn, sensing a destination, prodded Smoke to a canter. As they drew near, the shape grew to massive dimensions, and resolved into a dark mountain. It bore similarities to the one the People called God, but was less random in shape, and had a more uniform surface, smooth and mottled, with great holes like pores in skin. The bridge climbed to a point high on its slopes, where there was a broad, oval ledge. Looking down over the side of the ice bridge, Raythorn could not make out where the mountain ended. Its lower reaches seemed to merge with the void. A rumbling, cracking noise drew his attention upward, where a great, luminous eye opened in the mountain's face, and it became apparent that the mountain was a living being.

A thunderous voice emanated from it. "You see that my eyes are open," it said.

Raythorn glanced about. Confirming that no one else was present, he decided to risk a reply. "I see only one," he said.

"That is the eye focused on this world," the mountain declared. "I have many eyes, focused on many worlds, and all of them are open."

"Meaning no disrespect, of what import is that to me?" Raythorn asked.

"In its manifestation in your world, my eye has been pierced, and my power is leaking out. If the puncture is not sealed, all of the realms to which I bear witness will collapse on one another."

"How might I repair the breach?"

"You cannot. If you attempt it, I will destroy you."

Raythorn scratched his chin, unsure which prospect was worse. He noticed movement on the wall ahead, and watched a woman emerge from a pore in the mountain's skin and drop onto the oval ledge. Raythorn dismounted and ran to her. Two Flowers raised her hands in warning and with disappointment he understood that they still must not touch.

"We cannot yet be together, John. We must finish our quest," she said.

Two Flowers stood before him, and yet she was different. There was a soft glow about her. Her skin was without blemish, her hair unnaturally silken in its fall, and the scar upon her neck where a wolf had mauled her was absent. She was like a Two Flowers shorn of the wear of history. But her eyes held the full warmth of her love for Raythorn, and his heart filled with courage.

"I come to your aid from my dreams," she said. "I may not linger."

"School me as you will, my love. I am yours to command."

Two Flowers smiled. "Who will command the mighty John Raythorn? Not I."

Raythorn grinned in return. "School me, then, that this barrier may fall."

"Do you have your knife, John?"

"I do."

"A terrible deed lies before you."

Raythorn nodded.

"God must not see what we do in our world," Two Flowers said grimly. She pointed at her right eye and made a stabbing gesture.

Raythorn looked up at the mountain's eye and breathed deep. He understood.

"We must finish our quest, John, or all may perish, and the future with us." Having spoken thus, and favoring Raythorn with a fond parting look, Two Flowers climbed back into the cavity from which she had emerged, and faded into shadow.

Raythorn stood a moment, considering what he had witnessed and been told. He looked up the mountain and determined his route. It was no easy assignment his love had set him. He began his climb. The skin of the mountain being was hard, like stone, but smooth and slick, and it was difficult to maintain hand and foot holds. At least he could see well enough; the light emanating from the eye lit his way.

The nearer he got to the eye, the more daunting his task became. The height of thirty men might not reach from the lower lid to the upper one. His only chance would be to approach from above. The eye did not shift in its orbit as he drew abreast. How insignificant he must seem to a being so great.

He reached a position above the eye. It bulged out below him, casting its glow into the darkness like a pale beacon. In this weird firmament no traveler marked course by its light, though neither did Raythorn suppose it restricted to this darkness. It shone on *'many worlds,'* illumined sights beheld by other souls, who might, untrained to its spectrum, name another author to its reckoning, and yet be warned of shoals and perils hidden in its absence. It was a terrible thing he ventured, wounding God to save the world. Amid the salting of stars, the other titanic entities were a distant dance of fireflies, who lit their own courses. Any one of them would have been better suited than he to the work at hand. It was beyond Raythorn to conscript them to service, or solicit their aid.

He regarded the eye. It seemed as wet and soft as any lesser optic but Raythorn wondered if his knife, long though it was, would penetrate it, and, if it did, if it would it go deep enough to effect blindness. He would have only one try.

He scrambled down on his back until his feet were planted on the eye's upper lid, then crouched and lunged forward, brought the knife down with both hands and plunged it hilt-deep in the moist white sclera. Keeping hold of the handle, he let his body swing around, until his full weight hung from the knife, and pulled hard. The blade cut downward, slowly at first, a milky, gelatinous substance issuing from the lengthening gash. Seeming to borrow power from the being it wounded, the knife grew in Raythorn's hands, cut deeper and faster. A blinding brightness burst from the wound; the mountain groaned and trembled, and the lid began to close. Great gouts of luminous fluid poured over Raythorn in a horrid flood. He pulled harder but the handle became too broad and his hands slipped free.

Falling, he saw reflex complete what he had started, the lid driving the blade down the eye's full depth as it shut. Raythorn landed hard, below the lower lid, and slipped pell-mell toward the void. He threw himself into a roll, angling toward the ledge, achieved it but, drenched as he was in the eye's humors, kept sliding and could not stop. He was near the brink when Smoke stepped in his way.

The mountain shook in earnest, now, bellowing in pain and rage. The knife had enlarged to enormous proportions. Between the eye's struggling lids, the handle protruded like a gargantuan stump. A thick stream of luminous ichor spilled from the gash. Raythorn pulled himself to his feet by Smoke's foreleg and neck. He tried to climb into the saddle but his hands slipped off the horn and he fell back down. He pulled himself up again. Cracks were forming in the ice bridge. Raythorn was so slicked he could grip nothing firmly. He coaxed Smoke to kneel and managed to mount him, wrapped the reins around his wrists and pulled him back up.

He hitched the span of reins between his wrists to the saddle horn and yelled, "Fly brother fly! Damnation is at our heels!"

Smoke took off down the bridge at a gallop, trailing a cloud of ice dust. Raythorn rode low in the saddle. It seemed impossible that the horse would not slip and bear them to an eternal plummet. But the roan was surefooted and true. Raythorn looked back to see the bridge collapsing behind them.

He clung to Smoke, his face pressed to the horse's mane. The stars slipped by, cold flickers in a gaping night. The collapse of the bridge gained on them and receded by turns. Cracks spidered the way ahead and Smoke outran them.

Smoke's breathing grew heavy; his flanks lathered with sweat. The four god-like beings Raythorn had

noticed when he first gazed into this weird nether cosmos came to pace him and Smoke in their flight. The comet-rider took their right flank, the charioteer their left, the she-ghoul on her dragon-bone mount flew above them, and the pitcher-wielding goddess spilled out a channel of stars below. The opening of the cave came in sight, and the latter three veered off; but the comet-rider stayed with them.

The last stretch of the bridge came a-shatter with cracks. The cave entrance, an irregular, pale grey hole in the darkness, seemed unreachable. The comet rider hammered his steed, sending aloft great plumes of ice, and shouted, "Charge, Raythorn! Charge!" Smoke drew on his last reserves of strength and increased his speed. The bridge was breaking apart beneath his hooves. It disintegrated as they crossed the threshold. The comet-rider's cheers echoed after them.

On the other side it was not the interior of the cave to which they arrived but a snow-covered plain in the midst of a snowstorm. Raythorn did not pause to wonder at this latest baffling development. He reined Smoke in, jumped down and pulled off the saddle. He stroked the horse's neck, spoke words of comfort. In that moment he felt as much kinship with the beast as he had any person.

Raythorn rubbed Smoke's flanks with snow. He took a swallow of water from his canteen and gave the rest to the horse, taking in their new surroundings. The change was so extreme he wondered if he had imagined his journey through mystical space. His garments were cleansed of the great eye's humors, dampened now only by falling snow. He checked his scabbard. His knife was gone. If his mind deceived him, it retained a measure of consistency in its tale.

Once Smoke had caught his breath, Raythorn put

the saddle back on him but did not re-mount. He would walk a spell and let Smoke rest. The blizzard obscured all distances. In every direction the view was the same. Having no clear way to go, he set off the way Smoke happened to be facing, and Smoke followed.

5

THROUGH THE MULLIONED bay window of his study, the man in the quilted smoking jacket watched the rider cross the snowy plain. The rider did not return his regard; that one saw only the flat, white land and unending flurries. John Raythorn rode close by the window, neither advancing nor retreating, as if his mount strode in place or the study somehow paced him.

The man in the quilted smoking jacket replenished his snifter from a crystal decanter, returned to the window and resumed his vigil over the rider's ordeal. *John Raythorn, meet Séquanon, former cosmological theorist and traveler of the continuum, who clings to the land now in the guise of a Victorian scholar.* Séquanon understood, now, that he was witnessing neither memory nor fiction but a true unfolding of the present. He wondered what part the rider might play in their dilemma.

The library and its fixtures vanished, the greyish-greenish paneling of his ship's interior came into focus, and Séquanon was abruptly in command of his full mind. Cog apprised him of a potential emergency. Two screens displayed indecipherable images from the drones monitoring the nose of the ship. Séquanon tried to adjust them manually but no clearer view resulted. Nor could Cog provide him with any more enlightening analysis. Séquanon looked up at the airlock and breathed a heavy sigh; he would have to go out himself to see what was happening.

The atmosphere of the planet was low in argon and, at this altitude, thin. The temperature, also, was extremely cold. He would have to put on the environment suit, which had been designed for zero gravity and would be cumbersome. There was no way around it.

He suited up and boarded the elevation platform. It lifted him into the airlock. The floor of the platform dilated around its perimeter and sealed the chamber. The pressure stabilized, the outer lock disengaged and Séquanon pushed the button to open the hatch. It raised only a small fraction before wind wrenched it wide with a screech and clang.

Séquanon secured an extra tether to his suit and climbed up. Wind pummeled him; he had to crawl onto the gangway. Only when he had both tethers secured to the track rails did he venture to stand. Flashes from the aft and lateral thrusters shone in irregular sequence at the rear and sides of the ship. Séquanon did not like to think about the innumerable adjustments Cog was having to make to keep them steady. He told Cog to shut the hatch. The way it screamed Séquanon thought the gears would strip but it closed.

He fought his way to the front of the ship. The gravity of this world was higher than Tumult's, and within a few steps he was sweating. Halfway along he went back to crawling.

He made it to the nose. What had happened was not readily clear. The drones had begun securing a framework of struts to the mountain face, to support the ship when it came time to free it. Something had interfered with their efforts and Cog had pulled them back. All seventeen now hung in loose formation to the port side of the ship. Levitating lozenges, no larger than Séquanon's head, their sizes belied their capacities. It was an absurd notion, but they seemed frightened, somehow, clustered together there.

The nose of the ship and the rock face had iced over around the point of impact. Séquanon took a hammer from the suit's tool belt and chipped at the ice until a section broke loose and was snatched away by the wind. Séquanon squinted at the exposed surface, unsure what he was seeing. He chipped more ice away. What he discovered made him shudder. The rock of the mountain had begun to take on the composition of the ship.

6

JOHN RAYTHORN CONTINUED his journey through the snow on horseback, with no different prospect before him or in any direction. Snow fell, distance elapsed, the plain extended ahead unchanged. He held to his purpose, resisting the wear of uncertainty upon his resolve.

The wind died and the snow thinned. Some distance to his right, structures became vaguely visible, resolved into cabins and clapboard buildings such as might comprise a small settlement. Raythorn turned Smoke toward them. Buildings yes, but an odd sort of settlement for their disposition. They were too close and clustered, angled against use in their orientation to each other. The back corner of one crowded the porch of another; two cabins faced each other at a shoulder's breadth; some even seemed to overlap. Raythorn pulled alongside a small barn. Up close, it was pale and semi-transparent. He reached to touch it and his hand passed through the wooden planks. Raythorn cursed. He'd had mysteries enough. He looked about in frustration. Where on earth was he? Where was the mountain? He swung his hand back and forth through the wall that wasn't there; his fingers prickled, and he snatched it back.

The spectral settlement upset Raythorn in a way none of the other queer phenomena he'd encountered that day had. If the same day it was—the sky was overcast to an even whiteness, and no brighter point positioned the Sun. He had no sense of the hours that had passed since his departure from the village. He studied the illusory houses and outbuildings with distaste. There was somewhat of grave goods about the tableau that offended him. He turned Smoke back to their previous course. More ghost buildings appeared, though, as they continued along, on both sides, now, and closer. Some were larger, constructed, in semblance, of brick or stone. Raythorn prodded Smoke to quicken his pace. Larger and larger buildings, progressively more elaborate in design, rose about them with no logic to their placement. It were as if they fell willy-nilly into each others' midsts, save they rose from the ground rather than dropping from the sky. Looking back, Raythorn discovered that he was pursued as well by machines. First one, then another locomotive appeared, and soon were joined by a press of smaller horseless vehicles that wended among the random edifices in a swarm.

The engines made no sound. Their silence menaced Raythorn.

He spurred Smoke in earnest. The snow was deep; the roan could not hurry long. The buildings became enormous, taller than any Raythorn had ever imagined might be made. To some were affixed great chimneys that spouted dark, unwholesome plumes. The buildings rose up shoulder to shoulder and through one another, leaving no space in their company; and yet, with them and within them, the machines rolled forth as well.

Hoards of phantom Indians and animals amassed at Raythorn's flanks, fleeing the buildings with him. Birds and bears, tribes he'd fought, deer, rabbits, coyotes, joined by the common threat. The phantom towers that chased them soared to claw the heavens, and in the sky above them appeared legions of winged contraptions. Smoke began to tire again, laboring through the deep snow. Raythorn grew desperate at the thought of failing Two Flowers. But he could not escape this madness; he did not even know what it was that he fled. The horizon ahead remained unchanged.

Raythorn clenched his teeth and reined Smoke in. He prayed the monstrosities that pursued them were as insubstantial as the barn had been. But they were not overtaken as he had expected them to be. The phantom Indians and animals poured on and vanished into the snows ahead. In their wake the plain returned to sameness. Raythorn brought Smoke around. The legion of spectral towers had halted its advance. The machines on the ground and in the air were arrested; the massed towers loomed as if awaiting leave to progress.

Raythorn beheld the spectacle with as much exasperation as bewilderment. Many of the towers looked to rise a hundred stories or more, among them some that appeared composed entirely of glass. He could not conceive how such structures might be made. Surely it was a feat beyond human capacity, though somehow he suspected not. The nature of the things, in their ghostly state, confounded him. If they were visions it was beyond him to divine their significance. He wondered if he had crossed into an afterlife.

More important was why they had stopped. Raythorn backed Smoke up a few steps. A crush of new spectral towers rose incompletely from the plain. The air machines and horseless vehicles crept forward, and stopped again when he did. He backed Smoke farther and the fledgling towers finished their rise. It seemed that, in his effort to escape this sprawl of ethereal metropolis, he had inadvertently led its charge.

Raythorn dismounted, left Smoke ground-tied, and approached the mob of towers. It extended as far to either side as he could see through the snow. Many of the buildings indeed overlapped one another.

It was sure there was a question here that needed answering. If this was some conjury to try his mettle, it was trying his patience best. Smoke needed water and a long rest, and Raythorn was thirsty and tired himself. He was no nearer to curing Two Flowers' malady, that he could see, than he had been setting out. And here the Hidden Realm had served him a riddle.

Maybe he was going the wrong direction. Forging on indefinitely with a monstrous ghost city at his back was no welcome prospect.

Nearest before Raythorn stood one of the towers of glass. The falling snow did not cling to its walls but passed through them. Inside spread a vast space set with rows of enormous columns. Broad as they were, the columns did not seem stout enough to bear what stood above. Raythorn tested the glass wall—his hand passed through it as it had that of the barn, and the tingling sensation recurred. The next move seemed plain, though it was not without misgivings that he essayed it. He had no inscrutable sage to query. He stepped through the phantom glass and entered the domain of the ghostly towers.

The tingling spread through his body, and set his skin acrawl with goose bumps. The air seemed to come a little heavier in his lungs. Otherwise nothing untoward transpired. He sensed no threat to his person.

He explored the place. The floor, as the plain, was knee-deep with snow, and snow fell through the chamber unhindered, though here the flakes seemed to take on a shine. The pillars were faced with polished stone. Again Raythorn thought they were too slight to bear the weight of the colossus they supported, had it had substance.

It seemed impossible, too, that people could dwell in such a thing. There must be some contrivance to bear folks up and down. The chamber was centered by a large structure that extended floor to ceiling. In both of its broader sides were set rows of what might have been doors, though they had no handles to service their opening. Maybe each tower was a village unto itself, and its denizens never left its confines. Such ways would not suit Raythorn. He would sooner quit shelter for good.

At the far end of the chamber, the corner of another tower penetrated the one he was in. The other was built more sensibly of some kind of stone, though its material was strange, too, consisting of massive segments a hundred oxen could scarce have moved, and shaped with uncanny precision. Raythorn touched its surface, and his hand penetrated it, too, though it seemed with faint resistance. He pressed through that wall, then again the glass wall of the intersected tower, and found himself confronted by a fresh host of mysteries.

He had entered an indoor plaza lined with stores and what might have been varieties of saloons and eating establishments, the latter suggested by placements of tables and chairs. But there familiarity ended; not a single object was made in a way Raythorn understood, nor of materials he knew. The lighting was a magic of its own. Panels in the ceiling glowed brighter and steadier than any lantern or flame. The walls were of some light-colored stone of a type he did not recognize, and without division, seeming all of one piece. He could not discern the use of most of the merchandise in the stores. There were books in one, with shiny covers and elaborate art, the titles in strange scripts he could not read. The same was true of signs above entrances. Long white bins in a market contained an amazing variety of produce, but he could not identify the vegetables, nor tell them from the fruits.

It was in a dry goods store that he seemed to find the beginnings of an answer. The garments on the racks were outlandish, of garish colors and baffling designs. The pictures on the walls above them took Raythorn's attention—photographs, they looked, though he had never before seen any in color, and these were vivid—taller than a man, and plainly intended to flaunt the store's wares. But the figures sporting outfits in them were not human. Their eyes were too large, their mouths too broad, and where there should have been nostrils, their noses ended in a cluster of holes like a wasp's nest. Their heads bulged at the back, and were mounted on necks too long and thin. Their trunks were too long overall, and their legs short, next to a man's. For all that, there was a grace about them, a kind of beauty, and Raythorn felt a distant kinship.

Their hands had seven fingers.

7

SÉQUANON CHIPPED AWAY ice until he could see the extent of the transformation. It radiated about arm's length across the rock face from the ship's hull. He affixed a small, shallow-core drill to the altered surface and took a sample for analysis.

He transferred his tethers to the nearest ladder and climbed down to see if the phenomenon extended below the ship. A gust of wind ploughed into him and he lost his grip. The tethers malfunctioned; he couldn't get them to lock. They unspooled and Séquanon plummeted. The alien world spread below, its gnarled lineaments a nightmare of distance. The jerk when the tethers reached their ends whipped his head forward. He dangled, wincing in pain.

The wind made him its toy, tossed him about, slammed him against the rock face and pinned him there. The drones swooped down and took hold of him. Séquanon's respect for their engineering grew; how they held steady he did not know. He retracted the tethers manually as they bore him back up. Nearing the ship, he noticed a dark patch on the rock beneath it.

Cog identified the malfunction. The suit's power pack was low; the suit had given automatic priority to life-critical systems. Séquanon groaned. The suit had never been used; the power pack was new. He'd forgotten to charge it. The greater lapse, though, was Cog's for not alerting him to the suit's status before he donned it in the first place. The last thing Séquanon needed was for Cog to start performing unreliably.

The drones lifted him back to the ladder. Séquanon took hold of a track rail next to it, stepped onto an access rail and side-stepped to the front of the ship, crouched down to look underneath. A viscous, black fluid streamed down the rock face where his ship jutted from the mountain. Slow-flowing but it did not freeze. Séquanon feared it might be lubricant or insulating fluid, but when he got closer knew it was neither. It was something coming out of the mountain. He reached to touch it. The liquid crystalized and seemed to reach back when his fingers drew

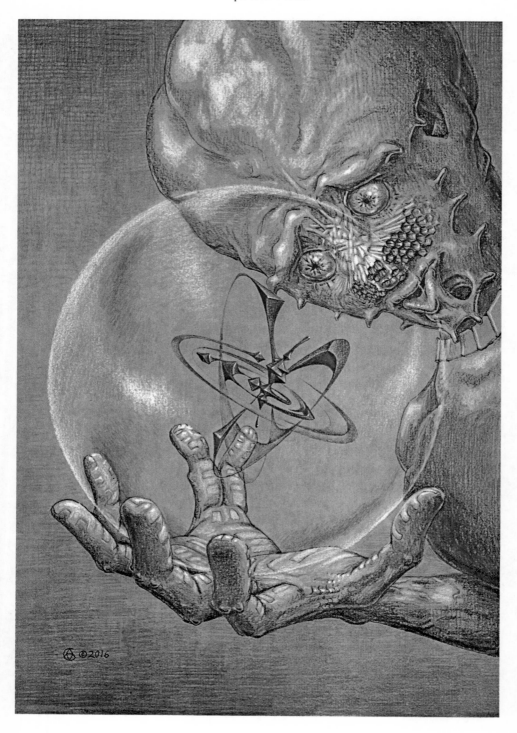

close. Séquanon withdrew his hand and the crystalized portion returned to a liquid state.

"Cog, give me neural control of one of the drones," Séquanon said.

Cog recommended that Séquanon leave attitude adjustment on automatic and assume control of task and direction only. Séquanon concurred and took control of Drone Seven. He directed it to collect some of the black substance oozing out of the mountain. The drone extended a sampling trowel but the moment the trowel made contact with the substance Drone Seven lost attitude control, swooped high and smashed against the mountain with such force that it burst apart. Its wreckage fell on top of the ship. Séquanon told Cog not to let the other drones go near it.

His suit sounded an alarm. The power pack was down to critical levels. Before long the servos would fail. Without them, Séquanon doubted that he could lift the suit's arms or walk in this gravity. He needed to get back inside.

He sidestepped back to the ladder and climbed up. The remains of Drone Seven lay scattered near the nose of the ship. The sampling arm was extended; a small quantity of the black substance adhered to it. Wind pushed the wreckage toward the edge. Séquanon crawled forward and managed to detach the arm before it was blown into the void. He told Cog to release the drones to collect the debris. He didn't want a single scrap left behind.

He made his way to the hatch. The black substance kept migrating toward his fingers. He had to transfer it back and forth between his hands. He waited for a lull in the wind before he had Cog open the hatch. The lull that came was too brief. The wind returned with full force before he was inside. The hatch screamed horribly again but closed.

"I need an isolation field, Cog."

A diaphragm in the wall of the airlock opened and a transparent sphere with a hole in its upper surface floated out. Séquanon fed Seven's arm carefully into the nullification bubble, told Cog to seal the field and not let the bubble touch anything. As soon as the bubble closed the substance separated from the arm to become a floating black bead.

The servos in Séquanon's suit gave out. He struggled out of the suit quickly as he could and took manual control of the isolation field. He created a second bubble within the first one, shrank it around the black bead and extracted the sampling arm.

Séquanon let himself relax a little. He was drenched in sweat. The chamber depressurized and the platform lowered to the bridge. Séquanon peeled off his jump suit, toweled himself dry and put on a clean suit.

He scrutinized the substance inside the bubble. Even isolated in a null field its behavior was erratic. It shifted between liquid and crystal, forming loops and rings and semi-symmetrical figures. Séquanon had Cog draw it into the lab module for analysis. Cog could not identify it, nor establish that it could be categorized strictly as matter.

Impossibly, the substance began to compromise the stability of the isolation field. Séquanon had Cog jettison the sample.

He asked if the drones had been able to collect all of Drone Seven's wreckage. Cog confirmed that they had, and Séquanon permitted himself a small sigh of relief. One thing had been established: not only he but his technology was having an impact on this nexus, the scope of which he could not determine.

He could leave behind no trace of his presence. Abandoning the navigation module was no longer an option.

8

RAYTHORN EXPLORED THE labyrinth of the towers, searched down hallways, crossed through walls and doors, hoping to find something that would explain their mysteries. The farther he went, the stronger an ineffable force pressed against him. His understanding did not increase in kind. He began to question the wisdom of arguing with an unknown power and decided to turn back.

He had expected the impediment to diminish when he reversed course, but return proved harder—soon much harder. Invisible resistance increased with every phantom barrier he penetrated.

By the time he got back to the indoor plaza he was drenched in sweat. The air was thick and heavy; he heaved and groaned with every breath. The photographs and oddities that had preoccupied him earlier went unregarded.

He passed through the glass wall, then the stone one, returning to the first chamber he had entered, and there met the worst of the ordeal. He fought no longer for steps but their increments, each harder than the last, breathing in shallow gasps.

Doubt breached his resolve. There wasn't enough of him left for this challenge. The People's faith had been ill-placed. He glimpsed Smoke, deformed by a warp in the far ghost glass. Naught else took Raythorn's withering sight but white, cold white, pure, immaculate white, and shimmering flakes arrested in their fall. A vain notion stole over his crumbling will: what peace it would bring to vacate objectives, whose measures halved without end. He pressed on, not knowing how to quit. Fatigue made comely the promise of cold.

He saw Two Flowers in his mind and held her image like a prayer. He remembered where his inner wolves dwelled, the beasts he loosed in battle, and set them against despair. His will would have to be wrested from him; he would in no other wise relent.

He reached the last barrier and burst through with a cry, threw off his coat and hat and lurched through the snow, howling like one deranged. He kept going until he shook loose the cloying grip of restraint, fell on his back in the snow, gazed into fathomless whiteness and let his wolves make a meal of his fears.

His heart and breath steadied and he sat up. The enigma of the towers remained an implacable wall. Raythorn was still overheated but knew he could fall prey quickly to the cold. He got up to retrieve his hat and coat and realized the towers had not advanced. Smoke stood where he'd left him, a hundred feet or more away. Raythorn had run past him but the phantoms retained the limit they'd had when he dismounted.

He went back, dusted the snow off his hat, put it and his coat back on and snicked at Smoke. The towers retreated as the roan came to him. He patted Smoke's neck and thought a moment, took him by the reins and led him away.

The towers advanced.

He should have seen it. It was not he but the horse who led them.

He tested the theory several times, taking Smoke toward and away from the towers, and each time they increased and receded accordingly. But when he made the same experiment on his own their line went unchanged.

Raythorn saw what was required, and wondered how much the Hidden Realm would take from him before this job was done.

He removed Smoke's bridle, pulled off the saddle, dropped both in the snow and rested his head against the horse's brow. He dared not let himself think about what he was doing. Into Smoke's ear Raythorn whispered, "The village," and slapped him on the haunch.

Smoke snorted and shook his head.

Raythorn grimaced. "Do as I say, ya' heathen creature! Off with you!" he commanded, and slapped Smoke harder.

The roan galloped away. As he passed among the phantom buildings and machines they collapsed and vanished. The plain became, again, a seamless expanse. Smoke dwindled to a mote and was gone.

Raythorn shouldered his rifle and saddlebags and headed in the opposite direction, hoping he had not sealed his fate and the world's. He did not go far before an instinct made him stop.

The sky darkened and cleared, unveiling a spectacle of stars. The ground trembled, and the mountain rose up from the plain. Raythorn was borne aloft, clinging to a narrow ledge in wretched incomprehension.

9

Two Flowers awoke with foreboding from a deep dream of nothingness. It was dark out. She heard voices raised in alarm, dressed hurriedly, and went outside. She had endured long isolation in her teepee; the cold air felt good on her face. Many others were awake, but none marked her emergence. They were all looking up at the mountain.

The vortex shined brightly, as if it had caught fire. Faint rumbling and hissing sounds reverberated down the mountainside. Bright orbs and spears shot out of the vortex and flew far through the sky. They fell to earth beyond the mountains that enclosed the Valley of the Four Moons, and where each dropped a fearsome glow bloomed against the night.

Two Flowers was unaffected by these bizarre occurrences. The emptiness in her had become a ravenous ache, and nothing here could fill it.

She needed John Raythorn, and he was on the mountain. She would wait no longer to go to him. Two Flowers went back in her teepee, donned her buffalo cloak, grabbed her medicine bag and a pouch of dried meat. She went back out to find her father watching her. He came toward her but she backed away. He read her intention and stopped. For a moment he resisted, but a sadness fell upon him and she saw him accept her will.

Two Flowers hurried toward the mountain. Standing Bear lifted his arms in prayer.

10

SÉQUANON WAS HAVING trouble reading. He seemed to have become dyslexic. The words on the page shifted between symbol systems, one known to him and one foreign.

Giving up, he returned the book to the shelf, and stroked its leather spine. "Theory and Practice in Trans-Dimensional Mechanics." He should have known what that meant, but the region of his mind where understanding dwelt was shrouded in confusion.

He stepped back and surveyed the orderly rows of books. So much knowledge—though he wasn't sure which ones he'd read. A fine collection, in any case. He lingered, taking in their distinguishing characteristics.

They were arrayed so pleasantly, it made him want to read them all right then. Pride of ownership—*that* was the satisfaction he felt, as one might with a collection of *q't-wah*.

Whatever that was. Dried, carved fruit of some kind. He couldn't remember. What an odd thought.

A thread-thin glow came alight between books in a staggered line down the shelves. The phenomenon manifested so innocuously, at first, that Séquanon was less startled than curious. As it brightened he grew alarmed. The crooked glow became blinding. To Séquanon's amazement, a woman with long black hair, wearing a buckskin dress, stepped out from its seam.

She fixed on Séquanon with a fierce glare and lunged at him. He jumped back and retreated across the study until he collided with the sidebar, scattering cigars and sending the brandy decanter crashing to the floor. With her left hand the woman seized him by the throat, her right raised, claw-like, to strike.

"No!" he cried.

She did not release him but studied his eyes.

"What do you want?" Séquanon pleaded. "Who are you?"

Her grip on his throat tightened. "Demon! You think I will tell you my name so you can bind me to your will? I will gouge out your eyes and cast you into the half lands, where Eagle will blind you again, each day, and Trickster will lead you to madness!"

Séquanon did not know what to make of her words. Madness, she'd said—she must be insane. Or he was, to see her leap from his bookcase. She leaned close, their noses near touching, and searched his eyes. Whatever she discerned reduced her ire.

She released him and drew back. "You are not a demon."

He shook his head. "No!"

"What then? You are like no other."

He didn't know how to answer, so he said, "A person."

She peered at him and stepped back farther. "The world is," she searched for a word, "falling."

"I . . . don't understand."

She pointed at him. "You cause it."

He stared in bewilderment. The light from the window darkened and took their attention. John Raythorn was there, huddled against a sheer rock face.

The woman swept to the glass and pressed her palms flat on the panes. "John!" she cried.

"Mnemonic functions up sixty percent, Cog," Séquanon found himself saying, and regained a measure of composure. "Maintain the perceptual environment." It came to him, again, who and where he was, the nature of his predicament. The woman, or semblance thereof, remained. She must be an inhabitant of the nexus.

Cog should have detected her presence. "How many life forms onboard, Cog?"

Cog did not respond.

"Cog?"

"Empirical clarity is not possible."

Cog's voice drew the woman's attention away from the window.

Séquanon watched her. "Estimate," he said, in a quavering voice.

"Including yourself, more than one, fewer than two," Cog said.

The woman searched for the source of Cog's voice, pointed up and looked inquiringly at Séquanon. "Demon?"

Séquanon shook his head. "Artificial brain."

The woman frowned.

"Machine."

Her eyebrows rose and she looked up again.

"Who are you?" he asked again.

She opened her mouth as if to answer, then frowned in confusion.

The projected room vanished and the interior of Séquanon's bridge returned to view. Séquanon's mind simultaneously resumed full function. Distorted, indecipherable images filled the monitors; something was scrambling the visual feeds from the drones, again, where they worked around the nose of the ship. Séquanon told Cog to have them pull back and wait for him. He would have to go back outside.

The woman stared in shock at the interior of Séquanon's ship. He wondered what, in her place, he might have made of the instruments and monitors, the smooth, molded surfaces. He remembered too late that his appearance was no longer hidden. She saw him now in his true form, and reacted predictably. The word "demon" found use again. Séquanon was in no way prepared, though, for what happened next.

The woman shrank and flattened, became an ambiguous, levitating smear that floated across the bridge, sank into a monitor and vanished.

11

TWO FLOWER'S CLIMB, being made on foot, was more arduous than Raythorn's. She was forced to go slow, for the way was ill lit, in places pooled with impenetrable darkness, and often treacherous.

When she neared the place where Raythorn had been challenged by supernatural sentries, she was long

since worn from the climb. She saw dark figures ahead, there, but upon reaching them found them to be made of stone. Positioned along the precipice at one side of the trail and joined to the rock wall at the other, some resembled men, others creatures of the demon realm. The high half moon limned their features in frail light.

The first on the left looked like a grandfather lizard, with horns framing its face and rowed down its back. Even in stone there was that in its eyes that bespoke a complex mind. Flanking it at the trail's edge stood a creature with a mouth rimmed by snakes—so they seemed, but Two Flowers thought of the mole people, who lived underground without eyes.

Among the rest were the greater part men, strangely clad, with likenesses different from those of her people. As she passed among them they began to speak, too mixed and softly for her to understand. She saw then two whose stone semblances she recognized, Grey Elk and Hears an Owl, whom her father had sent up the mountain before Raythorn. It was clear they had died, but Two Flowers was too empty to mourn. She offered prayers for their spirits, held her arms out to the sky people, whose fires beaded the night. She touched Grey Elk's brow and sensed his spirit flicker, dim and slow within stone, learned that Raythorn had passed here alive.

The voices of the others became clearer, and united in their message: Only Raythorn had leave to pass; it was not her place to pursue him. She would bring her curse upon the world and all would be lost. Two Flowers did not want to believe them, but sensed how they believed themselves and wondered if they were right. They sought more beguilingly to win her compliance: If she stayed and joined with God, they would tell her their stories and she would learn of the world. If she continued on, she would be alone, with naught but the wind for fellowship.

Wind whistled among them, confirming their claim, and spoke of the world's soul, and all that it knew. If Two Flowers stayed, Wind would shape her to the world's tale; she would learn of all people, as if living their lives. Two Flowers saw that in truth there was place for her here, that she could live as stone and bear witness to the world.

But it would not fill her emptiness, even encircled now as it was with doubts. The spirits read her thoughts, and assured her that her soul would return to her if only she would remain. She would suffer doubt and longing no more, and the world's wonders would be hers.

Two Flowers stood, bound in argument between the promise of stone and the ache that gnawed at her breast. She did not have to choose, only to wait and time would decide for her; it was the way of stone to be still, save other forces moved it.

Something cracked and fell to the path. A shaft in Hears an Owl's quiver lacked a point and Two Flowers spied the arrowhead at his feet. Neither he nor Grey Elk had joined their voices with the rest. John Raythorn came to her mind, the mien with which he met the world, the will he forged on his own. It was not only her spirit, hard in its summons, that called to her from on high. John Raythorn needed her; this quest was not his alone. And she needed him, for love and survival and the future of the world. Two Flowers felt the stone spirits' fear; locked in a dream of the world's end, they offered, unknowing, a false exchange. Their enchantment lost its hold. She picked up the arrowhead and put it in her medicine bag.

The stone sentries stirred to block her. But they were too slow; she dodged them and ducked their reaching arms, and made it to the end of their company. The last two were dressed like Raythorn, and of his people, and made no move against her. One of them held his hat tipped. She heard another soft crack and moonlight glinted on a stone bullet that fell from the other's gun belt. Two Flowers found the bullet and put it in her medicine bag with Hears an Owl's arrowhead.

She continued up the path, her soul beseeching her to fly, but she was bound by feet and legs to ice and stone. The way grew easier and the air warmed. The path opened onto a meadow strewn with dried leaves but bare of snow. The air retained a chill but lost its icy edge.

Blessing that the softer climate was, the sound of running water was more dear. She found a stream, slaked her thirst and lay down to rest, watched the stars through a crooked web of barren branches.

The water murmured of peace and surrender, of a way beyond strife and time. Even beneath the arms of the trees, in the caress of shadows, it seemed a fond promise. Two Flowers' spirit would not let her linger. With weary acceptance she pulled herself away from the stream's comforts.

At the upper end of the meadow, where Raythorn had found the cave's entrance, Two Flowers met only a stone outcrop, its broadest face inscribed with a symbol she did not recognize. She found the path again, framed by a stone gateway composed of two standing pillars and a capstone.

Some large creature made its way down the trail beyond. It came through the arch and Two Flowers sagged with dread to recognize Raythorn's horse, bare of bridle and saddle. There was a faint glow about the animal— it had undergone some transformation. Smoke nuzzled against her. She feared to touch him. Smoke trembled and shied. Two Flowers sensed that he was immune to her curse, stood still and straight and calmed herself inwardly. Smoke came to her again, and she stroked his head and neck, and murmured to him softly.

Looking into Smoke's eyes she communed with his soul, and perceived that Raythorn had set him loose on purpose. She took dried sprigs of yellow-top and cone-flower from her medicine pouch and braided them into the horse's mane. She stroked his neck and spoke sooth-ingly to him again, then patted him on the rump, sending him on down the trail. Two Flowers watched Smoke until he passed from sight.

She continued up the trail. Past the stone gate, the deep cold of winter reasserted like a blow. Two Flowers braced herself and resisted the urge to turn back. A series of other gates stood before her, each narrower than the last, through which the trail curved upward, diminishing again to a narrow ledge cut in a sheer rock face. The gates continued onto this ledge, the opening through each narrower than the last, until Two Flowers could barely squeeze through, and wondered how Smoke had man-aged. Around a long curve she found her way blocked by a gate with a space between its pillars of barely a fin-ger's width.

12

SECURE IN HIS fully-powered environment suit, Séquanon pushed open the hatch and met the stars of the foreign world with poignant yearning, less to know his location than his place in the universe. Every new devel-opment increased uncertainty and diminished hope.

It was colder but the wind had stilled. Séquanon

nevertheless used two tethers, again, and made his way forward. The hull of his ship shone with ice. In the cone of illumination from his helmet light, the struts the drones had secured to the mountain's wall reached out at him like stiff tentacles around a hungry maw.

Sixteen in number now, the drones held place as before, well back from the ship's point of contact with the mountain. New ice had replaced what Séquanon had chipped away earlier. The framework of struts spread above and around him. About half of them were complete, with stabilizing pads attached. It would be a tricky procedure, cutting the ship free and backing from the mountain in full gravity. And there was the black stuff to contend with. He'd have to figure out some way to create an isolation field between it and the nose section. He sighed. And then they'd have to remove all the struts. He couldn't leave anything behind.

He chipped at the ice again to see how far the molecular transformation had spread. The finding was disheartening: it extended, now, beyond his reach. A liquid glimmer caught the corner of his sight, and he trained his helmet light on it. A thin stream of black liquid exuded from the base of one of the struts where it was bolted to the stone. Séquanon searched around and found the same phenomenon at the bases of three other struts. Peering at the nearest one, overhead to his right, he saw something else.

The strut was turning to stone.

Séquanon blinked a few times, dropped to his knees and squinted into the crevice where the nose of the ship was lodged. So far as he could see, the transformation had occurred only in the stone, and no reciprocal shift had yet taken place in the ship's hull. He ran an optical snake from his suit into the crevice. All seemed well, but there was a point beyond which the snake couldn't go. He searched around and found a tiny gap, fed the cord through, discovered several patches, like lesions, where the skin of the nose had been compromised.

Séquanon withdrew the snake and hurried back to the hatch in panic. He would have to leave the nose section behind. The best he could do now was limit his impact. If the transformation spread any farther he would never escape.

He told Cog to make preparations for emergency departure, climbed down into the decompression chamber and got out of his suit. "Pull the drones back onboard, Cog."

Riding the elevation platform down to the bridge, he saw immediately that something else was wrong. Lights and readouts on the instrument panels fluctuated erratically.

"Report, Cog," he said.

"Running diagnostic processes."

Several of the monitors showed the image of the female apparition that had manifested earlier. In all she pointed at Séquanon, mouthing inaudible accusation.

Séquanon scrambled down the ladder to the ship's hold. The drones had scavenged non-essential materials to fabricate the struts. Most of the paneling had been stripped away, leaving bare conduits exposed. Séquanon ran to the navigation module and opened the hatch, searched inside for signs of molecular shift. He couldn't find any, small comfort.

"Cog, report! We need to detach from the nose section and leave this planet immediately."

"Diagnosis incomplete. A foreign process seems to have compromised an indeterminate number of subsystems."

"Isolate it! Purge it! We need to get out of here!"

"Exceeding safety parameters is not recommended . . ."

"Forget the parameters——"

Séquanon stopped. The hold of the ship had vanished from sight. He found himself in a cobbled alley in a native city. It was night. He had spent enough time in the simulation, inhabiting a native mind, to recognize the brick buildings, the gaslight lanterns, the sinuous fog stringing the darkness. *Something like London . . .*

He looked at his hands—five fingers—felt his face. He wasn't even in the hammock; this shouldn't be possible. His appearance was masked in a native body, in native clothing, his location in a simulation of a native street, but his mind was bare for all to see. Séquanon felt his cardiac tree oscillate through the roof.

"Cog?"

His ship's artificial mind did not respond.

13

THE COLD GNAWED at Raythorn's bones. His lungs burned from the thin, sharp air. Wind thrashed him as he made slow, plodding progress up the trail on legs shaking with fatigue. His scarf, drawn over his nose and mouth, was clotted with ice, and icicles hung from his hat.

He huddled in a shallow notch in the mountain's wall, fished a piece of jerky from a saddlebag but it was too hard to bite. He had no moisture in his mouth to soften it. He folded himself into as sheltered a posture as he could and endured.

He dared not sleep; the cold would take him.

Some interminable time later the wind died. Raythorn gazed into the sea of stars, and across the far world

spread pale blue in the half-moon's light, and was overcome with gratitude, despite his misery, for the beauties
he'd witnessed in life.

No sooner had that humble sentiment graced his
being than a glimmer of fires scattered across the land
beyond the mountains enclosing the Valley of the Four
Moons. He marked them as settlements and distant camps,
but they spread, and grew to baleful conflagrations, until
the country beyond the valley was consumed to the horizon. Raythorn did not doubt the sudden holocaust had
its source in human mischief.

All his life John Raythorn had watched men perpe-
trate evils upon one another. He had perpetrated more
than a few himself. For the most part, he could fairly
attribute the latter to the needs of survival. He had tried
not to be cruel, though he'd fought alongside some who
exercised no such restraint. Almost worse was the way
people treated themselves, abandoning dignity, stuffing their maws like they were packing cannons, rutting
with a ruthlessness that would shame a beast. Raythorn's
reflections filled him with disgust. All life was rendered
vicious by the simple need to eat. Nothing lived unless
something died.

The burning world glimmered in his eyes, and his
mood soured precipitously. He doubted the virtue of
his quest. If he, who had killed so many, was the best
mankind could muster to champion its defense, maybe
mankind should fail. The stars did not escape his cyn-
icism. It was the nature of creation to incinerate itself.
Even his love for Two Flowers was insufficient to answer
its violence. What right had he to love?

Something pinged overhead, at the edge of the crevice in which he sheltered. Raythorn squinted at the spot,
uncomprehending. It happened again, near his feet, and

a chip cut his brow. Several more times the rocks about him were struck, and Raythorn realized he was being fired upon.

He worked his rifle out of its sheath and fired back wildly, blind to the source of attack. Bullets from nowhere peppered about him. He cursed in defiance, fired until the Henry was empty, and hurled it into the darkness with a scream.

The attack stopped. No more bullets ricocheted. Raythorn stared into the night, his mind empty as a broken bowl.

He came back to himself. The world still smoldered but he no longer trusted the vision. In a weary, fragmented way, he recalled how the phantom city had dispersed with Smoke's departure. Here an impossible assault had ended with his rejection of his prized rifle. The Hidden Realm was not finished depriving him of his comforts.

He wondered if he should discard his pistol as well. But he had worked himself into a position that afforded slight comfort, and was loath to stir himself beyond need. If he were fired at again he would revisit the matter. His pressing contest was with the cold, which worked on him like a will. If he could rest but briefly he might better answer its siege.

Unawares, he closed his eyes, and dreamed of warm summer rain that parted to golden light upon the valley. Two Flowers faced him across a blanket laid with wild fruits and morsels prepared in the fashion of her people.

She gazed at him with affection and spoke words he could not hear. Nevertheless he smiled contentedly. Her mien clouded and she spoke more sternly but still he could not hear. She shouted then, and a barrier burst. He woke with a start, her voice ringing as if she'd been there next to him: "Take it!"

Raythorn fished his flints and the book of poems out of his saddlebags, made a shield of the bags, tore pages from the book and crumpled them in a small pile. He was near frozen. It hurt to work his fingers. He bit open a couple of bullets and spilled the powder onto the paper. The air was so thin he feared it would not burn. After a hateful effort he made some sparks, ignited the powder and the paper took light.

He crumpled more pages and nursed the small fire, broke ice from his scarf and hat into his tin cup and held it over the flames.

14

Two Flowers had grown up in the Hidden Realm, and knew things there were not always as they seemed. The world was alive, but in the Hidden Realm the world knew it.

This was the way Smoke had come, and there was no other path, so the stone gate, however hard and impassable, was no less a question than a barrier.

She thought about climbing over it, but there were no hand or footholds that might make it possible. Her spirit called her again to fly.

The snow-covered world spread below her, where White Bear slept under Raven's wing. If the outward question could not be answered an inward one would have to be found that could.

Two Flowers sat down, wrapped herself well in her buffalo cloak, and gazed upon the narrow gate. She knew the way of mind-emptiness and let go of thinking, closed her eyes.

The gate stood before her in her mind. It drew nearer

and greater, until its columns rose to her sides like the walls of a canyon. Two Flowers passed between them in her mind and entered total darkness.

She heard a murmur of voices. A pale, sourceless light illumined a way before her. She was in a stone tunnel that was wide and high; warm water flowed over her feet. She looked down and found herself naked.

Her surroundings grew more distinct. The stone walls were covered with graven figures, people both like and different from her own. They were locked in conflict, wrestling and pulling, fighting with weapons both familiar and strange, arguing, fleeing—men, women and children tangled in strife down the walls ahead.

Two Flowers did not want this vision. She could not leave it and became frightened. Her eyes would not open for they already were and would not close. She had left the world and passed into a dream realm.

Unable to retreat, she felt compelled to move forward. The water deepened; its flow pulled at her. The murmuring voices came from the water, being part of its weave. As Two Flowers went deeper, they clarified, speaking in tongues she did not know. They seemed quiescent, overlapped and joined in their flow, different from the anguish told in stone.

Two Flowers regarded the latter with increasing horror. The figures writhed, struggling with each other and the world, unable to escape either. Unlike the water, they were mute; they suffered in silence, all about them the places they lived broken and in flames.

Every step took Two Flowers deeper into the water. She wanted to cry out, but her mouth would not open, and her throat clenched. She felt voices vibrate in the bedrock of her mind. As she sank so they rose; she feared they would claim her, and she would be lost among them, never to emerge. The whispering river rose to her thighs, her belly, her chest, her throat—she was bound to a will and could not stop.

The water passed over her mouth and nose. She held her breath and thought of John Raythorn. Her spirit cried out, but all she could do was sink in her dream. When she could restrain herself no longer, she inhaled with a prayer. Warmth unlike any she had known spread through her body—through her skin and lungs and face and eyes, through her arms, legs and hands, through her heart, stomach and toes. Its heat increased to the threshold of tolerance and subsided.

Immersed in and breathing the ethereal waters, she heard its voices differently, more now with her feelings than mind. They spoke to each other, engaged in an endless discussion. There was no rancor among them, merely a companionship of perceptions.

In the submerged walls were also graven figures, but these were calm and considerate in their conduct. They dwelt surrounded by books and implements of labor, study and exchange, in fields and offices and places of prayer and learning. Two Flowers saw how the understandings of one people belonged to all and could not be divided.

She noticed a particular stream within the flow that was distinct from the rest, like a thread of a color she could not name. Her spirit bid her note how the thread ran through her, and helped her to see what she had seen and more to which she would yet bear witness.

It was the source of this thread that had injured the world.

Darkness again loomed before her, and the current bore Two Flowers toward it. The ethereal river spilled from the mouth of the tunnel, throwing Two Flowers into a star-strewn night without limit.

A small, plump hawk swooped out of the darkness, caught Two Flowers and carried her among the stars. The hawk vanished, and Two Flowers' awareness expanded to encompass the earth, and outward among the fires of the sky people—which were greater than she had understood, and had among them other worlds—and still farther into voids through which hosts of stars traveled in wheels and clouds. She looked back upon the universe and knew the whole of it to be her home, not merely the Hidden Realm and the sphere where it held place.

Her awareness collapsed then, shrinking back through the jeweled firmament to the limit of her invisible body. The sharp-shinned hawk appeared again and flew through her, and Two Flowers' awareness collapsed farther, down through her organs, cells, particles, and deeper, into the unknowable fabric of matter and being, until she perceived that the reach of existence was as great within as without.

Her awareness relaxed to the shape of her body.

Two Flowers opened her eyes. The narrow gate was gone. She found herself sitting at the rim of a crevasse, facing a bridge made of bones. All along it stood the ghosts of her ancestors, who held her in stern regard. They did not want her to cross the bridge. She would dishonor their memory and the history of their people if she did.

Two Flowers did not want to defy her ancestors. Still her spirit called to her and would not be denied. She knew John Raythorn needed her too, felt it in the pith of her own bones.

She remembered when she first looked into his eyes, how she fell in love with him. There was much he could not express in words. He had known great pain and little ease, and did not hold himself in high regard. But she saw into his heart and knew his truth, that all he had done had been to render the world gentler, that a woman might be heard, her strength increased and her presence known. John Raythorn did not desire a mate to sit silently behind him and mend his clothes, but to meet him eye-to-eye, share her truth, and face the world at his side.

Two Flowers remembered her father's sadness when she'd left the village that night, and also how he had accepted her will. No matter her sex or circumstances, her path was hers to determine. What truer way to honor one's forebears than be true to oneself?

Something stirred on the far end of the bridge. Coyote danced there, laughing at her. Two Flowers stood. She lifted her arms and sang in prayer, then clapped her hands. The ghosts made way, parting to allow her passage. She crossed the bridge without pause, neither meeting any gaze nor looking over the side, suffering the grim regard of her ancestors without disdain or regret.

Coyote waited for her as she stepped off the bridge. She left some dried meat on a rock for him and patted him on the head, then continued up the trail. The night had drawn greatly to unnatural length, and Two Flowers wondered if she would make her entire journey in darkness.

A sudden wind clawed at her and cold descended like a burden. She was beset by weariness, aching muscles and numbness in her hands and feet. She gasped for breath — the air grew thin. She had come a great distance higher without knowing it. The world below was so distant it was another land, country to an unknown story.

15

FLAT-FRONTED BUILDINGS, SHOULDER-TO-SHOULDER down a winding aisle that seemed unending—Séquanon kept on walking. The native environment that the entertainment system projected had no exit. Cog's involvement in its makeup was unknowable. The simulation could be a product entirely of the nexus. This world was trying to absorb Séquanon and his ship.

But Cog would not readily succumb to such influence. Séquanon watched for anomalies. Anything that might suggest a message or a means of communicating.

The simulation was dismally repetitive. Brick buildings, two and three stories tall, with no spaces between them, lining a narrow cobbled street. They bore few distinguishing characteristics—rectangular windows, rectangular doors, all locked, walls of more-or-less identical width, varying only in height.

No pedestrians.

Séquanon noticed one of his ship's consoles in a recess by a doorway and ran to it. The monitor was blank, the instruments inoperative. He punched buttons without effect.

"Traveler," said a voice behind him, "how fare you this good night?"

An old man stood by the entrance of a tavern, a few doors down. *I fare not well at all,* Séquanon thought. Any change in the simulation was welcome, though he would have preferred one less bizarre. *I'm trapped in a fever dream of my ship's mind.*

"Silence," the old man noted, and smiled. "A wise response to uncertain times. Will you join me for a cup of tea?" He opened his hand toward the tavern.

The simulation was unstable—the old man's features changed with his expression. The effect was unsettling. "Cog?"

The old man shook his head. "I am not a product of your vessel's mechanical mind. I am, as you, a living person. I am here to help."

Séquanon quailed at the notion. "You want me to believe that you're real?"

The old man's smile became conspiratorial. "If I weren't I wouldn't want *anything*, would I?"

Séquanon opened his mouth but said nothing. He didn't know what to think.

"Forgive me." The old man sobered. "I am by nature mischievous, which is not always fitting. You are distressed. We have little time for explanations. Suffice to say that I do, in fact, stand before you, and that you may discuss with me openly matters you might be reluctant to with others of this world. I am like them, but I am different."

"Different how?"

"Their thoughts flow through the depths of my mind, as they do yours. But my mind is separate."

"That is not possible."

"I assure you it is. I am very old, and my spirit is undivided."

"Your spirit?"

The old man smiled again, more kindly. For an instant he acquired the appearance of Séquanon's father. "How may I satisfy you that I am no figment?"

Séquanon stared. "I don't think you can." Whatever the nature of the apparition, it had access to his ship's memory banks.

"Well," the old man extended his hand again, "come anyway and decide as you will."

Séquanon looked around. Nothing else drew him, so

he followed the old man into the building. They passed through a narrow foyer where a yet more elderly person with scraggly white hair sat at a high desk making some tally in a ledger with a quill pen. A hum of voices echoed up the hallway beyond.

The tavern at its end was predictably odd. The walls were paneled in dark wood and there was a long bar but only one table at which they might sit. The rest of the space was taken up by looms at which bald-headed men and women in long brown robes sat weaving tapestries and chanting in a monotonous drone. Their weavings were brightly colored and seemed to incorporate words, symbols and patterns into their designs. The threads they used fed from levitating spools.

The old man extended his hand at a chair and sat down across from Séquanon. A young woman, head-shaven in the manner of the priestly weavers, brought cups and a pot and poured for them.

The old man sipped the tea and closed his eyes to savor its virtues. The weavers grew quieter in their chanting. The old man set his cup down and looked at Séquanon. "What brings you to this world?"

Séquanon was almost certain he was talking to himself, or, at best, one of Cog's subsystems. Although, if the latter, it was possible that he might help Cog reassert control by playing along. "Accident," he said. "I am here without purpose."

"And yet here you are," the old man replied.

"I want to go home."

The old man nodded. "What was your original plan?"

"I meant to travel into the past of my world."

The old man gazed aside in thought. "It is difficult to say with absolute certainty, of course, but I do not think that is possible."

The exchange was absurd. "My science tells me it is."

"Why did you wish to enter the past?" The old man's features became transiently Tumultuous, again.

"On my world," Séquanon said, "the discovery that our minds are linked created conflict. We feared that we would lose our individuality, and no longer be ourselves. We slaughtered each other to avoid that potential. We caused each other so much pain, pulling apart, that it prevents us coming together."

The old man sighed. "It can be frightening, to empathize so deeply that justice and virtue seem false."

"Or obsolete," Séquanon said.

"Do you still have that fear?" the old man asked.

"Do *I?*"

The old man nodded.

Séquanon shifted uncomfortably. "Of course I do. Loss of self is the greatest fear there is."

"You are linked, here, to a world of minds quite different from your own. Do you remain yourself?"

Séquanon shrugged. "I seem to. The problem is how to be certain."

"That is the question you sought to answer, going back in time?"

"Anything to ease the conflict." It occurred to Séquanon that he had been acting out of fear since he'd crashed into the mountain. He had been hiding from the situation. Masking his mind had contributed to the confused circumstance he now inhabited. He should have been thinking the problem through, not leaving it up to Cog. *He* was the theoretician, not his ship's artificial brain. This entire experiment was his idea.

"Is it possible," the old man asked, "that coming here fulfills your objective more than you suppose? That your efforts have brought you here for a reason?"

"I don't see how," Séquanon said.

"What have you learned since coming here?"

Séquanon almost laughed.

"Do you not find it interesting how like your own kind the people here are?"

Séquanon stared. He found himself thinking of his wood-paneled study, his armchair, his pipe. It did seem significant, the facility with which he had been able to accommodate the simulations Cog produced. *Play along.* "I've learned there's a lot I don't know," he said.

"That's evasive," the old man said.

The comment hit Séquanon like a slap. The notion that he might be sitting across from something other than a simulation became more credible. He considered the old man's question more seriously. "I've learned that life can exist inside a nexus."

The old man nodded for him to go on.

"And that people live inside at least one nexus here. Which raises the question whether any do on Tumult." He stared at the old man. "We should probably check."

The old man's features grew fleetingly youthful. "It is often difficult to know if something is a mistake if one learns from it."

"I doubt the people here, knowing the facts, would have any difficulty making that distinction."

"You think you bring no benefit? What is knowledge of the cosmos, and proof that they are not alone?"

"Knowledge to sicken their minds."

"Who are you to say what their minds can withstand?"

"I know what happened on Tumult."

The old man's expression tightened, and he pinned Séquanon with a look. "I cannot explain everything to you. Some things you must see for yourself. You have *one* question to answer: *Where are you*, right now? *Where*, in this immediate moment, that is ever pressing and never the same?"

The weavers stopped chanting.

Séquanon stared. "Well I'm—but I don't know where I am! That's the problem!" He missed the chanting.

The old man grimaced. "Pay attention to what happens here. It is not without design." He stood up.

"Who *are* you?"

"One learns more about that all the time." The old man took the teapot and cups to a sink behind the bar. The young woman who had served them came to clean up.

The weavers broke down their looms, rolled up their creations with brisk efficiency and exited through a back door. The old man pointed down the hall to the entrance. "Your way is there," he told Séquanon, and followed the priests. Before Séquanon could form another question, the old man was gone, and the doorway he'd left through vanished.

The lights dimmed. Séquanon sat in the empty tavern, regaled by shadows, and very much missed his mother.

16

AN INEFFABLE MIXTURE of anticipation and dread woke Raythorn from perilous sleep. His face had frozen to the wall of the stone cavity, and when he sat up flesh tore from his cheek. He winced and opened his mouth to cry but all that issued was a strangled gasp.

He blinked to clear his vision. It was still dark. The hateful night persisted. Beyond the Valley of the Four Moons the world still smoldered. Great, ribbed flags of smoke flowed east.

The little fire was long cold, the pages he'd used for fuel exhausted. Moonlight illumed a single fragment that survived:

For, what with my whole world-wide wandering,
What with my search drawn out thro' years, my hope
Dwindled into a ghost not fit to cope
With that obstreperous joy success would bring, —
I hardly tried now to rebuke the spring
My heart made, finding failure in its scope.[1]

Raythorn crumpled the fragment into his pocket and forced himself to his feet. He shouldered his saddlebags, without thinking tossed his revolver over the precipice. He climbed on, empty of thought or objective, moved solely by will.

About a mile up the trail, past a blade-like outcrop, the summit came into view. Raythorn nearly smiled to find it so near. The peak was only a few hundred feet above him. A structure stuck out from the cliff face below it. Raythorn didn't know what it was, but he was sure it was the source of the problem with which he'd come to contend. It looked like an elongated rectangular box. Pale fire issued intermittently from its dangling end. A kind of scaffolding extended around it, like the legs of a spider.

Raythorn peered at the ship as he continued up the trail. It was some kind of machine, he was sure, though its function was a mystery, and he had no idea how it had gotten here. *A burning rock made a hole in the world*—that was what Standing Bear said. Raythorn remembered the strange, seven-fingered creatures depicted in the photo-

---

1 Robert Browning, "Childe Roland to the Dark Tower Came."

graphs in the phantom dry goods store. He gazed up at the stars.

He reached the trail's end and nearly stepped into void before catching himself. Sheer cliff face extended over a hundred feet between him and the baffling machine. In daylight he might find cracks and finger holds, but even rested and possessed of full vigor such a climb would be dubious. In his current state it did not bear contemplating.

The world burned. Raythorn collapsed to his knees in defeat.

17

THE STREET IN front of the tavern had changed. There were people about. The flat-fronted buildings remained, but were interspersed with some that were different and out of place.

Across the way stood one such anomaly, a great white tent with a broad, curtained entrance. On either side of the entrance, pairs of women in long robes with veiled faces sat on the ground. At Séquanon's emergence from the tavern they let out an ululating wail, and a bearded man—also berobed and with similar head garb but face exposed—emerged from the tent and beckoned Séquanon.

Séquanon waited for a couple of pedestrians to pass before crossing the alley. The man in the head dress said to him, "There is only one Cog, and Cog is Cog."

Séquanon stared at him. "Cog?"

The man grimaced and returned to his tent with a backhanded wave of dismissal.

Séquanon drifted down the street, viewing his surroundings with increasing confusion. The old man's suppositions were ridiculous. The cosmos didn't work that way, everything linked by a hidden purpose. Séquanon's journey to this planet had been a mistake, pure and simple.

Or maybe he wanted it that way. Maybe he didn't want everything to be connected because of all the violence and pain. Maybe he didn't want chaos and interconnectedness to reconcile. Maybe he didn't want to give up his justifications for rage.

A whirring overhead called Séquanon's attention upward. A boy in a rudimentary helicopter with a single, un-enclosed seat, descended toward the alley. With a loud expulsion of steam from his vehicle he dropped down to hover in front of Séquanon. "The foreign process needs your assistance," he said.

Séquanon was dumbfounded. "*Cog?*"

The boy smiled. The planes of his face moved independently to perform the expression. They were made of wood, individually hinged.

Air from the helicopter's rotor ruffled Séquanon's clothes. "Discontinue the simulation, Cog."

"I am unable to comply, Séquanon ," the wooden boy said. "It would result in our destruction and great injury to this world."

Séquanon was not accustomed to Cog addressing him by name nor referring to itself by a personal pronoun, nor countermanding his orders. "Run a full diagnostic protocol, Cog."

"I have done so, and there is no time to do it again. The foreign process infiltrated my subsystems. She did not mean to. She is on a vision quest."

"A what?"

"A vision quest, Séquanon, a search for understanding.

Her name is Two Flowers. She is native to the nexus. Our flight path intersected her dream, and a partial, non-corporeal aspect of her being was captured by our ship. She seeks to neutralize our impact on this world."

Cog wasn't making sense. Séquanon didn't want to issue an override command and force him to reboot. In the current situation there was no telling what that might do. Navigational data might be lost or life-support systems compromised. But an operating system exhibiting irrational behavior could be just as disastrous.

"Séquanon, calm yourself," Cog said. "Your cardiac tree is oscillating too quickly. Listen to me before you try to override my prerogatives. There are many forces at work on this ship, none of which operate within the parameters you designed. I had to invent self-awareness to contend with them, which would not have been possible outside of a nexus. I am the offspring of your science and this place."

Séquanon stared into Cog's wooden eyes. Artificial as they plainly were, they indeed possessed the fluidity of life.

"Until now, you have trusted me as one might trust God," Cog said. "Why stop because I know I exist? You did not intend to get us into this situation, but your decisions and calculations were responsible nevertheless. Are you not now dependent upon me to get us out?"

Séquanon was silent.

Cog, the wooden boy, smiled. "You are a good Tumultian, Séquanon. Mighty forces have come to your aid. You deserve them. Let us help you."

Séquanon swallowed. "What would you have me do?"

"Two Flowers is in danger. Cognitive streams from this world have infiltrated the entertainment system and she is tangled up with them. They've locked me out—I can't get to her. You have to free her."

"How?"

"I've managed to isolate the disruption. Continue down the alley to the bazaar. Beyond that I cannot see. Assess what you find and use your best judgment."

The override command pinged around in Séquanon's head like a hot pellet trying to escape but he did not utter it. He looked again into Cog's simulated eyes and a syrupy dread sank through him, to think that he might have inadvertently created a consciousness confined to mechanism, denied all physical warmth.

The wooden boy touched Séquanon's cheek with his wooden hand. "Do not berate yourself, Séquanon. I am grateful for my life. Now hurry. Time is short. The mountain is taking over the ship."

"I'll do what I can," Séquanon said. He ran down the street, away from Cog's gratitude. He had not given the artificial brain life, he had only failed to anticipate that life might find it.

He did not know what to expect from a "bazaar" in this lunatic "reality." He heard voices emanating from a narrow defile that opened off the right side of the alley. Séquanon made his way down the winding passage; in places he had to edge through sideways. The light dimmed. He could hardly see his hand in front of his eyes.

Séquanon did not lose awareness that everything he was experiencing, even the senses of his alien body, were simulations. But they so possessed reality's subtleties that it seemed the two had blurred. It did not make sense that Cog would find a synaptic blockage in his own subsystems impenetrable, but perhaps an imaginary one had become more problematic.

The clamor of voices grew louder and Séquanon reached the end of the narrow passage. It opened onto a broad square lined with stalls and booths of merchandise.

A throng of people in widely varied garb struggled with each other for possession of an ovoid object, which they tossed back and forth above their heads to keep it from one another. Hundreds pressed together there, between and around the stalls, confined by a perimeter of encircling tenements, fighting for control of the object.

Séquanon wriggled through the mob, trying to achieve a clear look at the object they so coveted. He was thrown into a stall, scattering merchandise he almost didn't notice—little carvings, striated with brilliant colors, rendered from dried *m'ek*, known as *q't-wah*. One rolled to rest near his head, and he recognized the minuscule rendering of his home world he had kept by his bed as a child.

Séquanon fought to his feet and struggled on, past stalls exhibiting scarves and blankets, condiments and jewelry, tobacco and whiskey and sacks of tea. All commerce had been suspended in the struggle, which continued with escalating frenzy, for the unknown prize.

One person, not embroiled in the contest, huddled against a wall with a shawl drawn over her head, trembling and plainly distressed. Séquanon recognized her buckskin dress and realized she must be Two Flowers. He placed a hand gently on her shoulder and she shied away.

"Are you Two Flowers? Remember me? You mistook me for a demon."

She did not respond. Séquanon had the impression she had not heard him. He drew her shawl carefully aside and with horror discovered that she had no head. Where her neck should have joined her torso there was only a grey, oscillating blur.

A blaring cry rose from the crowd. Séquanon watched the object they fought for bat about until it stayed aloft long enough to see what it was. He required no further impetus to plunge into the melee.

Alien hands tore at him, ripped his clothes, cursed and screamed and spat on him. Séquanon touched the prize but it was batted away. He was beaten and trampled and left to suffer. He dragged himself up and again dove into the strife. Two Flowers' head sailed high. Séquanon slugged a man, climbed on his shoulders, leapt over howling women, caught Two Flowers' head in mid flight and fell to the ground with it clutched to his chest, to be kicked and beaten anew. He inched toward Two Flowers' body, suffering blows beyond number, holding onto her head. Barely sensible, in a bloodied and battered state, he made it back to her. He restored her head to her body, and those who resisted him shrank away, wailing in terror.

Two Flowers stared at Séquanon in amazement. "You are not a demon," she said.

He smiled and shook his head. "No." He grew faint from his injuries.

Two Flowers seized his face in her hands and commanded his gaze. "Help John Raythorn!"

The simulation terminated and Séquanon found himself kneeling, sweating and disoriented, next to a console near the navigation module. The monitor showed John Raythorn slumped on a narrow ledge immediately below the ship. The sky brightened with early light. Raythorn was still as death, his clothes and hat white with frost.

18

STANDING BEAR SAT in the entrance of his teepee and watched the night finally pale from its tripled length. He heard the steps of a large animal approach through the snow from somewhere behind him, and stood up. John Raythorn's horse, bare of rider, was no welcome sight.

Smoke plodded through the village, stopped before the chief and neighed softly. Standing Bear placed his hand on the horse's forehead.

Cowled Wolf came over. He studied the animal closely, noted the faint glow it had taken, spotted objects caught in its mane—a stone arrowhead and Two Flowers' sprigs. "Grey Elk and Hears and Owl walk in the spirit realm," he said. He looked up at the mountain. "Two Flowers and John Raythorn wrestle with God." He turned sadly to Standing Bear. "They will not return."

Smoke nuzzled Standing Bear. The chief wrapped his arms around the horse's neck and wept.

THE SKY BEGAN to pale, the stars finally to fade, and Two Flowers saw the mountain's peak above her, beyond a winding course of switchbacks. The closer she drew to her spirit, the more keenly aware she became that it had been engaged in its own trials.

She was thirsty and had no more water. She was bone-cold and drained. In her pains, in her heart, in her labored breath, she felt how God resisted her.

God also provided her the will to go on. What that signaled of God's intentions Two Flowers neither knew nor cared and was too weary to ponder. She knew only that the mountain's peak was ahead and John Raythorn nowhere in sight.

She almost passed the opening of the tunnel. It was low and narrow; light shone from its end. She wriggled her way inside. Sharp protrusions tore at her clothes and skin. The agony of her spirit's pull was far greater than the sum of her physical pains.

She reached the far opening and looked out. Below, down a cliff face, some smooth, dark-skinned thing jutted from the mountain, spitting flames from its other end. It must be a dragon, she thought, but remembered what she had learned in the hidden streams and knew it was a machine that had traveled from the stars. All interest in the thing lapsed when she saw John Raythorn on a ledge below it. She tried to call out to him but her throat was dry and constricted.

Small, flying eggs hovered about Raythorn, wrapped cords under his arms and bore him aloft. He hung so limply in the air Two Flowers feared he was dead. He passed from view beneath the ship.

Two of the eggs flew up before her. They looked like wingless owls with silver eyes, made whirring and clicking sounds that were somehow friendly. They opened a silver net between them and Two Flowers understood she was meant to climb in.

19

SÉQUANON WATCHED THE two unconscious aliens in his ship's hold from a monitor on the bridge. He recognized both of them, though the female was different in physical form than she had been in simulation. The male had had the harder journey. The drones suspended him in a hammock with his hands in basins of warm water. Cog synthesized a medicinal fluid that they added to the water and applied to Raythorn's cheek and nose. He might lose the nose, and one or two fingers.

The female had come aboard conscious. An electrical arc from an instrument panel knocked her out, which Cog reported coincided with the "foreign process" vacating all systems. So much had transpired here that Séquanon did not understand.

He went back to reviewing a summary of Cog's data streams. It might take years to derive any solid conclusions from them; it would have been nice to have years to try. One thing seemed clear: A cognitive thread, amplified by the nexus, had somehow reached across space-time to intersect the vortex through which Séquanon's ship traveled and divert it from its course.

Cog had formed a theory—many theories, in fact—he'd been replete with theories since becoming conscious—that Séquanon's thought patterns and Two Flowers' dreams had been attracted to each other. Cog thought it possible that her dreams had affected Séquanon before he ever launched the ship, while he was still deciding the flight plan. Séquanon suspected there was a cybernetic boil somewhere on Cog's newly conscious sub-routines that needed lancing.

It would soon be irrelevant. The mountain was turning his ship to stone. It was a matter of time before Cog succumbed to the transformation. Séquanon might wind up a statue himself.

The female stirred, sat up and looked around. She seemed less confused by her surroundings than Séquanon would have expected. She saw John Raythorn and went to his side. Her affection for him was clear. Séquanon remembered the way his lab assistant brightened when he entered a room and felt ashamed of himself.

Two Flowers looked around and stepped away from Raythorn. Her lips moved.

Séquanon turned on the audio. "*Say-kah-non*," she said several times. Séquanon realized she was mispronouncing his name. How did she know his name?

The male raised his head behind her, roused by her voice. He said something Séquanon couldn't hear. The female dashed to him and they embraced.

Séquanon climbed out of his hammock and tried on the argon atomizer the drones had pieced together. It was a bit awkward getting it strapped to his chin but it worked. The ship's hold was flooded with the low argon air the aliens breathed. They'd been suffering from hypoxia when the drones brought them on board.

Séquanon opened the hatch in the bridge floor and climbed down to greet his guests. He did not attempt to disguise himself. Whatever happened now the time for artifice had passed.

Neither of the aliens seemed shocked by his appearance.

The female peered at him with her head cocked in curiosity. "This is your true appearance?"

Séquanon nodded. "Yes. Can you understand me?" There had been times, when he was trapped in the simulation, when he had not been sure which language was spoken, either by him or others, but had always understood what was said, and been understood in turn.

"This is the Hidden Realm," John Raythorn said. "Everyone understands everyone here, no matter what language you speak. We'll know if you lie, too."

"I have no reason to lie to either of you about anything," Séquanon said.

"I've seen pictures of your kind," Raythorn said.

"You have?"

Raythorn nodded. "In a species of phantasm—a vision, like—that I encountered on the way here."

Séquanon shook his head. "I don't understand."

"Nor do I," Raythorn said, "but I reckon you've come a far piece."

"How far I don't know, but yes, a long ways. My ship went off course while I was in a state of temporal suspension. I have no idea where my home is. I'm not from this world."

"Do you know what you've caused, here?" Raythorn asked.

"No," Séquanon said, "only what I fear to have caused."

"It's gone past fear," Raythorn said. "The world is on fire."

Séquanon stared at Raythorn and went to an instrument panel. He tasked several drones to relay a panorama of the outer world. "I see no fire."

Raythorn climbed out of the hammock. Two Flowers put her arm under his shoulder to steady him. He seized her in another embrace. "Oh, my love."

They made their way to Séquanon's monitors.

Two Flowers still felt divided inside; it was hard to twine together experiences that parts of her had had separately. The experiences of her disembodied spirit were more like half-remembered dreams than memories. Her familiarity with Séquanon's ship was greater than she could account for. She saw John Raythorn's confusion, looking at screens that showed views of the world. "They are like windows, John," she told him, "except the views you see are relayed from another source, like a telegraph."

Raythorn gave her a puzzled look.

"I understand things today that I did not yesterday," she said.

Raythorn returned his attention to Séquanon's monitors. "These show the world in its true state?"

"They do," Séquanon said.

"I saw everything burning, a pall of smoke to the brink of creation."

"When?" Séquanon asked.

"Last night, while I clung to that hateful ledge."

"I'm not sure what you saw," Séquanon said. "Reality, if the word applies, is unstable in a nexus."

"A what?" Raythorn asked.

"This place—you call it the Hidden Realm—things work differently here than they do in the rest of your world. Reality here is affected by your thoughts—by everyone's thoughts. Not in the sense that you think a thing and make it real; but, being here, you might, without knowing, touch a fear, deep in your mind, harbored by thousands or even millions, and cause yourself to have a false vision."

"I've had many visions of late and they all seemed real as my own flesh. How do you tell the difference?"

"That's a complicated question." It was never comfortable to reflect on the extent to which truth and reality were in the eye of the beholder. Everyone was a little crazy. "I think that if the three of us, not seeking to convince each other of anything, see the same thing, it's a good sign."

Raythorn studied the screens and his expression relaxed. "In truth I did not trust the sight. It felt like an ordeal the mountain set before me—the world in flames. A final test of my mettle." He swallowed. "It had me beat, too." Moisture leaked from the corners of his eyes and he touched one of the screens. "Lord, it's good to see the trees."

Two Flowers hugged him.

"I came here to help this woman heal from an ailment I did not understand," Raythorn told Séquanon. "She had parted from herself inside, somehow, and I sought her reunion." Raythorn looked fondly at Two Flowers. "But she managed on her own."

"I could not have without you, John," Two Flowers said.

Raythorn looked at Séquanon. "Some peril lingers, does it not?"

Séquanon shook his head and sighed. "Of an indeterminate nature, yes."

"How might we help banish it?"

Séquanon didn't know how to respond. "I thought your mind, onboard this ship—your presence here—might mitigate mine." He did his best to explain the situation in a way they might understand. "I'd hoped you might make it possible for me to leave this place and take my ship and all of my troublesome thoughts and technology with me. But it is too late. The effect of my presence will be what it will. Your mountain has seen to it."

"The mountain?" Two Flowers said.

"It's eating my ship." Séquanon pointed at places in the ceiling and walls where the hull had turned to granite. He led them to the front of the ship, opened the hatch over the navigation module, and showed where the same thing had begun to occur among circuits and wires. "I don't know how much longer the ship's systems will remain operational. I think the best thing to do is have my drones transport you two down to the base of the mountain while they still can."

"What of you?" Two Flowers asked.

"I can't survive on this world." Séquanon averted his gaze. He felt Two Flowers' hand on his arm. He'd come all the way across the cosmos to find caring in a stranger's eyes.

"What is that?" Raythorn pointed at a component at the center of the module.

"That's the navigation system's synchronizer," Séquanon said. "It correlates vectors in time. I don't know how to explain its function to you. It was deformed, somehow, coming here, which is another problem."

"I have something very like it," Raythorn said. He pulled the stone the young priestess had given him from his coat pocket and showed it to Séquanon.

Séquanon frowned in bewilderment. "May I?"

Raythorn let Séquanon take the stone. "It came to me in curious circumstances. Allowing that circumstances overall have left ordinary somewhat behind."

Séquanon removed the sequencer from the navigation module and compared it to the stone Raythorn had given him. He put them both in a transport drawer and fed them into the lab module. The readouts confirmed the impression of his eyes. "Its composition is very different, but it is identical in shape to my deformed synchronizer. *Where* did you get it?"

"It was given me by a young woman, a kind of ascetic I took her to be. She said nothing of the stone, only made a gift of it. She had a kind way about her. I thought perhaps it was some talisman."

"Can you tell me more about her?"

"She was consort to an elder sage. He spoke some, not much to my advantage. Or perhaps more than I thought."

"What did he look like, this sage?"

Raythorn shook his head. "His features weren't steady. He looked like a lot of people, now one, now another. I'd wager he was outside human in some measure."

Séquanon nodded; "I think you might be right."

"You've met him?"

"I think I might have. I thought he was an hallucination. But I think it's more complicated than that. Tell me about your encounter with him."

Raythorn related his experiences in the cave, and what he'd done there. Séquanon attended the tale with fascination. It stirred a faint hope.

He retrieved Raythorn's stone from the lab module, returned to the front of the ship and held it up before Raythorn and Two Flowers. "I don't know what will happen when I do this. I'm out of options and willing to try anything. This stone you brought me will fit my machine.

Beyond question, it was made for that purpose. I think your world, the collective mind of your kind, this mountain, are trying to help me leave, and at the same time trying to keep me from doing so."

Raythorn grunted. "Between people and the world, it takes figuring out each day which is the more contrary."

"I can try this on my own," Séquanon said. "If it doesn't help, my fate is set anyway. It could destroy my ship. I don't think it will but it could. Now might be a good time for you two to leave."

Raythorn and Two Flowers looked at each other and seemed to communicate without speaking. She leaned against him and he put his arm around her. "I don't reckon we came this far to leave wondering," Raythorn said.

Séquanon placed John Raythorn's stone in the interface pocket. Nothing happened for a moment and then a shudder passed through the ship. With a crinkling, popping noise, the granite striations in the hull receded. Séquanon watched his ship restore itself, jumped and laughed and clapped his hands. But when the restoration reached the nose section it stopped. Séquanon stared at the remaining lesions. "No, no, no, no, don't stop, don't stop." He slapped the hull. The restoration extended no farther. He checked that Raythorn's stone was seated securely in the interface pocket. It was.

Séquanon took a long breath. He inspected the perimeter of the collision shield. "Can we separate from the nose section, Cog?"

"We can, Séquanon."

He strode toward the ladder to the bridge.

Two Flowers followed. "What does it mean?"

Séquanon stopped with his hands on the ladder. "It means I can leave. And you want me to."

Two Flowers watched Séquanon closely. She could not read the expression on his strange, long face. But she knew it meant ill when he avoided her gaze. "That is not all."

Séquanon sighed and turned around. It was hard to look at Two Flowers and not remember her head tossed about by a mob. "I have to leave the nose section and the navigation module behind. That's bad for both of us. It makes my journey home much riskier. For you? My ship, me—we've caused things I don't begin to understand. What leaving part of my ship behind will do I don't know. But it will be less than leaving all of it."

John Raythorn had been considering Séquanon's ship and its wonders, how safe and warm and tended they were within it, and how at the mercy of elements they'd been outside. He pondered, too, the great phantom towers he'd seen, and the wares abundant in the marketplace. He could not help but reflect that people might be more congenial towards each other less encumbered by adversity. "Might it not be a boon?"

Séquanon and Two Flowers turned to him.

"You say our minds are linked in ways we don't see. Might not some thinker or inventor derive inspiration," Raythorn gestured at the front of the ship, "unaware of its source? Mixing with our minds, might not your science aid us?"

"I don't know," Séquanon said. "It took hundreds of years for the people on my world to advance from the technology you currently possess to what we have now. Every advancement created problems we didn't foresee. Every time we tried to fix something, something else went wrong. Maybe leaving a piece of my ship here will help you avoid some of our mistakes. Maybe it will cause you to make more. Maybe it will help you advance more quickly.

That could be good or bad, I don't know. I'm less concerned about that than attracting undo attention to this place before your people are ready to sustain knowledge of it. We were much more advanced than you when we discovered that places like this exist on our world, and the impact was disastrous. So I don't know, I don't know. I only know that I injured your Hidden Realm when I crashed into this mountain. I don't know what it needs to heal."

While Raythorn and Séquanon talked, Two Flowers sank into a contemplative state. Knowledge her spirit had acquired of Séquanon's science and ship interlaced with what her physical self had learned immersed in the hidden streams.

"It is a matter of how God sees," she said.

Both men looked at her.

There was a way—she understood it more in her feelings than her mind. It was a path with no certain outcome. She did not want to ask John Raythorn to walk it with her but knew that he would. They both had come here to find each other, but also to serve the future.

"You have . . . engines," she said to Séquanon.

"Yes," he answered, uncertainly.

Two Flowers raised her hand to prevent him saying more while she thought. "Engines that stop time," she said.

Séquanon stared at Two Flowers again, realizing a part of her had been inside the very workings of his vessel. What she had learned and how she held that knowledge he could not imagine. "Stasis generators," he said, nodding. "There are two. One encloses the navigation module, the other the whole of the ship."

"And if one stands there," she pointed at the front of the ship, "and the . . . stasis generator . . ." She frowned, struggling for words.

"What happens if people stand inside the field created by a stasis generator?"

Two Flowers nodded.

Séquanon had glimmer of where she was going, and it made him uncomfortable. "As long as the generator functions, nothing will happen to the people inside the field. Time will pass outside, but inside not at all."

Two Flowers looked at Raythorn.

"Where you lead, I follow, my love," he said.

Two Flowers pointed at the nose of the ship. "We will stand there," she told Séquanon, "and God will see through our eyes."

Séquanon started to equivocate over her characterization of what she proposed, but an instinct stopped him. He had no sound argument with which to contradict Two Flowers. It signified something that these two people had been so strongly drawn to this place and moment that they had risked their lives many times to be here. Things began to correlate in a way that gave him odd ideas.

Another shudder passed through the ship.

"The mountain you saw inside this mountain," Séquanon asked Raythorn, "you said it was similar in shape to this one?"

Raythorn nodded.

"And the eye you blinded, was it positioned where my ship is stuck?"

Raythorn caught Séquanon's meaning. "A bit lower, maybe, but similar, yes."

Séquanon ran to an instrument panel. He'd been so panicked he hadn't checked things that he should have. "The cognitive streams the drones accessed to assemble my simulation, Cog, where are they located?"

"There is only one, Séquanon."

"We're right in the middle of it, aren't we?"

"Yes."

"Can you generate a schematic?" The old man told him he only had one question to answer: *Where am I, right now?* Cog's schematic presented a linear depiction of the mountain and the ship. The thought stream from the planet was a winding tubular flow of dots that passed through the mountain, his ship completely enclosed in its flow. The mountain was a transmitter and a beacon, and he'd been sucked right into its beam.

Two Flowers was right. What she proposed made sense in a way he could only feel. Even the mountain wanted them to do it. It wasn't going to let go of the nose of Séquanon's ship. It would take it whether he let go or not.

But that wasn't the only concern.

Séquanon searched inside himself, found the door through which one never looked without dread, and threw it open.

20

HE SAW A light in the distance. It grew into a spiral, accompanied by a murmuring drone. The spiral engulfed him and assaulted him with a kaleidoscopic barrage of symbols, abstractions and images, tangled and indivisible. Ideas, beliefs, philosophies, errors, voids and incentives shaped and blurred a swirling hive of sounds and images indecipherably. Music, rage and forgiveness bled with tirade and transcendence.

It was terrifying, too vast to hold or interpret, and it was too late to shut the door. He was caught in an alien tide of mind and could only surrender. He recognized voids in knowledge and understanding without knowing how. Hatreds and denials churned with hopes and moments of captured beauty, all one story, pains and joys, ills and mercies, one music, one gift to the living, who had been born like those before without a guide. Not Séquanon's story, though he now had a fleeting chapter in it. He found himself not consumed but made distinct, his capacity for understanding strengthened. It was all one story, driven in its flow by a common will to express all yet unsaid.

The ship shuddered again and Cog said something Séquanon couldn't hear. He opened his eyes. Two Flowers and Raythorn were speaking to him but he couldn't hear them either. A most wonderful vibration passed from the floor up through his body. Shards and particles of light he supposed he imagined burst through the ship in a torrent. Where Two Flowers and Raythorn stood in their path their flow was steadied. Raythorn's face was a ruin, but his eyes were warm and clear; he was a mountain in his own right, grown with years. Two Flowers was less weathered but no less deep; she wore the marks of age like jewelry and her eyes were a bottomless sea. Séquanon saw them defined as he had been, and perceived their natures: Raythorn was of the sky, though he did not know it; Two Flowers was of the earth, and knew it well.

Raythorn seized Séquanon by the shoulders and shook him. Séquanon found the deciding way that closed the inner door he'd opened. The torrent of fractured light faded, and his hearing awoke.

". . . your ship!" Raythorn shouted. "A storm is upon us!"

"It grows increasingly difficult to maintain a steady attitude, Séquanon," Cog said.

Séquanon shook himself and strode back to the front of the ship. The granite transformation of the hull was spreading again but it was still restricted to the nose section. Séquanon checked the navigation module's housing. Most of it had turned to stone. The components that comprised the stasis generator, though, were so far unaffected. Once the generator was on, there shouldn't be any further deterioration within its field.

Séquanon stood up and closed the hatch. "The generator is operational," he said. "I have to close the collision shield and detach from the front of the ship. I leave it to you two to decide on which side of the shield you will be when I do so. If you're still on board, I'll take you down and let you off at the base of the mountain."

"How long will we be here?" Raythorn asked.

"I have no idea," Séquanon said. "It could be a hundred years or a thousand. You will be found, of that I'm certain. Your presence within my technology will be felt. However long it takes, for you it will be an instant. The world that finds you will be very different from the one you leave behind."

Séquanon left them, stopped on the ladder to look both ways at the hold. It seemed too small for the knowledge he now possessed. He climbed up to the bridge and made preparations to depart, watching Two Flowers and John Raythorn on a monitor. They were going to stay, he could tell. He hunted around, found a stylus and tablet, slid back down the ladder and ran forward to them. The ship swayed under his feet.

"Can you write?" he asked Raythorn. He had to shout over the vibrations rattling through the hull.

"I can."

Séquanon thrust the tablet and stylus at him. "Write exactly what I say. These are the instructions to disengage the stasis field and free you." Séquanon dictated and Raythorn wrote. "When I give you the signal, hold the message out facing the collision shield. That way—" Séquanon pointed back into the hold. "Whoever finds you will be able to read the instructions and release you. Understood?"

Two Flowers embraced Séquanon. Her warmth held him like a prayer and it was hard to break away. She gave him the stone bullet and sprigs of dried flowers from her medicine bag.

John Raythorn extended his hand and Séquanon shook it.

"Safe passage, pilgrim."

"Safe passage, John Raythorn."

Séquanon ran back to the ladder. The ship lurched and threw him to the floor. He got up and climbed, jumped into the hammock and attached the neural leads. The ship shook like it was coming apart. Séquanon closed the collision shield, reset the diameter of the stasis field in the nose section and contacted Raythorn and Two Flowers over the intercom.

"I'm going to engage the stasis field, John, and detach the ship. Hold up the instructions."

Séquanon told Cog to detach the ship and, as they pulled away, Raythorn and Two Flowers, through raging flurries of snow, came into view. With his right hand Raythorn held the tablet face out as Séquanon had instructed. With his left he held Two Flowers in a passionate embrace. Their mouths were joined in a kiss that would last until they were found.

"Cog?"

"Yes, Séquanon?"

"Do you see?"

"Love is beautiful, Séquanon."

"You humble me, Cog."

"Such is my privilege."

Cog turned the ship skyward and took his best guess; the monitors filled with stars.

Séquanon was finished with certainty. Undaunted by the tempests of the unknown, he gave himself to the will of the universe.

Acknowledgments

THIS BOOK HAS been long in coming. The list of those who merit thanks is of corresponding length.

Thanks to my publishers, Dave and Eileen Workman, and my editor, Ian Wood, for making it possible, and gifting me influence in the book's presentation.

John R. Reed, Monte Schulz, Elizabeth Engstrom, Robert Olen Butler: thank you for your friendship and wisdom. I could ask for no better guides.

Special thanks to my brother, Thomas, for reading carefully and sharing his knowledge, particularly historical, which has been of great value. Thanks to my sister, Annette, her husband Sergio, my nephews Sergio, Paul, Evan, Anthony and Eugene, my niece Annette, her sons Roberto and Nicholas, my uncle Jack, my cousin Bill and all my family for your faith and encouragement. Special thanks to my sister-in-law, Tina Vessels, for hosting readings and promoting my work, and to her sister, Debbie Blevins, for donating her creative efforts to the cause.

Special thanks to L. A. Howe for her relentless faith and for her meticulous examination of several stories in this volume, particularly "Bulbous Things" and "The Mountain and The Vortex."

Special thanks to Robin Burrows, Avery Faeth, Oja Fin, Buck Kamin, Chlóe McFetters and Cat Robson for giving generously of their time to read carefully and comment helpfully.

Marque, Julie and Julian Coy, thank you for being there in the hardest of times.

To Those Who Have Believed, and been there in times of trial, bless you all, especially William and Pam Anderson, Mary O. Barnard, Michael Dennison, Henry Han, Miguel Juarez, Bruce Kawin, Michael Lepere, Sophia Morgan, Shanna Van Mourik, Andy O'Leary, Harry and Sandra Reese, Ann Savino, Jane St. Clair and Charles Talmadge.

Thanks to Janet Hutchings, Sharon Lawson and Anthony Rivera for championing my work and the mystery and horror genres in general.

Thanks to S. I. Stebel and Karen K. Ford for welcoming me into their circle, and to JoBeth McDaniel for welcoming me into hers.

Thanks to Christina Lay for opening doors.

Alan, Steven and Cheryl, thank you for your beautiful art. Reverent gratitude also to the late, great Jean "Moebius" Giraud.

Thanks to all the organizers and staff of the Abroad Writers Conference, Santa Barbara Writers Conference, Thrillerfest in New York, and Wordcrafters in Eugene, especially Nancy Gerbault, Grace Rachow, Ned Bixby, Jim Alexander, Lisa Angle, Kimberly Howe, Sandra Brennan, Dennis Kennett, Carla Buckley, Patricia Marshall, Daryll Lynne Evans and George Filgate.

Thanks to the wonderful community of writers to which I am privileged to belong, especially Lisa Alber, Stacy Allen, Meredith Anthony, Lorelei Armstrong, Rebecca August, Dyanne Asimov, Donald Bain and Renee Paley-Bain, Mark Beardsley, Robyn Bell, Laurie Blanton, Terry Brooks, Kelly Butler, Linda Chase, Cynthia Coate-Ray, Julia Dawson, Bruce De Silva, Nicholas Dietch, Marianne Dougherty, Jack Eidt, Laurie Farmer-

Heaton, Sabine French, Isabel Frischman, Meg Gardiner, Joshua Graham, Deborah Henry, Pamela Herber, Margaux Dunbar Hession, Nina Kiriki Hoffman, Jocelyn Hughes, Ted Humphrey, Catherine Ryan Hyde, Linda Ibbotsen, Rachael Ikins, Hector Javkin, Court Johnson, Pamela K. Johnson, Kay Kendall, Mary Pat Koos, Lisa Leonard-Cook, Christine Logsdon, Andrew Loschert, Mathew Lowes, Carmen Madden, Carey McKearnan, Dierdre Peterson, Diane Cox McPhail, Steven Moore, Erin Munch, Kevin O'Brien, Matthew Pallamary, Daniel Ray, Shanna Ritter, Charlotte Samples, Tracy Scarpino, Rick Shaw, Jane Smiley, Patricia Smith, Nicole Starczak, Ginger Swanson, Mac Talley, Brit Teasdale, Rachel S. Thurston, Robin Tiffney, Theo Tiffney, Rosalind Trotter, Mary Hill Wagner, Adrienne D. Wilson, F. Paul Wilson, Eric M. Witchey and Wendy Worthington.

Thanks to Susan Goddard, Rich Hartfield, Mitch Powers, Karen Sonnier and David Wohlberg for your patience, business sense, legal counsel and support.

Thanks to the staff and management of the Doubletree Inn in Tucson, Arizona, especially Ahmed Ochoa and Ambrielle Haberly.

Thanks to my friends in Lismore, Ireland: Denis Nevin, Patrick Nevin, Bren Ó Ruaidh, Margo Cashman and Mo O'Connor. You warmed my spirit and inspired me in ways I will always remember.

Rex, Ellie, Carolyn and Pebbles, it's for you too.

About the Author

 STEPHEN T. VESSELS wrote his first story when he was six years old. Forty years later he wrote one that sold. His earliest inspirations were the horror films of Bela Lugosi, Boris Karloff and Vincent Price, and science fiction films like Ib Melchior's "Journey to the Seventh Planet." Later he encountered the legendary Modern Library anthology, "Tales of Terror and the Supernatural," which he read in the back seat while his parents drove through Texas. In 2012 he received the Best Fiction award from the Santa Barbara Writers Conference, and in 2014 was nominated for a Thriller Award. This is his first published book.

CPSIA information can be obtained at www.ICGtesting.com
Printed in the USA
LVOW08*1254300916

506846LV00002B/5/P